Books by Nan Rossiter

The Gin & Chowder Club

"Christmas on Cape Cod" in *Making Spirits Bright*

Words Get in the Way

More Than You Know

MORE THAN YOU KNOW

NAN ROSSITER

KENSINGTON BOOKS
www.kensingtonbooks.com

KENSINGTON BOOKS are published by

Kensington Publishing Corp.
119 West 40th Street
New York, NY 10018

All Kensington titles, imprints, and distributed lines are available at special quantity discounts for bulk purchases for sales promotion, premiums, fund-raising, and educational or institutional use.

Special book excerpts or customized printings can also be created to fit specific needs. For details, write or phone the office of the Kensington Special Sales Manager: Kensington Publishing Corp., 119 West 40th Street, New York, NY 10018. Attn. Special Sales Department. Phone: 1-800-221-2647.

Kensington and the K logo Reg. U.S. Pat. & TM Off.

ISBN-13: 978-0-7582-8389-4
ISBN-10: 0-7582-8389-X
First Kensington Trade Paperback Printing: May 2013

eISBN-13: 978-0-7582-8390-0
eISBN-10: 0-7582-8390-3
First Kensington Electronic Edition: May 2013

10 9 8 7 6 5 4 3 2 1

Printed in the United States of America

In memory of all dearly missed,
irreplaceable, beloved Moms
. . . including mine.

WITH HEARTFELT THANKS . . .

To my editor, Audrey LaFehr, and my agent, Deirdre Mullane, whose thoughtful suggestions, patient guidance, and words of encouragement help make every story the best it can be; and to all the unsung heroes at Kensington who do their best to make every book a success; to my husband, Bruce, and our boys, Cole and Noah, who always keep me smiling and keep track of how many pages I've written; to my dad—my number-one fan—who tells everyone he meets about my latest publishing endeavors! To my friend and neighbor Carol Papov, who shared a real-life experience that stayed with me and inspired the beginning premise for this book; to my friend Carol Kent, who eulogized my mom with a wonderful letter—and then happily blessed my idea to use the same format in the book; and to all my reading friends whose kind words make me believe I can really do this . . . I am truly blessed!

PROLOGUE

Anyone passing by the Chesterfield Inn on that snowy November night would have felt drawn to the cozy warmth of the dining room's brightly lit windows. The flickering candles and the cheerful fire crackling in the fireplace made the elegant table settings sparkle invitingly, but Mia and Thomas Graham were the only ones enjoying the inn's charming ambiance and delectable fare that quiet evening. It was their fifth wedding anniversary, and despite the weather and Mia's protests about the expense, Tom had insisted they celebrate in style.

Savoring her last morsel of apple pie, Mia pushed her dessert plate away, contentedly closed her eyes, and rhythmically stroked her smooth, round belly. "We've got one busy girl," she said. "She's always on the move."

"She takes after her mom," Tom said with a gentle smile, reaching for her hand. "By the way," he asked, "how do you know it's a she? Maybe it's a he."

Mia looked into Tom's solemn gray eyes, sparkling in the candlelight. "Maybe," she teased. "You can always hope." She knew that her handsome, athletic husband would love nothing more than to have a son to mentor in life and on the playing fields. "But keep in mind, girls play sports too."

"I know, but our first two seem much more interested in dolls and dresses."

Mia smiled. "Well, I hope you won't be disappointed if it is another girl."

"You know I won't be. It would just be nice to have someone on my side when the going gets tough. I'm not sure I can handle a house full of women—especially when they're teenagers."

Mia laughed. "I'm on your side," she said with a smile.

"You know what I mean—my side of the gender gap."

"Oh, I'm sure you'll manage. They'll have you wrapped around their little fingers, and when the time comes, you'll be the one who's teary-eyed when you're walking them down the aisle."

Tom laughed, knowing she was right. He often thought Mia knew him better than he knew himself. He gazed into her cornflower blue eyes and reached out to stroke her smooth cheek, as if trying to memorize its soft curve. "I love you," he whispered.

"I love you too," she said softly. "More than you know."

Tom smiled wistfully, picked up his fork, scraped his plate, and licked the last sweet remnants of chocolate decadence. He'd never been very good at serious, intimate moments, so the shorter they were the better. "Well," he teased, his boyish grin returning, "have you two had enough to eat? Enough, at least, to get you home?"

Mia laughed. "I don't know. I might have to stop at the diner for another piece of pie." Tom stood to help her slip on her coat, kissed her softly, and then bent down and kissed her belly too. "Love you too," he murmured, gently laying his hand on the roundness. "Hey, maybe he has a basketball in there," he surmised, then felt a purposeful kick. "Or maybe he's a soccer player," he added brightly.

"Maybe," Mia said with the smile that always had a way of stealing his heart.

They nodded to their waiter and stepped out into the wintry night. Tom put his arm around Mia and guided her across the snow-covered parking lot. "Told you it would stop snowing," he said, pulling her closer and kissing her forehead.

She nodded and then almost lost her footing, but he held her tightly. "It's still slippery, though."

"I won't let you fall—I'll always look out for you," he said with a smile, helping her climb into the passenger seat and blowing on his hands as he walked around to his side of the truck.

"How come you didn't come out and warm it up for me?" she teased.

"I should've," he said apologetically, starting the engine, turning the defroster on high, and reaching for his scraper.

While she watched through the icy stripes of slowly defrosting glass, she thought of all the times she'd shivered in the passenger seat while Tom cleared snow off frozen windshields: from the time he was sixteen, clearing off his dad's Nova, to the cracked leaking windshield of the old Valiant her dad had given them when they got married, to tonight, through the window of his used, but meticulously maintained pickup truck. Intent on his task, Tom didn't notice Mia watching him; he didn't know she was thinking the years hadn't touched him; that he still looked like the slender, dark-haired high-school sophomore she'd fallen in love with ten years earlier; he didn't know she was considering how much more she loved him now, or that she was whispering a prayer, thanking God for giving her such a good man.

He climbed back in the cab, tucked the scraper under his

seat, adjusted the defroster, and held his hands over the heat. "Warming up?" he asked.

She nodded, admiring his rosy cheeks and then looking down at her wedding rings.

He put the truck in gear and slowly rolled forward, the tires crunching on the snow. "Look," he said when they reached the road, "all that worrying for nothing. The plows have already been through." Mia relaxed as he pulled onto the wet pavement.

"So," he said, turning the fan down a couple of notches and switching the setting from defrost to heat, "I keep meaning to ask you—have we settled on a name yet?"

Mia adjusted her seat belt so it didn't cross her belly and answered, "Well, if it's a girl, how about Beryl?"

"Hmm . . . is that the name of another amazing female author who's capable of doing anything she puts her mind to?"

"Mmm-hmm," Mia conceded with a grin.

"How'd I know?" Tom said with a laugh.

"Well, our girls are going to be remarkable women, so they should have remarkable namesakes."

"They'll be remarkable if they're anything like their mother—who, I might add, will be an amazing author in her own right someday." He paused. "But what if it's a boy?"

Mia looked thoughtful. "How about Thomas?"

"Oh, I don't know," Tom said, easing up to the light. "I think I'd rather give him a name of his own." The light turned green and he eased into the intersection. "I've always thought naming your child after yourself is a bit . . ." He looked over at her, trying to think of the word he wanted. Unexpectedly, he saw the color draining from her face.

"Tom, look out!" she screamed. He turned in time to see blinding headlights hurtling toward them, and slammed on his breaks, but it was too late—the careening car smashed headlong into the driver's door, pushing the truck off the road and down an embankment.

Mia felt her head hit the window, and heard metal and glass smashing as the truck rolled over and over like an out-of-control amusement park ride. Excruciating pain shot up her leg while the seat belt cut savagely into her abdomen and neck. Finally, the truck stopped, teetering precariously on its side and leaving her suspended by her seat belt. Gasoline fumes burned her nostrils and throat, and she felt something warm trickling down the side of her face. "Tom!" she screamed over and over . . . but there was only silence and darkness and dust.

In the days that followed, Mia read the accident report so many times it became etched in her mind. Their anniversary was scrawled in the upper right-hand corner in pencil: *November 15, 1968;* the rest of the report was typed. It stated that forty-eight-year-old Clay Davis had begun drinking when he left work; his blood alcohol level at the time of the accident was .25; the speedometer of his Buick Riviera was frozen at ninety-six miles per hour; there were no skid marks; and Clay Davis walked away from the accident virtually unscathed. The report went on to say that twenty-six-year-old Mia Graham received minor injuries, but her husband, Thomas, was thrown from his Chevrolet C-10 pickup and crushed by its rolling impact. He died instantly.

These words echoed through Mia's mind and tortured her endlessly until the image of her husband's body being tossed like a rag doll was the first thing she saw when she woke up and the last image in her mind before she finally fell asleep. But it was the very last words that haunted her the most: *He died instantly.* She kept trying to grasp this simple concept: Tom was alive in his body one second, but not the next. His spirit, essence, love, the sparkle in his dark gray eyes—everything that made him Tom—was all there one instant, but gone the next.

Where did it go? Where did he go? Mia had heard the words, *died instantly*, countless times, but now that they applied to someone she loved—someone who was her whole life—she found it impossible to comprehend.

It was weeks before she began to remember actually being in the accident, before the jagged images flooded her memory and woke her, screaming from her troubled sleep. If they'd only left a minute sooner or a minute later . . . if he hadn't had to clear snow off the windshield, or . . . if they hadn't gone out to dinner at all . . . he'd still be alive.

The doctor had given her a prescription to ease her torment and help her rest, but she worried she wouldn't hear the baby, so she refused to take it. Instead, she lay awake, night after night, her cheek, wet with tears, pressed against Tom's pillow, breathing in the scent that lingered there and knowing she would never again wash that old blue pillowcase. She slipped her hand over to touch the smooth, cool sheets on his side of the bed, and her heart ached with grief as she prayed that the baby, born that same tragic night, would wake so she'd have someone to hold.

Part I

*In thy book were written, every one of them,
the days that were formed for me,
when as yet there were none of them.*

—Psalm 139:16

1

Beryl Graham pulled on her North Face jacket and ran her fingers through her short dark hair as she walked around her pepper white Mini Cooper to open the passenger door for Flannery. The soulful old bulldog looked up at her and then eyed the distance to the ground warily. "C'mon, Flan-O, it's not that far. You can do it," she urged. The stout, short-legged dog edged cautiously to the door and tentatively reached her paw out over the gaping precipice before shaking her sloppy jowls and backing away. "It's not the Grand Canyon, you know!" Beryl teased affectionately, noticing that drool was now splattered across her dashboard. The homely face gazed at her forlornly and she couldn't help but laugh. "I know, I know, someday I'll be old and need help, too . . . although, honestly, I think I'd rather leave this earth before I need help!" She reached around Flannery's barrel-shaped belly, scooped her up, and set her gently on the ground. Without looking back, the compact canine waddled off, sniffing the new dandelions sprouting up everywhere across her old stomping grounds.

Beryl watched her go and shook her head. She opened the

trunk, pulled out two threadbare green bags, bulging with groceries, slung one over each shoulder, and then wedged the bag of Macintosh apples into the cardboard box from the package store. She hoped she'd remembered everything: two bottles of Toasted Head chardonnay for Isak, "and a Barefoot Pinot for good meshah," she murmured, mimicking her oldest sister's New England accent, and a bottle of Rex Goliath for Rumer. "The one with the roostah on it," Rumer had said, trying to trigger Beryl's memory; but when Beryl had stood in front of the red wines, she couldn't remember if Rumer had said Merlot or cabernet, so she'd finally decided on Free Range Red, knowing her organically minded middle sister would appreciate that the "roostah" had been allowed to wander.

Beryl hitched the box up into her arms, reached into the corner of the trunk for the small paper bag of beeswax candles and a fresh tin of English breakfast tea leaves, and tried to balance everything on her knee while she closed the trunk. "Not happening," she muttered. It didn't matter, she wasn't staying long. She just had to drop off the groceries, get Flan settled, and then head to Logan to pick up Rumer. She looked up at the old farmhouse full of memories. Its peeling white paint glowed in the melancholy light of late-afternoon sun, and its windows reflected the bright flames that were streaking across the azure sky. It looked as if an artist had dipped his brush in orangey pink water and swept it across the scene, washing it in the translucent warm hues of day's end, and then splashed bright, fiery orange on the windows. Beryl could almost hear her mom's soft, unassuming voice quoting one of her favorite writers: "The setting sun is reflected from the windows of the almshouse as brightly as from the rich man's abode." Beryl smiled, remembering how much Mia had loved Thoreau—she even named her cat after him—and then her smile dissolved, remembering that she'd forgotten to feed the famous author's namesake who, after thirteen years, still presided over Mia's tea shop. Oh, well, poor Thoreau would just have to wait.

"Stay around, Flan-O," she called over her shoulder. The pudgy dog nosed around under the tire swing that hung from a majestic, old oak tree but didn't look up. "No deer poop!" she warned, but Flan didn't hear—or else chose to ignore her—because she suddenly began to gulp down the new delicacy she'd found. "Okay, if you must. But please don't roll in it!" As if on cue, Flannery fell on her fat side and began wriggling around in the tall grass. Beryl shook her head and looked up to heaven. "Mum," she implored, "could you please get your dog to behave?"

She set the box on one of the Adirondack chairs on the front porch and fished around in her pocket for the key. Finally, she pulled the entire contents out of her pocket and realized, in alarm, that she was still carrying around her mom's wedding rings. She slipped them on her finger, found the key, unlocked the door, picked up the box, and went inside. Setting everything on the old Formica table in the kitchen, she took off her jacket, threw it over a chair, and opened the fridge. When the light didn't come on, she had a sinking feeling the power was out; then she remembered that she'd unplugged it after she'd helped her mom move into the nursing home.

Mia had just turned sixty-six when Beryl began to suspect that something was wrong. Initially, she told herself that her mom was just getting forgetful—perfectly normal for someone her age. But when she started having trouble remembering the names of people she'd known all her life and forgetting to take inventory and place orders—tasks that were necessary to keep her tea shop running smoothly—Beryl began to wonder if it was something more. She and her sisters had grown up working beside their mom at her shop, Tranquility in a Teapot, and at first, she tried reminding her mom what tasks needed to be done, but when that didn't seem to help, she just started doing the chores herself. She also began paying closer attention when Mia was helping customers and soon realized she was having trouble recalling where items were stocked on the shelves. It's so unlike her, she'd thought, Mum knows this shop inside out. But it wasn't until Beryl stopped by the house one evening after work that she'd really begun to worry.

As soon as she walked in, the smell of gas almost knocked her over. She rushed to the kitchen and found the oven on and a pilot light out! She immediately turned off the oven and pushed open the windows, but her mom, sitting in the next room, was completely unaware of the danger and only said that she thought something smelled funny. Later that night, Beryl called Rumer at home in Montana and mentioned the incident, and by the next morning, Isak was calling from California with the name of a neurologist. Beryl said she was sure old Dr. Hamilton could diagnosis the problem, but Isak had insisted Mia see a specialist, so three weeks later, on a bright blue sky September morning, Beryl had taken Mia to Boston.

They'd arrived early, hoping to have lunch in Quincy Market, and after perusing the menus of several outdoor cafés, they picked a sunny table and ordered Waldorf salads, mint iced tea, and a slice of peach raspberry pie to share. Afterward, they happily discovered that they still had time to look around in the shops. In one boutique, Mia had found a lovely silk scarf for Isak; at an outdoor stand, she'd purchased a pair of beautiful turquoise earrings for Rumer; and finally, in a little bookstore at the end of the building, aptly named The Bookend, she'd discreetly tucked away a small package for Beryl. Then she'd happily declared, "I've officially started my Christmas shopping. I only hope I can remember where I've put these things when Christmas gets here."

"Don't worry, Mum," Beryl had said, putting her arm around

her, "I'll remind you." As they'd turned to go, Mia bumped into a display of books, sending a whole stack tumbling to the floor, but when they knelt to pick them up, a friendly voice called, "Don't worry. It's my fault. I knew they were too close to the counter."

Beryl stood up, balancing the books in her arms, and when she saw the source of the voice, her face lit up. "Micah?"

A slender man peered at her over round horn-rimmed glasses, looking puzzled, and then smiled shyly. "Beryl!" He looked over her shoulder and saw Mia too. "And Mrs. Graham!" Happily surprised, he came around the counter to give them each a hug. Beryl hugged him back warmly, but Mia pulled away, looking startled and confused.

Beryl quickly came to her rescue. "Mum, you remember Micah Coleman. He worked at the shop when he was in high school."

Mia searched the tan face and ocean blue eyes and nodded. "My shop?" she asked uncertainly.

Beryl nodded and Micah took off his glasses. "Does this help?"

Mia studied his face again and shook her head. "Please forgive me. I'm having trouble remembering my own name these days."

Micah nodded thoughtfully. "It was a long time ago."

Beryl smiled. "It's so good to see you. How long has it been?"

Micah put his glasses back on and rubbed his chin thoughtfully. "Twenty-five years?" he mused, raising his eyebrows.

Beryl shook her head in disbelief. "It can't be—we aren't that old!"

Micah laughed. "You might not be, but I definitely am!"

"I didn't know you were in Boston. Have you worked here long?"

"When they let me. . . ." He grinned at the girl working the register. "Actually, this is my store."

Beryl looked surprised. "Wow! It's very nice. You've done a lot with a small space."

"Thanks," Micah replied, his shy smile returning. "All those years ago—working at Tranquility—inspired me to start my own business."

Beryl glanced at the clock above the register. "Oh, Micah, I'm sorry we have to rush off—we have an appointment." Micah nodded, taking the books from her.

Mia tilted her head politely. "It was very nice to see you again, Micah."

Micah smiled warmly. "It was very nice to see you too."

Beryl gave him a hug. "Can't believe it's you!"

"Me too," he said softly. "Hope you'll stop by again."

"We will," she promised.

Reluctantly, they'd left the shop and hurried to the doctor's office, the memory of the day and their chance encounter quickly slipping away—giving way to the anxious thoughts they'd been trying to keep at bay. They each whispered hopeful prayers that somehow all their worrying was for nothing. But later that afternoon, after a myriad of written and oral tests and a review of Mia's health records, the doctor gently confirmed that dementia—most likely Alzheimer's—was slowly stealing Mia's mind and memory. Mother and daughter listened quietly, nodded numbly, asked the few questions that came to mind, although there would be many more later, graciously accepted pamphlets and slips for new prescriptions, made another appointment for further testing, and escaped into the late-day sun to hold each other close and weep—never wanting to let go.

At last, Mia had pulled away gently and held her daughter's lovely face in her hands. Searching the glistening cornflower blue eyes that mirrored her own, she'd smiled sadly and said,

"Berry, dear, you'll just have to remember these wonderful days for both of us."

The decision to seek long-term care had been heartbreaking for all of them, but Beryl had struggled with it the most. Without hesitation, she'd offered to move back home, but Mia wouldn't hear of it, and Rumer and Isak agreed. They insisted that Mia would not want Beryl to take on such a burden for an indeterminate length of time.

"It's not a burden," Beryl had argued. "I want to do it. Besides, she's so young."

"And so are you," Isak had responded. "Who knows how long she'll need care. She's going to need someone around the clock, and there's no respite—or life—for a long-term caregiver."

"We could have a nurse come in too," Beryl had suggested, but her sisters had both been so adamant that she'd begun to wonder if they felt guilty because they weren't willing to do the same. Instead, they insisted it would be better to find a facility that specialized in caring for Alzheimer's patients. Beryl had strongly disagreed—they could not put Mia in a nursing home. They'd argued bitterly, tearfully, and in the end, she'd felt as if she'd had no say in the matter and wished she'd never told them about her mother's decline. Her heart had ached with regret and sorrow.

Beryl plugged the fridge in and it hummed to life, its cheerful light illuminating clean, white walls and bare glass shelves. She stocked it with the produce and dairy she'd bought: a head of romaine, cucumbers, carrots, celery, eggs, cheddar, milk, half and half, and then, in an afterthought, she slipped one of the bottles of chardonnay in the door. Rumer was coming in that night and Isak the next day. Together, they'd plan Mia's service and begin the overwhelming task of going through her belongings. They'd be staying at the house all week; then their families would arrive on Thursday or Friday. Beryl put the remaining bottles of wine on the counter and, beside them, lined up a fresh bag of Green Mountain Vermont Country Blend coffee, oatmeal, brown sugar, raisins, a bag of walnuts, bread, the apples, her tin of tea, two golden heirloom tomatoes, and the beeswax candles she'd brought from the shop. She washed her hands, remembered the rings, and climbed the worn, narrow stairs to the quiet bedroom that looked out over the front yard.

Golden sunlight streamed through the windows in long slants, creating a pattern of crosses on the wainscoting and across the faded Amish wedding quilt that had been on her mom's bed for as long as she could remember. Beryl sat down, held out her hand, and wondered for the thousandth time if she'd ever wear rings of her own. She looked at her tan, slender fingers and thought of her mom's hands. Over the years, she and Mia had often held their hands up palm to palm or side by side and marveled at their sameness: Not only were they the same size and shape, but they both had small bumps on their right middle fingers from holding their pencils too tightly, and they both kept their nails neatly trimmed, like crescent moons, and unpolished, except for special occasions, like the times they'd painted on clear gloss for Rumer's and Isak's weddings. The bride and the bridesmaid had both teased them, "You two are really living on the wild side!"

And it wasn't just their hands that were the same. Beryl wished she had a penny for every time someone had asked them if they were sisters. Mia had always been petite and athletic and, by the time Beryl was in high school, she'd grown into her mom's mirror image. It was only in recent years—as Mia's hair had become more salt than pepper, and smile wrinkles had crinkled around her friendly eyes—that there was a noticeable difference again. Beryl smiled at the thought; then an unexpected wave of grief swept over her.

"Oh, Mum," she whispered, "how am I ever going to manage without you?" Through the blur of her tears, she noticed the countless tiny bright polka dots dancing on the walls. She slipped off Mia's diamond and the dots spun and sparkled like fireflies playing in the shadows. She wiped away her tears and slipped off the wedding ring too. Squinting, she tried to make out the inscription, but it was too delicate and worn to read without her glasses. She walked over to her mom's bureau, slid open the bottom drawer of her jewelry box, and carefully placed the rings in the front corner. As she did, a ray of sunlight fell over the drawer and a flash of blue caught her eye. She stared at the shiny object: a large sapphire ring tucked in the back of the drawer. She picked it up and held it in the light; it was the same sparkling blue as Mia's eyes, but Beryl had no memory of her mother ever wearing the ring. She looked in the drawer again and saw a card. It was made from a folded piece of watercolor paper and on the outside was a beautiful painting of a tawny red female cardinal. Beryl studied the delicate illustration and then opened the card and read the long, elegant script:

> For my Mia,
> This stone reminds me of those amazing
> blue eyes that see right through me!
> Always, David

Beryl frowned and murmured, "Who is David?" In recent months, she'd sometimes heard her mom say that name, but she never knew why—the only Davids she knew were a long-lost uncle who'd actually been a family friend and a boy from Virginia who'd sat across from her in the third grade. She turned the card over, hoping for a clue, but the back of the card was blank. She studied the handwriting again and then happened to look out the window—just in time to see the stout little dog marching toward the pond.

"Oh, no," she murmured. "Oh, no, you don't!" she shouted, knocking loudly on the glass. But the determined canine trundled on purposefully, as if on a mission. Beryl dropped the ring back in the drawer and flew down the stairs, out the door, and across the lawn. "Flannery O'Connor, get your butt back here." To her surprise, the wayward dog, now standing shoulder-deep in murky brown water, had a sudden change of heart and plodded back through the mud to stand in front of her. Then she closed her droopy eyes and, like a slowly rumbling earthquake, began to shake her whole body—from her big, blocky head all the way down to her curly, pathetic excuse for a tail.

Beryl leaped back, but it was too late—her pink oxford was splattered with mud. She looked down at her blouse and then up to heaven. "You'd better not be laughing, Mum!" she said, admonishing the wispy clouds that were drifting across the sky. As she did, she noticed a flock of geese winging high above, barely visible, their ever-changing formation floating through the heavens like a shimmering silver strand of Christmas tree tinsel. Beryl watched in amazement, heard their faint honking, and suddenly realized that her beloved mom, who'd always smiled at adversity, would be having a hard time suppressing her laughter. Beryl could almost hear her cheerful voice, "I'm sorry, Ber, but you should try not to take everything so seriously. Life is much too short—and full of wonder!" Beryl shook her head and considered the possibility that her mom had somehow teamed up with God to strategically place that flock of geese—and Flannery—in her life to help her get through this.

She thought back to the rainy spring day, ten years earlier, when Mia first brought Flannery home. At six weeks old, she was so small that Mia had tucked her into the front of her raincoat to keep her dry, and when that sad, wrinkled face had peeked out over her zipper, Mia had grinned impishly. "I just had a feeling!" she'd explained. Beryl had taken one look at the homely face and teased, "What feeling was that—sympathy?" In retrospect, she couldn't help but wonder if that day had been part of a greater plan—God's tapestry, Mia had called it, firmly believing that nothing in life happened by coincidence. The thought made Beryl smile as she walked back to the house with the muddy, wet canine waddling beside her.

On the way, they stopped at the car and Beryl retrieved Flan's old L.L. Bean dog bed and a bag of Eukanuba. Then they continued to the porch, and she told Flan to sit and stay while she went inside to find a towel. When she came back out, the old dog was busy cleaning herself up with her hind leg over her head. Beryl cleared her throat and Flan looked up indignantly. "You really need to work on your manners," she said, kneeling down. Flannery sniffed the towel, pulled her rotund self up, and before Beryl had a chance to defend herself, leaned forward and licked her right on the lips. "Yuck!" Beryl exclaimed, falling back in surprise and wiping her mouth on her sleeve. She contemplated running to her car for her Purell bottle but just shook it off, regained her composure, picked up the towel, and started to dry, which prompted the old dog to arch her back, close her eyes, and groan pleasurably—her guttural sounds vibrating with every movement of the towel.

"Oh, my goodness, Flan-O, you have absolutely no shame," Beryl teased. Finally, she announced, "Good enough," opened the screen door, and Flan trotted in like the old dame who owned the place. "That's what I love," Beryl said, "a dog with attitude."

Flan trundled eagerly through the house, checking every room, her hind end wagging. "Flan, what in the world are you doing?" Beryl asked in dismay. Then it hit her—she was looking for Mia. Tears filled Beryl's eyes. "Oh, Flan, she's not here." But Flan, undeterred, painstakingly climbed the narrow stairs and, as Beryl watched, waddled hopefully from room to room, ready to announce her arrival. "Hon, she's not here . . ." Beryl repeated, but her words fell on deaf ears. Finally, Beryl sat on the top step, tears streaming down her cheeks, and wondered if she was going to break down every time she thought of her mom. She felt a cold, wet nose press against her arm and looked up. Flan gazed at her mournfully. "I'm sorry," Beryl whispered, putting her arm around her and pulling her close. "I wish you could understand." The old dog leaned into her, nuzzled her cheek, and licked her salty tears.

Finally, she carried her back downstairs, set her on the kitchen floor, scooped a cup of kibble into her bowl, and put the bowl near the back door next to her water. Flan sniffed it indifferently, took a little drink, found her old bed next to the stove—where Mia had always kept it—circled around several times, and curled up on its soft, fleecy cover. Beryl shook her head. "You've been living with me for three years, and yet, it's like you never left this place." She reached into her pocket to make sure she still had her keys and her phone, turned on the stove light, knelt down to scratch Flan's ears, and whispered, "Don't be sad, old pie! I'll be back soon with one of your favorite pals."

2

Rumer gazed at the Black Foot River as they neared Missoula. "Wake up, Rand," she said, reaching into the backseat of the pickup to give her ten-year-old son a nudge. "The sun's makin' the river look like a golden ribbon weaving through the city."

Rand sat up, his tousled chestnut hair sticking out in every direction. He blinked sleepily. "Mmm-hmm," he murmured, unimpressed, before slumping over again.

"Thanks for driving me," Rumer said quietly. She paused. "I'm still hoping you'll come. It would mean a lot to me if Rand—and you—were there."

Will nodded solemnly. "We'll try, Rumer, but I can't promise anything." He pressed his lips together and looked over at her. Her eyes glistened and he knew he was playing a big part in breaking her heart. He wanted to wrap his arms around her and hold her, but lately it felt like there was an invisible wall between them. "I'm sorry about your mom—you know that— but it'll be at least two grand for me and Rand to come—and we just don't have that kind of money."

Rumer blinked back tears, remembering the angry words

they'd hurled at each other the night before. "I know, Will, but this is his grandmother. You only go through life once and, believe it or not, there are things more important than money."

Will sighed in frustration. "Rumer, honestly, I wish things were different, I really do. I wish I could give you everything you want. I wish money wasn't always an issue with us, but construction is the only thing I know how to do and no one is building anything in this damn economy. Working for a modular home company is not what I had in mind either, but at least it's a job. The problem is—no matter how many hours I work— it's never enough."

"Maybe we shouldn't have moved out here," Rumer said quietly.

Will looked over. "Maybe we shouldn't have—maybe you and Rand shouldn't have."

Rumer stared out the window, tears stinging her eyes.

Will glanced over. "I'm sorry, I shouldn't have said that. I just don't know what the answer is anymore."

Rumer didn't know what the answer was either. Her profession had changed, too; with so much art being generated by computers, it was even harder for a freelance illustrator to find work. She'd been reduced to waitressing and catering as often as she could—and she hated every minute of it.

Will pulled up in front of the airport terminal and Rumer got out. She reached into the back of the truck for her bags, and Will pulled the seat forward and shook their son's knee. "C'mon, Rand, wake up. Mom's leaving and you need to say good-bye."

Rand climbed sleepily out of the truck. "Bye, Mom," he said, yawning.

Rumer put her bags on the sidewalk and gave him a long hug. He was as tall as she was. She held him out at arm's length, searched his face, and tried to smooth down his hair. "Be good for Dad," she ordered. "And do your homework—before PlayStation!" She looked at Will. "That's the rule now."

"Got it," he said with a wry smile—it was a rule he'd been trying to establish for years.

"Are you two going to be okay?"

"We'll be fine—right, sport?" Will said reassuringly, putting his arm around Rand's shoulder, pulling him closer. "Maybe we'll even go fishing."

Rand gave his mom a thumbs-up and Rumer eyed them suspiciously. "Promise me you'll eat something besides pizza and McDonald's."

Rand grinned. "Yup, we'll have Burger King and Wendy's, too—right, Dad?"

Will teased, "Maybe we'll even throw in some Chinese for good measure."

Rumer frowned. "All that eating out won't be good for your precious budget," she said with a hint of sarcasm, but as soon as the words slipped out, she saw Will's smile evaporate and she regretted it.

"Whatever."

"I'm sorry," she said, shaking her head. "Just take care of yourselves. I'll call when I get there."

Will nodded. "Say hi to your sisters."

Rumer slung her backpack over her shoulder and turned to walk away but suddenly remembered their two-year-old black Lab. She turned around and realized her two men were still standing there, watching her go. "Don't forget to feed Norman," she called, "and, Rand, walk him when you get home from school. Pam said she'd take care of him if you decide to come. And, Will, please try to get Rand a haircut."

Will nodded and Rand waved. Rumer smiled wistfully, waved back, and realized that a tall man wearing a Red Sox shirt was holding the door for her. She turned and hurried inside.

Standing in line, she rifled through her backpack, making sure she had everything—license, money, boarding pass, phone. She handed her pass to the attendant, slipped off her Keen mocs, dropped the shoes and the contents of her pockets into the bin, and walked through without incident. On the other side, she retrieved her belongings, slipped on her shoes, and looked around for a Dunkin' Donuts. Will had been so early picking her up, she hadn't had time for a cup of coffee—and she knew he wouldn't have wanted to stop, so she didn't even ask. Rand, on the other hand, who was now fully awake, would press his father until he gave in. In fact, her growing son was probably already wolfing down an Egg McMuffin and a carton of milk—because Will would say the OJ was too expensive.

Rumer spied a Dunkin' Donuts at the end of a line of storefronts and waited in line. When she finally reached the counter, she'd decided on her usual, a medium hazelnut with cream, and, gazing at the donuts, asked for a plain cruller too. She found a seat, put her backpack between her feet, and broke off a small piece of the donut. Taking a bite and a sip of her coffee, she decided that plain donuts were, by far, the best to have with coffee; she couldn't remember the last time she'd had one. She looked up at the departure board, realized her flight had been updated, and groaned. It was three hours late—What happened? She pulled her phone from her bag and texted Beryl. Then she leaned back in her seat, watched the cargo handlers loading a plane with luggage, and wondered what she would do for the next three hours. She looked out at the clear blue sky, watched the shimmering dots in the distance evolve into landing silver planes, and thought about Will. She shook her head sadly. Things had certainly changed—he didn't even hug her good-bye anymore.

Rumer had met William Josiah Swanson III at a frat party when she was a freshman at the Rhode Island School of Design and he was a sophomore at Brown. She'd been watching him from across the room as he manned the keg at the Alpha Epsilon Pi luau, and he glanced up and caught her looking. Carrying two red plastic cups overflowing with foamy beer, he'd walked over and held one out. She'd hesitated; her experience with drinking up until that night had been passing around a bottle of Boone's Farm with Isak and her friends in the woods at the end of their road—and the next morning, she'd had such a wicked headache she'd sworn she'd never drink again. But on that mild autumn night, the handsome undergrad with the friendly smile and dark eyes had caught her attention, and she didn't want him to think she was just a kid—who didn't drink—so, ignoring the alarms going off in her head and feigning nonchalance, she'd accepted, and then followed him out onto the porch where she continued her ruse by leaning against a railing that felt like it might give way at any moment.

They'd talked easily, the beer quickly having its effect; she discovered he was from New Hampshire, too, but was only in college to please his parents who were alums of the Ivy League school. She told him she had just started her foundation year at the art school down the hill and she hadn't declared her major yet, but she was leaning toward illustration. She vaguely remembered that he'd replenished her cup once . . . twice? And then he'd started talking about going to the beach. In her tipsy state, she thought he meant the RISD beach—which was the grassy area in front of the freshman dorms where everyone hung out on sunny days—so she wondered why they would need a car to get there.

As they drove out of Providence, the mild, breezy air and swirling lights reminded her of the county fair back home, and the wind that drifted through the open windows of the car smelled like the cool, gray ocean. The next morning she woke up—uncertain of where she was or how she'd gotten there. Bleary-eyed, she'd looked around and noticed that all the furniture was draped in white sheets—except for the bed on which they lay—which was covered in a blue quilt. The smooth tan skin of Will's back was uncovered and she realized she was wearing his shirt—thankfully, it was over her shirt. She wondered how much more of him was exposed under the quilt and tried to remember. When he woke up, he teased her for not remembering; but finally, with a long sigh of regret and a heart-melting grin, he revealed that she didn't need to worry—nothing had happened.

Later, they'd closed up his parents' beach house, stopped at Box Lunch for breakfast wraps and coffee, and walked along the deserted beach, watching the sandpipers being chased by the waves and listening to hungry seagulls begging for handouts. As the sun slipped from the sky, they'd finally made their way back to Providence and he'd kissed her good night under a streetlight on Benefit Street and promised to call.

The next several months had been a whirlwind. As the attraction between them grew, their strong-willed personalities surfaced—and the results were often tumultuous and tearful. So when Will proposed to Rumer three years later, on the night she graduated from RISD, everyone who knew and loved them held their breath and wondered if their fiery relationship could last.

Well, it had lasted, Rumer thought, sipping her coffee, for almost twenty-three years; but it hadn't been easy. And now it looked as if the naysayers might have been right after all. Maybe they didn't have what it takes to make it. The only thing holding them together was Rand. Tears stung Rumer's eyes. At least her mom hadn't lived to see them fall apart. She would've been heartbroken.

3

Beryl was lost in thought when she turned onto Route 3, and at least ten minutes passed before she realized that the last remnant of the day's bright sky was over her left shoulder, and not her right. She groaned. "What did I do?" Anxiously, she searched for the next highway sign and, sure enough, she was headed north toward Manchester. "What's the matter with me? I've traveled this road a thousand times." She shook her head; even though she was just shy of forty-five, ever since her mom's diagnosis, she'd become increasingly aware of her own mental blunders and "senior moments"—and the more aware she was of them, the more they seemed to happen. "I'm going to be right behind you, Mum." She pulled off the next exit, praying it wouldn't take her around Robin Hood's barn. "Thank you," she murmured, turning off the ramp and immediately seeing a sign for 3-South.

Her thoughts turned to Rumer and she prayed her sister's flight would be on time. She looked at the setting sun, now on her right side, and knew that was the direction from which Rumer was coming. Suddenly, she caught herself beginning to imagine tragic scenarios; then she heard her mom's voice echo-ing in her head: *"Beryl, why don't you allow yourself the joy of look-ing forward to someone's visit instead of worrying that something bad is going to happen while they're traveling?"* It was true—her mom knew her too well. It was almost as if she could read her mind. She glanced at the clock and realized she had plenty of time but felt bad knowing the lost minutes could have been spent stop-ping by the shop to feed Thoreau. She pictured the gray tiger curled up on the armchair alone and recalled how often he'd nestled on Mia's lap, purring contentedly. Somehow, that wise cat had sensed the quiet change taking place in his old friend, and although he'd always been affectionate, he'd become in-creasingly attentive during those last several months.

After her diagnosis, Mia had continued to manage at home with Beryl keeping a closer eye on her, but her forgetfulness had become increasingly worrisome. Isak and Rumer had flown home in the spring, and together they'd visited several facilities, but the one they'd liked best didn't have a room and it had a long waiting list. Surprisingly, Isak and Rumer had agreed it would be better to wait than confuse Mia by moving her twice. They'd helped Beryl move some of her things back home, and Beryl had felt as if she'd been given a reprieve and been anxious to prove that caring for their mom at home was the best solution.

But Mia's health had deteriorated quickly and her care be-came all-consuming, just as Isak had predicted. It was almost as if her diagnosis had accelerated her decline. Bathing, feeding, and keeping tabs on her kept Beryl busy all the time. She never told her sisters how many times she found Mia walking down the road—talking about going home, but headed in the oppo-site direction. One time, she was missing for more than an hour before Beryl found her sitting by the pond.

"Oh, Mum," Beryl had cried in thankful relief. "I'm so sorry you got lost. You really scared me."

"I was going to our cabin at MacDowell," she said, "but I couldn't remember the way."

"Mum, you haven't worked at MacDowell in years—and we never owned a cabin."

Mia's eyes had clouded over with confusion.

On top of everything, Tranquility in a Teapot's hours had become sporadic at best and business suffered. Everyone in town knew about Mia's decline and they'd tried to rally around the Grahams, but it had still looked like the little shop might close. Beryl had been beside herself. She'd wanted to hire help, but she hadn't even had time to interview anyone. She'd tried to open every day, at least for a couple of hours, and on good days, Mia had seemed to enjoy being at the shop; but most of the time, she'd just sat in her armchair, gazing out the window with Thoreau on her lap. Beryl had missed the old days, when they'd cheerfully worked side by side, laughing and helping customers select and sample specialty teas; and she missed pulling down the shade at the end of the day, sitting at one of the café tables, chatting with her mom over a freshly brewed pot of Darjeeling tea, and munching on raisin scones or almond biscotti. Mia had no longer wanted tea; its heat surprised her and made her wince with discomfort.

So it was a somber day, ten months later, when the nursing home called to say they had a room for Mia, and Beryl, in spite of her deep commitment to care for her mom at home, had felt sadly relieved. The burden had been much more than she'd imagined, and she was physically and emotionally exhausted. On top of that, she'd felt utterly hopeless because nothing seemed to slow the steady progress of the awful disease that was stealing her mom away. She'd called Isak and Rumer to let them know, and they'd each asked, hesitantly, if she thought she could handle the transition alone. Beryl had said she could—after all, it was just a suitcase and some pictures.

But, as it turned out, it wasn't just a suitcase and some pictures—it had been the most heart-wrenching thing she'd ever done. Tears had filled her eyes as she promised she'd come every day, and Mia had nodded trustingly, trying to understand. Beryl had clung to her and Mia had held her daughter close, trying to be a comfort. When Beryl left, she'd turned around at the end of the hall, and Mia, looking lost and small, had smiled, trying to be brave and waving uncertainly. Beryl had waved back, tears streaming down her cheeks and feeling as if she had just betrayed the one person she loved most on earth.

There was very little traffic headed into Boston that early May evening and Beryl breezed down 93 onto 90 and zipped off the airport exit without incident. She found a spot in short-term parking, hurried into the terminal, and scanned the arrival/departure screen. Immediately, her heart sank—Rumer's flight was delayed by three hours! She pulled her cell phone out of her pocket and realized she'd missed two calls and one text. She read the text and realized that her sister had written to tell her she was going to be late. *That's what I get for not checking this stupid phone,* she chided herself.

She sat down in a chair and listened to her first message. It was from Isak: *"Hi, Ber. I'm catching an earlier flight tomorrow, but don't worry—you don't have to pick me up. As much as I'd love to ride up to New Hampshire in that cool Mini, I'm just gonna rent. Love ya!"* Beryl smiled, picturing her oldest sister—tall, feisty, and redheaded. Of course she was going to rent; she had points, money, miles—she traveled all the time—Beryl was sure the Hertz guy would be waiting for her, holding her keys when she got off the plane. That's how life was for Isak—if she told the earth to stop, it would come to a shuddering halt, its axis swaying with the unexpected pressure.

Rumer, on the other hand, was not as worldly as Isak, but she'd definitely seen more of it than Beryl. Like Beryl, she didn't have points, money, or miles, but she had spent a semester of her junior year traveling abroad, and she'd finally broken the bonds of home and moved to Montana. But Rumer never cared about having a car when she was home. She was a free spirit and went wherever the road took her or, in this case, wherever her little sister drove her—and she loved being met at the gate by someone more dear to her than the Hertz guy.

Beryl sighed and pushed the button to hear the second message. *"Hi, Beryl, it's Micah—Micah Coleman. I know—I probably don't need to clarify that—how many Micahs could you possibly know? Anyway, I'm sure you're wondering how I got this number. Well, I tried to call the shop, but there was no answer and my mom saw this number on an old Tranquility business card. She told me about your mom and I'm . . . I'm so sorry. Your mom was a wonderful lady. Anyway, I just wanted to tell you . . . and find out if there are any plans for her service. Listen, I'm home, and by home, I mean New Hampshire. You have my cell number now so—if there's anything you need—anything at all—call me. All right—talk to you soon."*

Beryl pushed replay to listen to Micah's message again and smiled at his question about how many Micahs she could possibly know—it was true, she only knew one. She hesitated, her finger hovering over the button with the green phone icon—it was serendipitous that he should call when she'd just been thinking of him. She hadn't seen him since that fateful day three years ago and, ever since, she hadn't had time to think of anyone but her mom. She'd been overwhelmed with—well, life! She stood and slipped the phone into her pocket. She'd call him when the arrangements were set. Her stomach growled and she realized she hadn't eaten lunch or dinner. She wandered through the terminal, looking for someplace to grab a bite, and wondered what she was going to do for the next three hours. She could almost go home, feed the cat, and come back before

Rumer arrived. She saw a Dunkin' Donuts and bought a small black coffee and an egg-white veggie wrap, found a seat near the window, and stared out into the darkness.

The last several months of Mia's life had been a blur of despair and uncertainty. "I just don't know if she's going to pull through," Beryl had told her sisters on the phone. They'd been through it all before: Mia had had an undiagnosed urinary tract infection in October, and she'd been so sick and unresponsive that the aides had started giving Beryl consolatory hugs. Beryl, in turn, had tearfully reported to her sisters that it didn't look good and they'd flown home immediately. But by the time they'd arrived, the antibiotics had kicked in and Mia was rebounding. "I'm sorry," Beryl had said. "If you'd seen her, you would've thought she was at death's door." Isak and Rumer had insisted it was okay; they knew she was carrying the lion's share of their mom's care and they were just thankful she was there.

A mild winter had followed, bringing nagging colds to the nursing home, and although Mia only ended up with a cough, it had lingered annoyingly. In early spring, the respiratory ailments had resurfaced. Everyone had been coughing and sneezing again—so much so that Beryl had started carrying a bottle of Purell in her pocket. She'd sat with Mia in her room, carefully trimmed her nails, rubbed Purell on her hands, and then smoothed them with Curel hand lotion. "They should combine these two products," she'd said with a smile, gently rubbing the cream into Mia's hands. "Cu-Pu-Rel!" She'd laughed and Mia had gazed at her with a half-smile, not understanding. Beryl had gently rested her forehead against her mom's, gazed into her blue eyes, and whispered, "I love you so much, Mum."

Slowly and softly, Mia had murmured back, "I love you— more—than—you—know." Tears had filled Beryl's eyes. She hadn't heard her mom say those words in a long time. She left that day feeling lighthearted, but when she returned the next day, her heart filled up with fear—Mia was still in bed, her breathing labored and raspy, and her gaze unseeing. The nurse said she hadn't eaten anything and, within hours, she was rushed to the hospital with possible pneumonia.

Beryl had sent another cautionary alarm out to her sisters. "She's on antibiotics, but I don't know if she'll respond this time. She's very weak and she doesn't open her eyes. It's almost like there's something else going on . . ." She hesitated. "I hate to make you fly home again for no reason, but I just don't know . . ."

Beryl had called her next-door neighbor to take care of Flannery and stopped by the shop to feed Thoreau. When she'd returned to the hospital, there was little change. A nurse had offered to wheel in a cot, but Beryl had declined.

"She can hear you if you talk to her," the nurse had said gently, bringing her a cup of coffee and a sandwich. "Their hearing is the last to go. . . ."

Beryl had looked up in surprise. "The last to go?"

The nurse had searched Beryl's eyes. "Hon, if there's anyone you think would want to see her, you'd better give them a call."

"Isn't there something we can do?"

"Oh, hon, there're feeding tubes and breathing tubes that can prolong life. . . . But do you think that's what your mom would've wanted?"

Beryl had been stunned—this wasn't her decision to make . . . *alone*. She'd stroked her mom's lovely face, now thin and drawn, as tears had filled her eyes. "Oh, Mum, what would you have wanted?" she'd whispered.

She'd called Rumer and Isak again, and they said they'd come right away . . . and they'd both assured her that Mia would not want to be kept alive with tubes. Through that night,

Beryl had dozed on and off in the chair, but she'd never let go of her mom's hand and, by the next morning, when she awoke with a start, she'd noticed that her breathing had changed again.

"Isak and Ru are coming, Mum," she'd whispered, touching her soft, white hair. "They're coming to see you." Tears had streamed down her cheeks. "Please don't go . . ." With her heart breaking, Beryl had gently kissed the hand that was so like her own and held it against her wet cheek. She'd gazed at the lovely face and whispered, "Oh, Mum, I love you so much."

Within the hour, Mia had slipped away.

Beryl sipped her cold coffee and shivered. She looked up at the arrival/departure screen and realized that Rumer's flight had been updated. Her heart pounded—she'd be landing soon!

❧ 4 ❧

A wave of people poured through the gate, bringing chaos and noise to the quiet waiting area. Beryl spotted Rumer first, her blond head bobbing along in the sea of strangers. Although Rumer was twenty-two months older, she could hardly be considered a big sister. Like Mia and Beryl, she was only 5'2" ... *when* she was standing on her tiptoes and holding her head high. She was a blond version of Beryl, and she wore her wispy sun-streaked hair pulled back in a long, thick braid. Her cheerful, freckled face always had a ready smile, but as soon as she saw Beryl that night, her eyes filled with tears. The two sisters made their way through the crowd and fell into each other's arms—their grief spilling over like water over a breaching dam.

"I'm so sorry I wasn't here," Rumer whispered into her sister's wispy dark hair. "I'm sorry you had to go through this alone." Beryl nodded, trying to brush back her tears, but they just kept coming. "Oh, Ber," Rumer murmured, pulling her closer. "I'm so sorry."

After a while, Rumer pulled back and searched her sister's eyes. "You know what I was thinking?"

Beryl shook her head and Rumer continued, "I was thinking you were there for both Mum and Dad." She held Beryl's face in her hands and gently wiped away her tears. "You were there for Mum when Dad died, and yesterday, you were there when Mum needed you most."

Beryl considered her sister's words and Rumer nodded, smiling through her tears before wrapping her little sister in another long hug. When they pulled apart, Rumer looked down at her sister's mud-spattered blouse and smiled. "What happened?"

"Don't ask," Beryl said, shaking her head.

Finally, with their arms around each other, the two sisters left the terminal.

"So, how's my nephew?" Beryl asked, opening the trunk for Rumer to drop in her old canvas duffel and the leather backpack she'd carried since high school.

Rumer smiled. "He's fine—fresh as ever!"

"I hope you have pictures."

"I do; they're on my old phone, though, so they're not very good. Honestly, he looks more like Will every day—same dark eyes and boyish grin. He's only ten and he already has girls calling him every night."

Beryl laughed, knowing her sister was going to have her hands full. "And . . . how's Will?"

"He's okay—busy. I hope they come."

Beryl closed the trunk and looked up in surprise, not realizing there was a chance Rumer's family wouldn't come. "Why wouldn't they come?"

"Will wasn't sure he could get away, and I didn't want to take Rand out of school for a whole week—he'd fall so far behind. Not to mention the expense . . ." Her voice trailed off, sounding sad, and Beryl searched her face. In the glow from the dashboard, she could see her sister's eyes were glistening with tears.

Beryl reached for her hand. "Ru, what's wrong?"

Rumer sighed. "Oh, Ber, I wasn't going to say anything . . ." She paused tearfully. "Will moved out a month ago. . . ."

"Oh, Ru, I'm so sorry. Why?"

Rumer shrugged. "You know us. We fight all the time, and it's been no better out there. Money is tight and it puts Will on edge. He works as much as he can—so much that he never has time for Rand—or me. We fight about that—we fight about not having any money—and now that he's moved out, it's even harder to get by. Paying for two more plane tickets will absolutely sink us."

In the darkness, Beryl nodded. "You know, I hate to say this when Mum's not even buried yet, but you should remind him that once we sell the house, you'll be able to pay for the plane tickets . . . *and* probably a lot of other things."

"I know, but who knows how long that'll take—estates take forever to settle and we need the money now."

"Well, I'm sure you could borrow it from Isak."

Rumer laughed. "Blueberry," she said, using their mom's childhood nickname for her sister, "do you have any idea how much money I already owe Isak?"

Beryl shook her head and Rumer sighed. "Pretty soon, I'm gonna have to give her my first-born son!"

"Well, I'm sure she wouldn't mind having Rand around. After all, I don't think she enjoys having an empty nest. Having only Matt to talk to at the dinner table is definitely putting a strain on their marriage." Rumer laughed, knowing Isak wasn't adjusting very well to having both kids in college—not to mention that her fiftieth birthday was looming.

"If anyone is material for a midlife meltdown, it's Isak," Rumer surmised with an affectionate chuckle.

Beryl nodded in agreement. "It was one thing when Tommy went off, but now that Meghan's in college, too, she's pretty lost." The sisters were quiet for a while, considering how time marched on, sparing no one.

"I know it's late," Beryl said finally, "but we have to stop at the shop."

Rumer, who'd been fiddling with the radio and just settled on a country station playing a Kenny Chesney song, looked over at her little sister with raised eyebrows. "Did you forget to feed Thoreau again?"

Beryl laughed. "Hey, I've had a lot on my mind. You're lucky I remembered you!"

"By the way, did you get my message?"

"I did—after I was at the airport."

"Oh, Ber, don't you check your phone?"

"Sometimes . . ."

Rumer shook her head. "How are Thoreau and Flan-O?"

"They're fine for two old coots! Flan is as flatulent as ever and, when it happens, she looks back at her hind end curiously like she doesn't have any idea where the sound came from . . . or the wonderful smell. She's too funny. When I brought her to the house today, she marched in like she owned the place."

"Has she adjusted to living with you?"

Beryl laughed and shook her head. "Of course, nothing fazes that dog. She takes everything in stride—I should say waddle." She paused. "Did I tell you I used to bring her to the nursing home?"

Rumer laughed. "No . . ."

Beryl nodded. "Yup, she'd trot down the hall, saying hello to everyone. The patients loved her. Even Millie, who never acknowledged anyone, always whispered hello to Flanny—that's what she called her. She was such a character." Beryl paused, then added softly, "I guess she still is. . . ."

Rumer looked over at her sister. "It was great that you could bring Flan."

Beryl nodded, thinking of all the patients who had always

been lined up in their chairs or wheelchairs along the hall. "They're going to miss seeing Flan," she said, suddenly realizing that her absence might actually affect the lives of the remaining residents. "Smiling John, and Ethel, who always bickered with Ruth, but stopped when she saw Flan coming along; and Millie, who always saved a cookie for her; and George, who paced the halls; Frank and Jim and Betty, who never had any visitors." Tears stung Beryl's eyes and her sister looked at her in amazement.

"Ber, you know all the other patients' names?"

Beryl brushed back her tears. "Silly, isn't it?"

"No, sweetie, it's not silly—it's so you!"

"Well, they're going to miss seeing Flan. . . ."

"You can still take her to see them. After all, it seems Flan enjoyed her role as therapy dog."

Beryl nodded. "You're right, maybe we will. Otherwise, Millie will end up with a whole pocketful of cookie crumbs just waiting for Flan to come see her."

"You are too funny," Rumer said, shaking her head.

Beryl parked under the streetlight outside the shop and Rumer looked up at the sign over the door. She had designed and painted the wooden teacup with the word *Tranquility* floating steamily above its rim, and given it to Mia for Christmas the year she'd opened the shop; and although she'd given it a fresh coat of paint in recent years, it definitely needed another one. Beryl followed her gaze and read her thoughts. "Maybe while you're home . . . ?"

"Maybe," Rumer said with a smile. "Although we're going to be pretty busy."

Beryl sighed in agreement. "You're right." She unlocked the door to the shop and turned on the light. Thoreau looked up, blinking his eyes. "Sorry, buddy."

Rumer closed the door behind her and Thoreau, spying his old friend, hopped down and brushed against Rumer's legs, purring loudly. Rumer knelt down and scratched his head. "How are you, old pie?" Thoreau jumped up, lightly placing his paw on Rumer's knee, and greeted her, nose-to-nose. "Thanks for the warm welcome in the middle of the night," she whispered, stroking his soft fur. The old cat purred happily while Beryl looked on.

"Hey, you, where's my hello?" she teased.

Rumer grinned and whispered, "It's okay if you don't want to say hello to her. I know she forgot to feed you—again! I'd ignore her too."

While Rumer and Thoreau got reacquainted, Beryl went behind the counter and filled his bowl. Thoreau heard the sound of kibble hitting plastic and darted after her. "Wow! Good thing we came by. Are you sure you fed him yesterday?"

Beryl paused, trying to remember. "I think so—these last few days have been a blur."

"Speaking of food . . ." Rumer began.

Beryl looked up in surprise. "Have you eaten?"

Rumer shook her head. "I wasn't very hungry—especially for airplane food."

"You should've said something. We could've stopped." She looked in the refrigerator. "I can warm up some croissants."

"That sounds good."

Then, in her best *Downton Abbey* accent, Beryl asked, "Can I interest you in a spot of tea?"

Rumer laughed. "What do you have in mind?"

"We have a new Lemon Myrtle."

"That sounds good too. Need help?"

"Nope," Beryl answered, filling the teakettle.

Rumer plopped down in the warm spot Thoreau had just vacated and looked around. The shop was exactly as she remembered.

Once home to a small market, the little storefront had sat empty for many years until Mia, seeing its potential, gathered her meager savings and what was left of Tom's insurance and bought the space outright. She'd sold the two big freezers and, with the profit, completely transformed the interior.

Donning face masks and coveralls, they'd pulled down the cracking plaster walls and swept up the debris; then Mia had hired a local contractor to Sheetrock, tape, sand, and install wainscoting. Keeping the wide oak floor had been the easiest decision; Mia had rented a sander and refinished it herself, and although the finish had since worn through in the entrance and around the counter, most of it had aged to a warm honey hue. They'd painted the new walls and the original tin ceiling a creamy white, and offset it by painting the wainscoting a lovely ocean green. When it came to furnishings, Mia had finally settled on a classic arts-and-crafts style of café tables and chairs. Rumer still remembered poring over the catalogue with her sisters until they'd finally convinced her to buy the style she liked best. Even though it had been more expensive, it had obviously been a good choice because the cherry finish—wiped down thousands of times since then—still glowed in the soft, warm light of the lamps that hung over each table.

On the far end of the room was an old tile fireplace that Mia had always dreamed of having restored. She'd gotten as far as having an oak mantle installed above it and decorating it with tiny white Christmas lights woven into a faux garland of red berries. The effect was festive and cozy, and she ended up keeping the lights up year-round, adding stockings and ornaments at Christmastime. Above the fireplace hung a beautiful landscape painting, and beside it was a tall wooden bookcase where gift items—mugs, teapots, linen napkins, beeswax candles, and bluebird houses that a local craftsman sold on commission—were displayed. There was a second bookshelf with a sign above it that said BOOK EXCHANGE; this was a favorite draw for the regulars who liked to drop off their latest read and peruse the ever-changing selection for a new one.

There was a glass case in front of the counter that was usually full of tarts, pastries, croissants, and cakes, but Rumer noticed it was empty and decided her sister must have cleaned it out and put a hold on orders. The shelves displaying every kind of tea imaginable, however, were neatly stocked and arranged by country of origin. Finally, on the wall behind the counter, painted in mission-style lettering, was one of her mom's favorite Thoreau quotes: *"Go confidently in the direction of your dreams! Live the life you've imagined."* It was the one last touch—along with some stenciled paintings of teacups and steam—that Rumer had painted.

Beryl peered over the counter, interrupting her sister's thoughts. "Mug or china?"

"Mmmm . . . mug."

A moment later, Beryl came around the counter carrying a tray on which was a sunny yellow teapot, two croissants oozing with melting chocolate, and two sea green mugs with the word *Tranquility* painted inside their rims. She put the tray on a table and Rumer joined her.

"Ber, did Mum ever tell you where she got that painting?"

Beryl looked up at the beautiful old painting above the mantle and shook her head. "She didn't, but sometimes I saw her gazing at it for a long time—seeming to be lost in her thoughts." The evocative painting depicted a rosy sunset filtering through lazy autumn leaves. Long shadows contrasted against long angles of sunlight that stretched across the canvas, drawing one's eye to a small cabin tucked back in the sun-dappled woods. Beside the cabin was a tremendous oak tree that must have been centuries old. The windows of the cabin glowed warmly, and wisps of white smoke drifted from its chimney. Beryl had always been drawn to the scene. Who lived in that cabin? And what did he do with his time?

"I guess we'll never know . . ." Rumer mused as Beryl scooted into the chair across from her.

"I guess not," Beryl agreed with a sigh. She leaned back wearily. "I've missed doing this."

Rumer looked up. "Doing what?"

"Sharing a pot of tea at the end of the day. I can't remember the last time . . ." She stopped in midsentence. "I take that back. I do remember the last time—Mum was sitting in the armchair by the window and I handed her her favorite china teacup and saucer from the set that had belonged to Gram. I should've known better. She took one sip and the heat of the tea must have startled her, because she pulled it away from her lips and the cup slipped from her hand, shattering it. She was very upset." Beryl shook her head sadly. "Oh, Ru, I wish I could've kept her home. Then none of this would've happened."

"You can't think that way, Ber. You don't know that. You did the best you could."

Beryl looked away, her eyes filling with tears. "I miss her so much."

Rumer reached for her sister's hand. "I miss her, too, but you know she didn't like depending on other people for everything . . . and not being able to remember anything."

"I know—it's absolutely the worst thing that can happen to a person."

She shook her head sadly as she poured tea into the mugs. Then she nodded toward the croissants. "Eat one—while it's warm."

Rumer took a bite out of a croissant and chocolate dripped down her chin. She reached for a napkin and grinned. "Mmmm, you make the best chocolate croissants."

"It's Mum's recipe, silly."

Rumer rolled her eyes. "I know, silly."

5

Isak slipped quietly out of bed, showered, smoothed Oil of Olay onto her face and neck, brushed out her thick auburn hair, lightly swept her lashes with waterproof mascara, dressed in the Elie Tahari slacks and blouse she'd laid out the night before, and tiptoed down the stairs. She dropped in a Keurig cup and, while it brewed, jotted a few words on a sticky note: *Didn't want to wake you. I'll call when I land!* As she poured the steaming coffee into her travel mug, she heard a sound and turned to see Matt leaning against the door frame, wearing sweatpants and a faded Columbia Crew sweatshirt, his blond hair tousled from sleep.

"No good-bye?" he asked.

"It's Saturday. I thought you'd like to sleep in," she answered, unflustered by her husband's unexpected appearance.

"I could drop you off. . . ."

"Don't be silly. I'll just do long-term—it's simpler." She paused and looked up. "Thank you, though."

"Where are your bags?"

"In the car."

He sighed. "So, Tommy and I fly into New York on Thursday?"

"I think so—but we haven't finalized anything, so I'll have to let you know."

"But we're picking Meghan up, right?"

"Yes, her last exam is Thursday morning, so it should work out perfectly—if the timing of a funeral *can* be perfect," she added, her voice edged with irony.

He nodded. "You gonna be okay?"

"Me?" she said with a laugh. "Always okay."

"Yeah," he said, "always good at putting up a formidable front."

"No . . ."

He pulled her into his arms. "The Isak Graham-Taylor I know never lets her guard down—she's as tough as nails."

Isak smiled and pulled away. "I've gotta go . . ."

Matt held up his hands and backed off in visible frustration. "Go," he said, nodding toward the door.

"I'll call when I get there."

"Fine."

She looked up, surprised by his tone. "What's the matter?"

"Nothing."

She shook her head. "All right . . . bye."

He nodded, stood in the doorway, and watched as her black Beemer pulled away.

Two hours later, Isak slid her Gucci carry-on under the seat in front of her, pulled down her tray, and wondered if they served Bloody Marys on the early-morning flight—she could use one! As the plane taxied to the end of the runway, she discreetly checked her iPhone one last time. There was a text from Meghan: **have a safe trip, mom. love you! see you soon!** ☺ She wrote back quickly: **love you, too, honey! can't wait to see you!** Then turned off her phone and clicked her seat belt. She was glad the seat next to her was empty—she didn't feel much like chatting. Superficial conversations with strangers about reasons for travel and family backgrounds always left her feeling weary and empty—and today would have been especially hard. She didn't want to explain the reason for her trip or thank a stranger for their sympathy. She just wanted to be left alone. She leaned back in her seat, looked out her window, watching the California skyline and highways disappear, and thought about Matt.

Isak couldn't pinpoint the exact moment when "the big chill," as she called it, had settled on her twenty-four-year marriage. She'd met Matt in the spring of her senior year at Barnard—the college their daughter, Meghan, now attended—and at that point, she'd been thankful for finally meeting someone—anyone—of the opposite sex before graduating from the famous all-women's college. She'd been working in the library and he'd come in looking for a medical journal. She could still see him standing there—blond-haired, blue-eyed, tan, and probably wearing the same sweatshirt he'd had on that morning. He'd been pretty darn cute—in fact, he still was—but in that hooded sweatshirt, faded Levi's, and Docksiders with no socks, he'd had that carefree, preppy look she'd loved so much when she was younger. He'd signed out the journal—and she'd tried not to stare as he walked away. The next day, he'd returned with the journal and shyly asked her if she had time for a cup of coffee.

They'd found a small café near campus and he'd impressed her with the woeful tales of his premed days at Harvard—and now at Columbia, preparing for residency. She'd revealed that she was finishing her business degree and hoped to someday travel the world. They'd talked until the owner came over and told them he was closing; then they'd moved to a college bar across the street and ordered drinks and a plate of calamari. By the end of the evening, Isak—who'd never fallen for any guy—was falling for a medical student named Matt Taylor.

They'd married while he was still in residency and then

moved to California, where he quickly became a well-respected heart surgeon, and where she climbed the corporate ladder of an up-and-coming software company. She was twenty-nine when Tommy was born; Meghan had come along twenty-two months later. Their lives had been busy and full; the kids' activities filled their days with soccer, basketball, and baseball, dance and swim lessons, PTO meetings, dinners on the run—and little time for each other. But then the kids had suddenly graduated from high school and left for college—embarking on lives of their own—leaving their parents alone with too much free time. Isak missed the busyness of having the kids around; she missed looking in on them as they slept—and, most of all, she missed being needed. She tried to fill her time with work and travel, but the empty void the kids had left was almost too much to bear—she'd never felt so irrelevant and lonely.

Isak looked out the window at the floor of puffy clouds and the bright blue sky above it as tears spilled down her cheeks. She'd give anything to talk to her mom once more. There was still so much she wanted to say to her, so much she wanted to ask: *Had she ever felt this way? How in the world had she managed after their father died? How had she filled the aching emptiness?* "Oh, Mum, I have so much to be thankful for—why do I feel this way?" she whispered. She closed her eyes and realized that she hadn't thought twice about moving far from home . . . and she'd never looked back or considered how her mom had felt about it—and now it was too late. She'd never again get to tell her how much she loved her . . . or say how sorry she was for not making it home more often.

6

Flan was lying on her bed with her legs up in the air, snoring loudly, when Beryl came into the kitchen to make coffee. She knelt down and scratched the exposed, round belly. "Position is everything in life, isn't it, you silly ole girl?" Flan opened one eye, stretched her short legs straight out, and smacked her tongue contentedly. Gravity pulled her jowls back, exposing her teeth and making it look as if she was smiling. "You're so ladylike," Beryl teased. "Do you need to go out?" Flan rolled over, scrambled to her feet, shook, yawned, and looked up expectantly. "Come on, then," she said, pushing open the screen. Flan waddled down the two steps and promptly squatted in the leaves with her head up, sniffing the early-morning air. Then she started to snort her way across the yard, but Beryl reminded her it was time for breakfast and she turned around and trotted back up the steps, licking her lips.

As Flan wolfed down her breakfast, Beryl reached for the coffee and gazed out the window. It had been after midnight when they'd finally gotten home and the stars had sparkled brightly, but clouds had drifted in overnight and the muted sun hung weakly in the milky white sky. She hadn't seen a forecast in days, and as she filled the perk pot and copper kettle with cold water and measured coffee, she wondered if it was going to rain. While the coffeepot sputtered to life, she put the kettle on, lit a match under it, and adjusted the ring of blue flame that sprang up, making the kettle shudder and click. For a moment, the queasy scent of gas reminded her of the event that had triggered the whirlwind of decisions she and her sisters had made. She opened the fridge to see what they could have for breakfast and then remembered the oatmeal. It was a perfect day for warm oatmeal with rivulets of melting brown sugar and cream, chopped walnuts, apples, and raisins—just like they'd had on school mornings when they were kids.

Beryl measured the oats and water into a small pot and lit another burner. When it came to a boil, she gave the oatmeal a stir and lowered the flame to simmer. Meanwhile, the kettle started to whistle and she scooped a teaspoon of loose tea leaves into the mesh infuser that hung over the stove. She dropped it into Mia's old teapot, poured steaming water over the infuser, swished it around, and left it to steep.

"You certainly are noisy," Rumer said sleepily, pulling a faded blue sweatshirt over her head.

Beryl eyed the sweatshirt. "There's a relic from the past."

Rumer pulled her braid out of the back and grinned. "I know, I found it in the closet."

"I think it's mine. You ripped the neck of yours."

Rumer frowned. "I did not."

"You did—remember when you were trying to get Jimmy Dixon to notice you?"

"Hmm . . . well, maybe. I guess that's possible; he was pretty cute—except for that gap between his front teeth."

Beryl rolled her eyes and Rumer laughed. She poured coffee

into a big blue mug and cradled it in her hands, breathing in the fresh aroma. "Thanks for the coffee," she said, peering into the simmering pot. "Mmmm . . . you're making oatmeal too?!"

"Yup. Want to chop up some walnuts and apple for it?"

Rumer looked around the kitchen. "Ber, I'm beginning to think that getting through everything that's in this house is going to take a lot longer than a week. Have you seen Mum's office?"

Beryl stirred the oatmeal while Rumer chopped up a handful of walnuts and apple slices. "I know. It looks overwhelming, but I think a lot of papers can be thrown away. I don't know when it happened, but at some point, she started saving everything." She spooned the steaming oatmeal into bowls, sprinkled generous spoonfuls of brown sugar and raisins onto each one, and then drizzled cream on top. Rumer added the walnuts and apples, and they sat down at the old Formica table that had been the site of countless school projects and childhood meals. Flan, who'd been watching their every move, waddled over and curled up between them. Beryl tucked her feet under Flan's warm body, scooped a small spoonful of oatmeal from the inside edge of her bowl, and blew on it softly. "It's so strange to be here without Mum."

Rumer looked out the window and nodded. "It's hard to look around and see all of her things and know she'll never use them again. She'll never make apple crisp in her glass Pyrex dish or a pot roast in the big cast-iron pot she's had since the beginning of time . . . or wear her silly pink hat . . . or any of her blinking holiday earrings."

"Or, out of the blue, start quoting poetry or Bible verses," Beryl quipped. "I think she had a Bible verse for every occasion. Which reminds me—we need to think of some for the service."

"Have you talked to Reverend Peterson?"

"He came to the hospital and then stopped by my apartment to see how I was doing. He said he can meet with us anytime, so I told him maybe this afternoon."

Rumer nodded. "Are you keeping your apartment?"

Beryl looked up in surprise. "Of course, why wouldn't I?"

"I don't know—you could stay here."

"In this drafty old place?" She shook her head. "It's too big and lonely . . . and full of memories. My apartment is cozy and bright and just the right size for me and one stubborn old bull-dog." She rubbed her feet on Flan's side and Flan groaned, rolling onto her back.

After Beryl had graduated from Wellesley with a degree in English and the dream to author the next great American novel, she'd moved back home to help her mom in the shop—temporarily. But the years had slipped by and, except for an occasional journal entry, she'd found little time for writing. Gradually, she'd lost sight of her dream—and her hope of ever finding someone with whom she could spend the rest of her life. Finally, as her thirtieth birthday approached, she decided that being an old maid was bad enough—she wasn't going to live in her mom's house forever, too—so she started to keep an eye out for a place of her own. After several months of halfhearted looking, she noticed a small sign in the window of a newly renovated Victorian in town, and stopped to inquire. The downstairs apartment had floor-to-ceiling windows that were trimmed with lustrous dark mahogany, a huge fireplace with a stone hearth, and a claw-foot tub with a stained glass window over it in the bathroom; the kitchen had been updated with new appliances and granite countertops, which had made her think there was no way she'd be able to afford it, but the owner said he'd inherited the house, updated it, and was anxious to find someone responsible and neat to rent it so he wouldn't have to worry.

He said the price was entirely negotiable. That evening, Beryl had brought Mia back to see it, and although her mom had had mixed feelings about her moving out, she'd understood her need for independence and gave her blessing. Beryl had signed the lease that night, and a week later—with help from Rumer, Will, and her mom—she'd moved in. They'd celebrated with pizza that was delivered to *her* apartment and beer that had been chilled in *her* refrigerator. It had given her a wonderful feeling of new possibilities.

"I love my apartment," Beryl said. "Besides, this house needs so much work—I couldn't afford to buy you two out . . . never mind fix it up. It'll be sad to let it go, but hopefully the right person will come along and love it as much as we do."

Rumer looked around, trying to come to terms with the inevitable prospect of selling their childhood home. "I just wish we didn't have to sell it," she said sadly. She slowly stirred her oatmeal. "So, what time is Isak's flight?"

Beryl glanced at the clock. "She gets in around three."

"Are we picking her up?"

"What do you think?"

"Not . . ." Rumer said with a knowing chuckle.

They ate in silence and then Beryl stood to clear their bowls. "We can start without her, though—if you're up to it."

Rumer yawned and stretched. "I don't think I'm ever going to be up to it."

As Beryl filled the sink with hot, sudsy water, she remembered one other thing they needed to do. "The undertaker is stopping by this afternoon, so we need to pick out some clothes."

Rumer looked puzzled. "I thought Mum was being cremated."

"She is . . . but he said out of respect . . ."

"Oh, I didn't know . . ." Rumer said quietly.

"I know, I didn't either . . ."

They were both lost in thought as they washed and dried the

dishes. Finally, Rumer smiled. "How about her tan slacks and navy blazer with a white blouse? She always looked so sharp in that outfit."

Beryl smiled. "Yeah, that's perfect—she'll be the best-dressed angel in heaven!"

$\backsim 7 \backsim$

"We're going to need a lot of boxes!" Rumer groaned, looking at the mountain of clothes on the bed. "I'm beginning to think Mum kept everything. There are clothes in this closet that I wore when I was twelve!"

Beryl laughed. "Well, it's all your stuff and you didn't get rid of it either."

"We're going to have to hire one of those estate companies," she said, dragging a box out of the back of the closet and pulling open its flaps. "Hey!" she exclaimed. "Here are our games!"

Beryl looked over her sister's shoulder at the contents of the box. Lined up, side by side in their original boxes, were all the games of their childhood: Parcheesi, Clue, Scrabble, Checkers, Monopoly, and Yahtzee; there was also a plain black box with no name.

"There's our Ouija board! I always wondered what happened to that."

Rumer laughed. "Do you remember the time we had Sarah Jacobs over for a candlelight séance?"

Beryl sat down on the corner of her old twin bed—which was the only place left to sit—and grinned. "Yeah, we told her we were contacting old lady Johnson so we could ask her what really happened to her husband. Isak was so good at acting like she was possessed—even I believed it for a minute."

"Yeah, and Sarah was so scared she went down and told Mum she had to go home. I honestly thought she was going to wet her pants!"

"And Mum was so mad—do you remember?"

"I remember," Rumer said. "She said we were mean, but it was so funny—and Sarah deserved it."

"We were mean," Beryl said remorsefully.

"Ber, girls *are* mean—and manipulative. It's in their nature, except in rare cases—like you! Knowing how I acted at times makes me very glad I have a son."

"Well, Mum was right."

"I know, thank goodness we outgrew it."

"I wonder what happened to Sarah."

"She married John Winston and moved to Vermont. They have a dairy farm and something like ten kids—all under the age of fourteen."

"How do you know that?"

"Facebook. You should join. It's fun to see what old class-mates are up to—and what they look like!"

"Well, at least she got married," Beryl said gloomily, ignoring her sister's enthusiasm for Facebook.

Rumer looked up from where she was kneeling in the closet. "Ber, marriage isn't all it's cracked up to be—trust me! Besides, would you want to be married to John Winston and have ten of his kids?"

"No—but I'd like to find out for myself that it's not all it's cracked up to be."

Rumer sat down next to her on the bed. "You just haven't found the right guy yet."

Beryl shook her head. "Rumer, I'm almost forty-five and I have zero prospects—it doesn't look very promising—and having kids is almost completely out of the picture. Even if I was pregnant at this very moment, it would be risky, and I don't want to be an old mom."

Rumer sighed, knowing she was right. "You'll meet someone, Ber. I just know it. Remember what Mum used to say: 'God has a plan, and even when it doesn't look very promising, you just have to trust that He has something good in mind.' And, Ber, if anyone deserves something good, it's you! Besides, Mum's up there now and I'm sure she's pulling some strings."

Beryl laughed, knowing she was right. "I wonder why Mum never remarried."

Rumer shrugged. "It would've taken a very brave man to marry a woman with three little girls."

"That's true . . ."

"Besides, she used to say that Dad was irreplaceable and she didn't want to bring another man into our lives. I think she worried that it might not work out."

"I don't know, Ru. I've always had this feeling that there was something else that held her back, something going on in her life that she didn't talk about."

"What do you mean?"

"It's hard to explain. At first, I thought it was just a normal mother-daughter connection, but then, in recent years, it was as if I could feel what she was feeling—with the same intensity she was feeling it."

Rumer frowned.

"I know, it sounds weird. Maybe I'm crazy!"

Rumer shook her head. "You're not crazy. But I wonder if it has something to do with the accident," she offered. "Mum was pregnant with you when they had the accident—and it was so traumatic."

"Maybe. I honestly don't know, but the older I got, the

more I felt it. Anyway, I've also always had this feeling there was something in her heart that she never told anyone. I don't know what it was, but in the last year, as her memory declined, I heard her say the name *David* on several occasions. I couldn't figure out who she was talking about, and the one time I asked her, she just gazed out the window and didn't answer. I forgot all about it until yesterday when I was putting away her wedding rings and came across a different ring and a card in her jewelry box. The card was signed: *Always, David.*"

Rumer's eyes grew wide. "Really?!"

Beryl nodded. "Come see."

Rumer followed her sister across the hall and Beryl pulled open the drawer of their mom's jewelry box. The sapphire ring sparkled brightly. "Oh, my," Rumer said softly. Then her expression changed from one of amazement to one of puzzlement. "How come I never saw Mum wear this?"

"I don't know—I didn't either," Beryl answered, reaching for the card. "That's funny," she said, "the card's not here." She looked behind the dresser and then under the bed and found it surrounded by dust mice. "I must have dropped it when I ran outside to get Flan before . . ." She looked at her sister and shook her head. "Long story—anyway, that's it."

Rumer studied the delicate painting of the cardinal and then opened it to read the inscription. "I have no idea who David is . . . or was. Maybe Isak knows." Just then, a car door slammed and they looked out the window to see a red Ford Mustang parked next to the Mini. "Speak of the devil," Rumer said with a grin.

8

The morning clouds melted away as Mia's daughters stood in the driveway, embracing, smiling, and crying—all at once—their grief overwhelming them as they realized their beloved mom would never stand in the sunlight with them again—to hug . . . or cry . . . or laugh.

"Listen," Beryl exclaimed, pulling back tearfully. "Do you hear that?" Her sisters stopped talking and listened. "Peepers!" Beryl exclaimed, her heart lifting. "Mum loved that sound." A chorus of high-pitched chirping filled the air and Rumer and Isak smiled, remembering all the times they'd scooped clear, gelatinous eggs and pond water into jars and watched the little black centers of the eggs hatch into tadpoles. Then they'd pulled on their muck boots, marched dutifully back to the pond, and gently released the tadpoles into the cold, gray water. A month or so later, on a warm, sunny afternoon, they would trip down the driveway from the school bus and hear the cheerful, welcoming sound of peeping. And night after mild spring night, they'd drift to sleep listening to the wonderful sound of new life. "Mum is smiling too," Beryl said matter-of-factly, and Isak and Rumer both nodded, knowing it was true.

Suddenly realizing there was another new guest, Flannery trundled over from the direction of the pond and jumped up on Isak's tan slacks. "Oh, Flan," Isak groaned, leaning down to brush away the muddy smear. The old dog looked up and wagged her hind end, blissfully unaware of any wrongdoing. "I would've said hello to you. You didn't have to jump up," she said, scratching her big blocky head.

Beryl smiled and picked up Isak's suitcase while Rumer clicked out the handle of the rolling carry-on. Isak followed them, stopping to look up at the old farmhouse and then, with Flan at her heels, went inside.

They set the luggage just inside the door, and Isak ran her fingers lightly over the kitchen table and shook her head. "Some things never change . . ." she said wistfully as new tears spilled down her cheeks. "And some things will never be the same." Beryl put her arm around her and Isak leaned against her little sister. "And you had to weather the worst of it, Ber. I'm so sorry."

"It's okay. You got here as soon as you could," Beryl reassured her. "There was no way to know how quickly she would go."

"And . . . how bad was it?"

"It was sad . . . and really hard, but she wasn't in any pain, and I'm glad I was there."

Isak nodded, wiping under her eyes. She smiled through her tears. "Thank goodness for waterproof mascara and hemorrhoid cream." Rumer and Beryl both looked puzzled and she laughed. "Didn't Mum ever tell you? Hemorrhoid cream works like a charm for puffy eyes."

"Really?" Rumer asked incredulously.

Isak nodded. "Yup, just don't get it in your eyes."

"Mum never told me that," Beryl said. "We'll have to get some before Saturday."

"No need," Isak said as she reached into her bag and produced a new tube of Preparation H.

Beryl laughed. "Well, that's one less thing we have to think about."

As she spoke, there was a light knock at the screen door and they all looked up. Beryl immediately recognized the tall, thin figure standing on the porch and hurried over to open the door. "Hi, Mr. O'Leary."

She turned to introduce him to her sisters. "This is Mr. O'Leary—he owns the funeral home. He's also a faithful customer at Tranquility." The old gentleman smiled and reached out to shake their hands.

"I'm so very sorry for your loss," he said solemnly. "Your mother was a lovely lady." Isak and Rumer thanked him while trying not to notice his wayward appearance. Mr. O'Leary's khaki pants, held up by worn leather suspenders, were hitched well above his waist, making them three inches too short and revealing sagging wool hiking socks; his blue oxford shirt was threadbare and wrinkled, and his once-white-now-mare-gray undershirt was frayed around the neck. "Please forgive me," he said, apologetically, "I forgot my tie." As he spoke he reached up to close his collar with fingers gnarled by arthritis.

Beryl gave her sisters a warning look. "That's okay, Mr. O'Leary, we aren't dressed up either. Would you like some iced tea?"

"That sounds good," he said. She filled four glasses with ice, poured chilled tea into the glasses, and added a sprig of mint to each. He thanked her and they all sat down around the kitchen table of their childhood to discuss the burial plans for their beloved mother.

* * *

"He was very nice," Isak said after Mr. O'Leary had left with the bag of clothes for their mom—of which she had approved—and a check for four thousand dollars.

"He was," Rumer agreed, "and funny too. I never expected him to be funny, but I guess—in a business like that—you have to have a sense of humor."

"His wife passed away a year ago," Beryl said, eyeing them admonishingly. "I'm sure that's why he looked a little disheveled. He used to come in and buy Irish breakfast tea all the time—and he was always neatly dressed—but I hardly ever see him anymore."

Isak and Rumer nodded a bit remorsefully, and Isak commented, "Well, I'm glad he takes the body to the crematory himself—I don't want to end up with someone else's ashes."

"Are you sure you don't want to see her before . . . ?" Beryl asked.

Rumer shook her head. "I'd rather just remember her the way I do now." Isak nodded in agreement.

The phone rang suddenly, breaking the somber silence that had settled over the kitchen and Beryl stood to answer it. Isak and Rumer both listened quietly as she spoke. "Hi, Reverend Peterson. Yes, I think so. Hold on." She held the mouthpiece against her hand. "Are you guys all right with meeting at the church in an hour?" Rumer and Isak both nodded. "Yes, we can come," Beryl continued. She looked at the clock. "Five o'clock? That's fine—okay, see you then."

"I'm going up to change," Isak said as Beryl hung up the phone. She turned to get her bags.

"Well, before you do, we have a question for you," Rumer said, grabbing the carry-on and following her. Isak set her suitcase down in the hall outside their mom's bedroom and peered into the familiar sun-swept space as Beryl walked around the bed, opened the jewelry box, and picked up the ring. "Have you ever seen this before?"

Isak walked over, tucking her hair behind her ear, and Beryl dropped the ring into her sister's hand. Isak smiled slowly. "Not only have I seen it before . . . I've worn it."

"When?!" Beryl and Rumer asked in surprised unison.

"To my prom . . ."

Beryl and Rumer blinked in astonishment, and Isak continued, "Mum didn't know. I tucked it into my clutch before I left and slipped it on in the car, and then I put it back the next morning."

"How did you know about it?"

She shrugged. "Do you remember how we used to dress up and wear all of Mum's beads and clip-on earrings?" They nodded and she continued. "Well, one time I accidently pulled the drawer out all the way and I saw the ring . . . and I never forgot it."

"How old were you?"

Isak shrugged. "I don't know, seven or eight. Why?"

"Well, we were wondering how long she'd had it because we never saw her wear it."

Isak nodded. "I don't know why she never wore it."

"Didn't you worry you might lose it?"

Isak ran her fingers through her thick mane of red hair, fluffing it up, and grinned impishly. "Ber, when I was eighteen, I didn't worry about *anything*. Life was all about having fun and seeing how much I could get away with."

Beryl shook her head—it would never have even occurred to her to do such a thing.

Isak smiled, reading her mind. "Berry, how are you going to write the next great American novel if you don't live a little—if you never take any chances? What will you write about? Mum never wore this gorgeous ring—she never did anything out of character—and now, she's gone. Her life is over. Is that how you want your life to be?"

Beryl searched her sister's face, trying to wrap her mind

around what she'd just said, and when she answered, her voice was edged with anger. "Mum lived a good life, Isak. Maybe it wasn't as exciting as yours, but she raised three little girls all by herself, and she never lost her faith in spite of tragedy, loss, and heartache. She helped those who were less fortunate, volunteered at soup kitchens, helped little kids learn to read, and gave generously to her church. Mum made us her life, and I know she felt blessed. I don't know how many times I heard her say her cup runneth over." Tears had filled Beryl's eyes as she spoke. She couldn't believe she had to defend their mother's life to her own sister.

"I'm sorry, Ber, I didn't mean to upset you. All I meant was she could've lived a little."

"You've lived a little, Isak. You've snuck out of the house, run wild, traveled the world, driven expensive cars and hosted parties until the wee hours of the morning. Does that make your life better somehow?"

Isak swallowed hard and stared. Her youngest sister—so like their mom—wasn't fooled by her bravado. She had looked straight into her heart and seen the emptiness, and she had spoken with brutal honesty. "You're right, Beryl," she said, her voice edged with sarcasm. "I do feel like something's missing."

Beryl's mouth dropped. "I . . . I'm sorry, Isak," she stammered. She took a deep breath. "I'm just tired and stressed, and that didn't come out the way I—"

But Isak held up her hand and shook her head. "No, Ber. You're right. Mum did live a good, full life and I . . ." She stopped as tears spilled down her cheeks. "I just wish I could ask her her secret."

Beryl nodded slowly. "I wish I could too," she said softly.

Rumer, who'd been sitting on the bed, cleared her throat. "Well," she began hesitantly, "there's actually more to our question . . ." Isak looked up and Rumer handed her the card. "Did you ever see this?"

Isak opened the card and turned it over. "No—you know me . . ." she said with a weak smile. "Blinded by bling! All I saw was the ring." Her rhyming words rang true and they all laughed. Isak studied the handwriting again and slowly shook her head. "Who is David?"

Rumer shrugged. "We were hoping you would know."

9

"I think Mum would be happy with the hymns we chose," Beryl said, climbing into the back of the Mustang. "She always loved 'Here I Am, Lord'—and cried every time we sang it in church." She pulled the seat back for Rumer to get in and looked out the window. "She loved 'Spirit of Gentleness' and 'There Is a Balm in Gilead' too," she added softly.

"Those hymns are all perfect," Rumer agreed.

"I think Tommy might be willing to give a eulogy," Isak said, turning the key. The engine rumbled to life. "He has a lot of memories from spending summers with Mum when he was little. But I think we should ask someone else too."

"I wish I could say something," Beryl mused, "but I'm afraid I'd never get through it. Maybe I'll write something and let someone else read it."

"That's a good idea," Rumer said.

"I think Meghan would be willing to read one of the Scriptures," Isak added. "Would Rand want to?"

Rumer swallowed. "I don't know, Isak. He's kind of young

and his reading skills aren't the best, and I . . . I'm not even sure they're coming."

Isak looked over at her sister and just about drove off the road. "What? Why?"

"Hey!" Rumer said, reaching for the handle above her head. "Watch where you're going!"

Isak looked back at the road. "By the way, where are we going? Are you two hungry?"

"A little," Rumer said.

Beryl looked out the window. "I bought salad and stuff."

Isak glanced over her shoulder. "We have all week to eat at the house. Why don't we just go to Harlow's? It would be quick and easy—and my treat."

Beryl hesitated and then remembered the Avocado Bliss sandwich on the Harlow's Pub's menu. "Fine with me," she said. "But afterward I have to stop at the shop."

Isak and Rumer looked at each other. "Thoreau!" they said in unison.

"Why don't we just bring that poor cat back to the house for the week?" Rumer asked. "He's going to be lonely with the shop closed."

"Actually, I hadn't decided if I was going to close," Beryl confessed. She was already beginning to feel like she might need a break from her sisters, and the shop would be the perfect excuse.

"Ber, you have to—we have so much to do," Rumer said. "Just put a sign in the window. Your customers will under-stand."

Isak nodded as she parked near the restaurant. "One week won't break the business."

"It might."

"Well, if it does," she quipped, "you'll have more time for what you're supposed to be doing—writing!" As they got out of the car, she eyed Rumer. "Now, what do you mean you don't know if they're coming? It's his grandmother and he better be coming!"

"It's not that simple," Rumer said as she passed through the open door of the pub.

"It is that simple," Isak countered, smiling at the hostess. "Three, please."

The restaurant was crowded, but the hostess showed them to a table that had just been cleared. "Your waitress will be right with you," she said with a warm smile, handing them menus.

"Rumer, I don't want to hear some lame excuse about money. You're about to come into money, and if you need some until that happens, just say so."

Rumer shook her head. "Will does not want to bor—"

"Will needs to get over himself," Isak interrupted dismissively. "He always thinks he has to carry the world on his shoulders. There was a time when he was fun to be around, when he didn't take life so seriously—whatever happened to that Will?"

"I guess I happened to him," Rumer replied edgily. "You know, Isak, you're awfully quick to judge people. Not everyone has had the world handed to them."

Their waitress appeared. "Hey, ladies! My name's Lexie. Would you like to start with something to drink?"

Isak looked questioningly at her sisters, and Rumer quickly scanned the beverage list. "Hmm, I'll have a Sam Adams—Alpine Spring, if you have it." Lexie nodded and turned to Beryl.

"I think I'll have an iced t . . ." she started, but out of the corner of her eye, she noticed Isak shaking her head and quickly changed her mind. "I'll have a Corona with lime."

Isak chuckled and, giving their waitress a conspiratorial grin, said, "I'll have a Grey Goose and soda with a twist of lemon. Thanks, Lexie."

Beryl took a deep breath and felt like kicking her—hard! Isak was as overbearing as ever.

"Anyway, we'll make airline reservations on my card and you can pay me back whenever. And now that we know that it's definitely going to be Saturday, they can come out on Friday and they'll only miss one day of work and school."

Rumer sighed; she was already dreading the conversation she'd be having with Will.

Lexie returned with their drinks. "Ready to order?"

"I am," Beryl said.

Rumer groaned, "No, I haven't even looked." She reached up to tuck the loose strands of her wispy blond hair behind her ears and opened her menu.

"I guess we'll need a couple minutes," Isak said, reaching for her drink.

"No problem," Lexie said. "I'll come back."

Rumer looked up. "What are you having?"

"An Avocado Bliss." Beryl pointed to where it was on the menu.

"And . . . what are you havin'?" Rumer queried, looking at Isak.

Isak sipped her drink. "An Avocado Bliss," she said with a grin.

Rumer closed her menu. "You guys should've said so!" She took a sip of her beer, leaned back, and finally seemed to relax. Lexie came back and they ordered chips 'n' salsa and three of their famous avocado sandwiches.

Beryl squeezed her lime and pushed it down into the neck of her bottle. It dropped into the clear bottle and fizzed. She took a sip and licked her lips, savoring the lime juice on the rim.

Rumer glanced around the room and her eyes stopped at a table in the corner. "Ber, isn't that Micah Coleman?"

Beryl followed her gaze and nodded. "It is," she said with a smile. As she said this, Micah looked up and smiled at her; a moment later, he stood and reached for his jacket and an older couple and a little blond-haired girl stood too. Beryl watched the older gentleman hand Micah the little girl's jacket, and Micah knelt down and helped her slip it on. Then he reached for her hand and led the little girl across the room to their table.

"Hi, Ber," he said.

Beryl stood up, smiling, and gave Micah a hug. "Hi," came her soft reply. "I got your message and I was going to call you as soon as we finalized everything."

Micah nodded and looked over at Isak and Rumer too. "I'm sorry about your mom," he said. Rumer and Isak hadn't seen Micah in years, but they immediately remembered him as the quiet boy who'd worked in their mom's shop.

"Thank you," they replied.

Micah turned as the older couple came up behind him. "Do you remember Beryl?" he asked.

"Of course," they said, smiling and giving her a hug.

"We know all the Graham girls, Micah," his dad teased, winking at them. "You do remember that I taught English and coached cross-country at the high school they attended?" Isak and Rumer both laughed and started to stand, but Asa Coleman put up his hand. "Stay put. We just came over to say hello and how sorry we are. Your mom was a sweet lady . . . and she certainly knew her tea!"

Maddie Coleman smiled too. "Your mom was such a lovely lady and a dear friend. She used to come into school and help the first graders with their reading. She was a generous soul and we all miss her."

Beryl smiled and nodded. "Thank you, Mrs. Coleman," she said. Then she looked down at the little girl clinging to Micah's leg. "Who is your little pal?"

Micah scooped her up onto his hip. "This," he said with a grin, "is Charlotte."

"Hi, Charlotte," Beryl said softly.

The little girl blinked at her with solemn blue eyes and Micah asked, "Can you say 'hi'?"

"Hi," the little girl whispered, then buried her face in the collar of Micah's jacket.

Just then, Lexie came out from the kitchen with their appetizer and some plates, and Micah realized they hadn't eaten. "Well, I guess we'd better let you guys have your dinner."

Beryl smiled. "Micah, I'm not sure if you're planning to come . . . but the service is this Saturday at eleven."

"Okay, thanks."

They said good-bye and Charlotte waved shyly over her father's shoulder. Beryl waved back, and when she sat down, Isak and Rumer both looked at her quizzically.

"What?" Beryl asked.

"He called you?"

"Yup," Beryl said matter-of-factly, reaching for a tortilla chip and dipping it in one of the salsas. "He just wanted to say how sorry he was and find out about the arrangements."

Isak looked at Rumer. "*You* saw the look on his face, right?"

Rumer nodded. "Mmm-hmm," she said, reaching for a chip.

"What are you talking about?" Beryl asked, frowning.

"The way he looked at you," Isak said.

"Don't be silly," she protested. "Micah's married and owns a bookstore in Quincy Market."

Rumer shook her head. "Uh-uh," she said with her mouth full.

"Ber, Micah's wife passed away three years ago," Isak said. "She was diagnosed with cancer right after they found out she was pregnant, and she refused to have any treatment because she didn't want to jeopardize the baby's health. She died six months after the baby was born, and now Micah's raising that sweet little girl all by himself."

"He doesn't own the book store anymore either," Rumer added. "I think he's working for a small publisher."

"How do you know all this?" Beryl was incredulous. How did her sisters know more about Micah Coleman than she did?

"Facebook," Rumer said. "I told you to join."

Beryl groaned. "I have no interest in joining Facebook. I manage just fine keeping in touch with the people I care about."

Isak looked up. "And who are these people?"

Beryl took a sip of her beer and tried to think of some names.

Rumer grinned and teased affectionately, "Well, Ber, there's always Millie, Ethel, Ruth, Betty . . ." Beryl gave Rumer a wilting look that clearly said shut up and Isak looked puzzled, but Rumer quickly covered her tracks. "I was just teasing. . . ."

Lexie appeared with their sandwiches and asked if they needed anything.

"I'll have another drink, please," Isak said, eyeing her sisters' beers, which were still three-quarters full. "How about you two lightweights?"

"I'm good, thanks," Rumer said. "Ber, you know how to drive stick, right?"

"Yup," she answered with a grin.

"So," Isak said, ignoring the comment and eyeing Beryl curiously, "when was the last time you saw Micah?"

Beryl shook her head and held up one finger while she swallowed a bite of her sandwich. "Mmmm . . . the last time I saw him was when Mum and I went to Boston for her first appointment, and that has to be"—she looked down, calculating—"almost three years ago . . ."

"Well, the years haven't touched him. He's still cute and I love his glasses," Rumer commented.

"Just look at his father," Isak mused. "I had a wicked crush on Mr. Coleman when we were in high school, and now he must be in his early seventies and he's still incredibly good looking." She sighed. "Some men age like fine wine—they just get better. And it's genetic, Ber. Micah looks exactly like his dad did when I had him for English, so he'll probably be good looking when he's old too."

Rumer took a bite of her sandwich. "Did you and Micah ever date?"

Beryl shook her head and took a sip of her beer. "Nope . . . just friends."

"Didn't he have a crush on you, though? I vaguely remember hearing that he was going to ask you to the prom."

"I don't know where you heard that, but he never did."

"Who did you go with?" Rumer asked. "I can't remember."

Beryl took a sip of her beer. "Jimmy Dixon."

"Oh, yeah, now I remember."

"How could you forget?" Beryl teased. "You were just talking about how cute he was."

"Well, maybe that's why Micah didn't ask you—maybe Jimmy beat him to it." Rumer paused thoughtfully. "Did Micah even go to the prom?"

"I don't think so," Beryl said thoughtfully. "He was still working at the shop when I left to get ready."

"That explains it," Rumer announced with absolute certainty.

"Maybe it also explains how Jimmy Dixon turned out to be gay," Isak teased.

"No way!" Beryl exclaimed. "How do you know that?"

"How do you think?" Isak asked.

Beryl looked puzzled, but then saw the goofy looks on her sisters' faces and groaned. "Facebook . . ."

10

Beryl hung a small sign on the window of the door, switched off the lights, and, carrying a box of chamomile in one hand while cradling Thoreau in her arms, locked the door. "Don't you have a cat carrier?" Rumer asked.

"It's at my apartment and he hates it," Beryl answered, setting the old cat gently on Rumer's lap. "Don't worry, he likes riding in the car."

She walked around to the driver's side and got in. Isak was sulking in back because, after her second drink, they'd refused to let her drive. "That's all we need in the paper: 'Woman Returns Home for Mother's Funeral and Is Arrested for DUI.'"

"Especially with what happened to Dad, Isak, Mum would turn in her grave—and she's not even buried yet."

Isak had resisted but soon discovered she had no choice. "Whatever," she grumbled, climbing into the backseat.

As they drove, Thoreau peered over Rumer's shoulder, realized there was a third person in the car, and jumped in back to say hello. Isak spoke softly to him and stroked his head. "Do you think animals know when their owner has died?"

"I don't know," Beryl said. "Thoreau hasn't seen Mum in a long time, but he was definitely more attentive and affectionate with her before she went into the nursing home. It was almost as if he knew there was something going on." She paused. "It's hard to tell with Flan, though. She's had time to adjust to living with me—but she loved visiting Mum in the nursing home."

"You took her to visit Mum?" Isak asked in surprise.

"Yup," Beryl answered, looking in the rearview mirror and watching Isak gently stroking Thoreau's soft head. "Maybe you and Matt should get a pet to fill your empty nest."

"Matt and I should get something," Isak said, "but I don't think it's a pet. Counseling might be better."

Rumer glanced over her shoulder. "It can't be that bad. Matt's a great guy and he worships the ground you walk on."

"Maybe that's the problem," Isak mused. "I don't know," she said sadly. "Lately, I keep thinking I really need to eradicate the word *sad* from my mind, because it feels like it's becoming my daily mental mantra—sad, sad, sad. I never seem to look forward to anything."

Beryl eyed her sister with new concern. "Maybe you should mention this to your doctor; there are things that help with depression. Maybe it's not you and Matt—maybe it's you."

Isak shook her head. "I don't want to take anything."

"Isak," Rumer said, "you do know alcohol is a depressant, right?"

"Yeah, I know," she said with a yawn, "but I don't care—having a glass of wine at night is the only thing I do look forward to."

"Well, it sounds like you both just need some time to adjust to not having the kids around," Beryl said. "It's a shock to any marriage. You never know, you might enjoy it."

"I don't know about that. I still take out four plates when I'm setting the table—and Tommy's been in college for three years!"

They pulled into the yard and heard the familiar chorus of peepers, whose song had reached a feverish crescendo on the warm spring night. "That sound will always remind me of this place," Rumer said wistfully. "I wish we didn't have to sell it."

As they walked up to the house, they heard a long insect-like *beeeep* coming from the edge of the woods. Every few seconds, at regular intervals, it happened again—and then, from across the driveway, a second long *beeeep* replied. "What is that?" Isak whispered.

"It's a pair of woodcocks," Beryl said softly. "That was another of Mum's favorite sounds." She unlocked the door to let Flan out and the woodcocks grew quiet, but they soon resumed their conversation.

When she came back in with Flan, Beryl asked them if they'd like a cup of chamomile, but they both shook their heads and retreated—Rumer to the porch and Isak to her old bedroom—to call home. Beryl put the kettle on and plopped a tea bag into a large mug with the words *World's Best Mom* painted on its side. She sat down on Flan's bed and leaned back against the oven, waiting for the water to heat. The old dog immediately wriggled onto her back for a belly rub, and Beryl obliged and thought about Micah and the news her sisters had shared. It was so sad that his wife had died at such a young age, leaving him to raise their little girl alone. It was almost like her mom's situation.

The teakettle started to sing and she pulled herself up. She could hear Rumer on the porch, arguing with Will, and she whispered a prayer that her sister and her husband would find some way to work things out.

~ 11 ~

Beryl woke up to the sensation of four paws landing lightly on the bed and then a small, warm body curling up beside her. She looked down and saw Thoreau lying in a long shaft of early-morning sunlight, licking his front paws with his eyes closed in contentment. She reached down to stroke his head, and he pushed it up against her hand and purred softly. "You are such a mush," she whispered. They lay like that for a long time and she must've dozed off, because the next thing she heard was a flushing toilet. She looked down, realized Thoreau was gone, and rolled onto her back to stretch. Then Rumer came back in the room and threw a pillow at her.

"Gettin' up, lazy bones?" she teased.

"Mmm-hmm," she answered with a yawn.

"I always sleep best in this old bed," Rumer mused. "Maybe I'll have it shipped to Montana."

"That'll be good for your marriage," Beryl teased.

"Hey, after last night, who knows if he's ever coming back."

"He'll come around."

"I don't know," Rumer said, sitting on the edge of Beryl's

bed. "He was pretty p-oed when I told him Isak wanted to pay for their airline tickets."

"Well, I can understand how he feels, but Isak's right—your son should be here for his grandmother's funeral."

"Isak's right about what?" called a voice from the hall. She peered into their room with raised eyebrows. "When are you guys going to learn?" she added with a grin. "I'm always right!" Then she ducked as two large pillows careened toward her head.

"Ber, do we have eggs?"

"Yup."

"K . . . I'm making scrambled. Y'all interested?"

"Yup," they both answered with a grin. Rumer pulled on the sweatshirt with the torn neck that she'd found in her dresser drawer and shuffled down the stairs while Beryl headed to the bathroom.

When she joined them in the kitchen, the kettle was already clicking and Rumer was making coffee. "I hate to be the bearer of bad tidings," Beryl announced regretfully, "but another thing we need to take care of is Mum's obituary."

"Well, Ber," Isak said, "you're the writer. Do you feel like doing it?"

"If you want," Beryl said. Her writer's mind immediately searched for the words and phrases that would best describe their mom: generous, steadfast, faithful . . .

"Oh, and Tommy said he'd be honored to give a eulogy," Isak continued as she whisked the eggs, "and Meghan said she'd be fine with a reading. They're coming in Thursday." She looked up. "Ru, what did Will say?"

"He said he'd let me know by tonight," she answered cryptically.

"Okay, but no later, cuz we really need to figure this out."

After breakfast, they lounged around the table, sipping their coffee and tea, and Beryl rubbed her feet on Flan's belly. "Do you guys feel like going to church?" she asked hopefully.

Isak shook her head. "No . . . I don't think I want to see anyone before the service. Besides, going through this house is going to take at least the whole week and then some. Do you have any idea what we're going to do with all the furniture?" She tucked her hair behind her ear and looked around, shaking her head in dismay. "I honestly think we're going to have to hire one of those estate companies."

"That's what I suggested," Rumer said, looking at Beryl. "Really, Ber, we have no way to dispose of—or move—any of this furniture. What are we going to do with it all?"

"Well, I was hoping the people who buy the house might be interested in it. . . ." She looked around too. "Isn't there anything you guys want?"

"There are things I might want, but I'd have to arrange to have them shipped. Nothing is ever simple," Isak said.

"No, it's not," Beryl agreed, "not when you live thousands of miles away."

Rumer shook her head. "Well, I can't even begin to think of paying to have something shipped. Maybe we could get one of those storage units."

"That costs money too," Beryl said. "In this miserable market, though, maybe we don't have to worry, right away, about having the house completely empty. Who knows how long it will take to sell. But we're not getting anywhere just sitting here."

Rumer yawned, "You're right."

"We need a plan," Isak said, sitting up. "Breakfast dishes, showers, and you said we need boxes—any idea where we can get some on a Sunday?"

"There's some at the shop," Beryl said, "and maybe the grocery store. They have those boxes with the handles that eggs come in. And whoever goes to the store can get some of those big black garbage bags too." She paused. "You guys can shower first. I'll clean up."

"Go ahead," Rumer said, nodding to Isak. "You cooked. I'll help Ber."

An hour later, Rumer and Isak went to the store and left Beryl sitting on the front porch with her laptop open, Flan at her feet, and Thoreau curled up in the wicker chair beside her, basking in the sunshine. She began to work on her mom's obituary, distracted by the thought that her sisters would forget something. They had a key to the shop and instructions to retrieve the remaining chocolate croissants from the freezer, as well as any boxes that might be piled in the storeroom. "Don't forget the garbage bags," she called. Rumer gave her a thumbs-up as Isak peeled out of the driveway, leaving a cloud of dust floating across the yard. Beryl shook her head. "That girl will never grow up!" she said with a sigh, scratching Flan's head.

"Now, where was I?" she murmured, pulling her legs up under her and running her fingers through her still-damp hair. "Mum," she murmured with a sigh, "I don't think this will ever be a truly complete story if we don't figure out who David is . . ." She started to tap away on her keyboard, writing down their family history from memory. When she finally had a rough draft laid out, she stood to stretch her legs and went inside to make a cup of tea. While the water heated, she went into her mom's office to see if she could find something with her grandfather's middle name on it.

She sat at her mom's desk and looked around the room—there were papers everywhere. Feeling oddly intrusive, she pulled open the top drawer; it was filled with papers, too, but in an envelope in the corner she found a small key with a tag attached to it with string. The tag had something illegible scribbled on it. She looked at it closely; it was old and definitely not a house or car key. Just then, the kettle started to sing, demanding her attention, and she dropped the key back in the drawer and went to the kitchen. As she did, Rumer and Isak came through the screen door, laughing and clumsily carrying piles of flattened boxes.

"There's more in the car," Isak said, nodding in that direction while making her way into the living room. Beryl turned off the kettle and headed out to the car.

"So, how'd you make out with the obit?" Isak asked, coming up behind her.

"Pretty good, I think. You'll have to read it." She lifted out the rest of the boxes, and Isak reached for the sack with the croissants while Rumer reached for the rest of the bags.

"We bought lobster ravioli and vodka sauce for dinner," Rumer said with a grin. "And cranberry chicken salad wraps from 12 Pine Street for lunch."

"That sounds good, but don't forget I bought food too."

They carried everything inside and she dropped the flattened boxes on the pile in the living room. When she came back into the kitchen, Isak was sitting at the table looking at her open laptop with Rumer looking over her shoulder. "Do you know what Grandpa's middle name wa—" she started to ask, but Isak held up her hand.

"This is perfect," Rumer said softly, looking up.

When they finished reading, Isak nodded slowly. "It's great, Ber, very nice."

"Thanks. I just couldn't remember Grandpa's middle name . . ."

"It was Francis, I think—but you don't need it," Isak said.

"Okay, well, when I submit it online, they'll post it right away and then run it in Friday's paper."

"Sounds good," Rumer said.

Isak nodded in agreement. "Thanks for doing it." She paused. "You know, we also need to find Mum's will . . . or whatever she had set up."

Beryl nodded. "I think she had a trust, but I have no idea where it is."

Rumer opened the bag of wraps while Beryl put the croissants in the fridge and poured three iced teas. "Okay," she said, "so right after lunch we're going to get started, right?"

"Yup, right after my nap in the sun," Rumer teased.

"I don't know, Dad," Micah said, looking across the yard at the barn. They'd driven out to his parents' cabin after church. "I've always loved it out here; it's such a peaceful spot with the river and everything. But it's so secluded and there wouldn't be anyone for Charlotte to play with."

"That's fine, Micah. I'm not saying you have to stay here. I just had to come out to check on it and I thought you'd like to come along—and then it occurred to me that you might be interested in it. When it's empty, it's a big temptation for kids looking for a place to party. And the price is right—same deal I had with Linden Finch—just look after and maintain it. In fact, in his spare time, Linden built all those stone walls," Asa said, pointing across the meadow. "He had a whole menagerie of animals here, but when that old fellow from New York—the writer, can't think of his name just now—passed away, he left his farm in Dublin—the old Harris farm—to Linden. The old guy had no family, but he'd taken a liking to Linden."

"Lucky, lucky Linden," Micah said with a smile.

"Anyway, no pressure—you and Charlotte are welcome to

stay at the house with us as long as you need to. Heaven knows we have plenty of room, and your mother loves having you and Charlotte home. But in case you decide you'd like a place of your own, you're welcome to it."

Micah nodded thoughtfully. He hadn't wanted to move back in with his parents, but after Beth died, his world had collapsed around him and he needed some time to get back on his feet. "Let me think about it, Dad."

"That's fine," Asa said, putting his hand on his shoulder. "The offer stands—you might find you want some privacy and can't handle living with your old parents."

Micah laughed as they walked toward the barn and Asa unlocked the padlock and slid the doors open. As he did, an old owl flew out from the rafters through the open hay door above them.

"Atticus is still here?" Micah asked in surprise.

"He is, old fellow . . ."

Micah walked toward the back of the barn and lifted up the dusty sheet covering his dad's old Chevy pickup. "Dad, I think it's time we restored this old truck."

Asa smiled. "I hauled beach wood in that, took it to college—lots of memories in that old truck."

"Well, you have time to work on it now—and I have time. What do you say?"

"Maybe . . ." Asa said, nodding wistfully. "Maybe."

When they pulled into his parents' house in town, a black Labrador pushed open the screen door, bounded across the yard, and, wagging her tail, dropped a sloppy tennis ball at Micah's feet.

"Hey, Harper," Micah said, picking up the ball. He threw it as far as he could, and Harper took off after it.

"She sure knows a pushover when she sees one," his father teased.

"And you're the biggest pushover of all," Micah teased back.

"You're probably right."

Harper dropped the ball at Micah's feet again. "One more, and then it's time for lunch." He threw the ball into the field next to the house and she charged off, but when she came back this time, ready to go again, she was disappointed to find him holding the door open for her. "Come on in and get a drink." She sailed over the two steps and skidded into the kitchen, still carrying the sloppy green ball.

Charlotte was standing on a chair next to her grandmother, munching on an apple slice. "Hi, Daddy," she said with a big grin. "We're making apple crisp."

"You are?" Micah said, reaching for a slice.

"Mmm-hmm," Charlotte said, her blond head bobbing.

"How come you're making two?" he asked.

"So you can take one to Beryl," Charlotte answered.

"Oh, really?"

"Mmm-hmm. Grandma says it's the right thing to do."

"Well, Grandma would know."

13

"Okay, if we're going to find the will or trust—or anything of importance—I think we should start in the office," Isak said, crumpling the paper from her chicken salad wrap into a tight ball. She ran her fingers through her hair, fluffing it, and then tucked the stray strands behind her ears. Standing up, she carried as much as she could to the counter.

Beryl watched as her oldest sister filled the sink with hot water. No matter what, Beryl decided, Isak always carried herself with grace and poise—and she did a very good job of hiding her demons. She stood to help clear the remaining glasses and called through the screen, "C'mon, Ru, your vitamin D absorption session is over."

Rumer opened one eye and squinted. "Cute!"

Moments later, they all stood side by side in the sunny downstairs bedroom that their mom had converted into her office and surveyed her piles of papers. "This is depressing," Isak said gloomily. She walked over to a stack of boxes near the window and opened one. It was filled with cards and letters dating back decades. "What do we do with all of this?" she groaned. "I think Mum must've saved every card that was ever sent to her! And all the letters—our whole lives are here. What do we do with them? Throw them away?"

"I don't know," Rumer said, shaking her head. "What do people do with their parents' stuff? We definitely don't have time to read every letter, but I hate to throw anything away that might be important."

Isak shook her head. "Remind me not to do this to my kids. In fact, when I get home, the first thing I'm doing is renting a Dumpster!"

"Maybe that's what we need," Beryl suggested.

"Well, it might come to that," Isak said, "but let's start with those big garbage bags and some empty boxes and see how it goes." She and Rumer went to get the bags, boxes, and tape, and when they returned, Beryl had fished out the key she'd found that morning.

"If you come across anything that needs unlocking, this could be the key," she said brightly, holding it up.

Isak looked at it. "Did Mum have a safe deposit box?"

Beryl shook her head. "I honestly don't know."

"Well, if worse comes to worst, her attorney or accountant will know, right? Do we know who they are?"

"Hmm," Beryl mused with a funny puzzled expression.

"Gee, you're a big help," Isak teased. "You were supposed to find out some of these things before Mum forgot."

"You're right, I should've; but hopefully we'll find some clues when we go through her stuff."

They got right to work, quickly establishing a system: Each one had a box and a bag—saved items went into a box, and garbage went into a bag. Slowly, slowly, the piles diminished.

Every once in a while, one of them would come across a funny anecdote or an interesting tidbit and would share it. "Holy cow!" Rumer exclaimed in an astonished voice, holding up a faded document. "Guess how much Mum and Dad paid for this house in 1964?" Beryl and Isak looked up quizzically from behind their piles and Rumer read the figure out loud: "$17,500!"

"That's crazy!" Isak said. "You couldn't buy an acre for that now."

"Well, when we put it on the market, I don't think we should ask less than $300,000," Beryl said.

"We'll have to have it assessed first," Isak said with a sigh.

"By the way, Ber," Rumer said, looking up, "I've been wondering how we've been paying for the nursing home all this time. Usually people have to sell everything they own."

"Mum had a sizeable nest egg stashed away. I don't know how she did it, but it's almost gone now. There've also been regular deposits into her checking account all along, including a large sum at the end of last year, but I always assumed they were automatic deposits from a retirement account. I was beginning to worry that she'd run out and then we'd have to sell the house at a loss."

"It's odd that there was that one big deposit," Isak mused. "Usually when monies are coming from a retirement account, it's set up so it's always the same amount."

Beryl shook her head. "I don't really know. I guess I should have paid more attention to it."

They went back to their piles and once she'd gotten through a few layers of paper, Beryl uncovered her mom's old turntable and receiver. She traced the wires back to actual speakers and then discovered an old Rinso box full of 45's and 78's, and an L.L. Bean box full of albums. She looked up to see if her sisters had noticed her discovery, but they were so absorbed in their own piles they hadn't even looked up. Quietly, she flipped through the albums, slid one out, and gingerly placed it on the turntable; when it started to spin, she set the needle down and it crackled to life. At the familiar sound, Rumer and Isak both looked up, and then big band sounds filled the room along with

Frank Sinatra's smooth, unmistakable voice crooning "Come Dance with Me." Rumer and Isak smiled, remembering how their mom used to swing them around the kitchen when they were little, singing along to Ol' Blue Eyes; suddenly Beryl started dancing around the room like their mom used to do, singing at the same time. Laughing, Rumer and Isak joined in— surprised that they remembered every word. When the album ended, Isak looked for a clock. "Is it cocktail hour yet?"

"Nope, it's only four forty-five," Beryl said, changing albums and hoping they could get a little more done.

As Patsy Cline began to sing "You Belong to Me," Rumer leaned back in her mom's chair and groaned. "This drawer is locked. Do you think that key opens it?" The heavy oak desk had multiple drawers on both sides, but the bottom drawers were bigger than the rest. She leaned over to the other side. "This one is too."

"I never knew that desk locked," Beryl said.

"The locks are under the handles," Rumer said, fiddling with the key but having no success. "Maybe we should get some WD-40."

Isak knelt down in front of the desk, pulled the key back out, flipped it over, slid it back in, and turned it again. This time the lock clicked open. She pulled the drawer out and glanced through its contents. "More papers," she announced, "which can only mean one thing—it's definitely cocktail hour." She stood up and looked around the room. "We're getting there, though."

"I'm with you," Rumer agreed. "It's time for a break."

Beryl sat down in the chair. "I'll be there in a minute," she said. She pulled open the drawer, sifted through some of the loose papers on top, reached underneath, and pulled out an old manila envelope. It was tied closed with a red string wound tightly around a small cardboard circle. As she slowly unwound it, she pictured her mom's hands—the last to touch it. . . .

Beryl slid the contents of the envelope out onto the desk. It was a collection of fragile, yellow newspaper clippings. She looked in the manila envelope again to make sure it was empty and saw a crumpled piece of paper at the bottom. She pulled it out and unfolded it; it was a typed report, but the date was scrawled across the top in pencil: *November 15, 1968*—the day she was born!

With Patsy Cline softly singing "Sweet Dreams," Beryl carefully read the accident report that had haunted her mother's life, and with tears streaming down her cheeks, she felt, for the first time, the extent of her mother's grief. When she finished reading it, she turned to the newspaper clippings. There were two about the accident: One showed a picture of the demolished truck, and one showed a picture of her father smiling. He looked no older than a boy and the caption read: "Thomas Graham, 26, leaves behind a young wife and three small children." Paper-clipped to the article were three copies of his obituary.

Beryl wiped her eyes and glanced through the other clippings. There was an obituary for a man named Clay Davis. Mr. Davis, it said, had died on Christmas Eve, but it didn't say how he died; it only asked that contributions be made to the VA in his son's name. Beryl stared at the name, trying to remember where she'd read it before; then she looked back at the accident report and put her hand over her mouth in surprise. She continued to sift through the clippings, trying to make sense of everything. There was a clipping of a painting of New Hampshire's Old Man of the Mountain and its caption read: " 'Old Man and the Moon' as seen through the eyes of painter David Gilead, currently an artist in residence at Macdowell Colony, 1969." There were several more articles about the artist and the shows he would be having—New York, Paris, Rome. One article showed a photograph of him standing beside a landscape. Beryl looked closely at the photo—he was very handsome and, even in the faded newspaper photograph, his eyes were striking. Finally, Beryl looked at the last clipping. It was torn, but it looked like it had been repaired with tape—tape that was now yellow with age and had lost its adhesiveness. The photo was of a woman wearing an elegant gown, and the caption read: "Catherine Gilead at a New York City Catholic charity fundraiser"; the year, *1980,* was scribbled next to the picture in pencil.

Beryl squeezed her eyes shut, trying to absorb what she was reading. Why had her mom saved these clippings? And why were they kept together with the clippings about the accident and her father's obituary? What significance could they possibly have?

~ 14 ~

"Ber, Micah's here!" Rumer called from the kitchen. Beryl looked up, startled, and realized the needle had never lifted from the album—it was still gliding across the smooth black inner circle, hitting the label and jumping back, making a scratching sound. She stood up, leaving all the papers on the desk, set the arm of the needle on its stand, clicked the turntable off, and hurried to the kitchen.

"Hey!" she said with a smile when she saw Micah standing in the kitchen with Flan sitting on his foot.

"Hey," he replied.

"I see you've made a friend!"

"Yup," he answered with a grin, leaning down to scratch Flan's blocky head. "What's her name?"

"Flannery . . . Flannery O'Connor," Beryl answered with a smile.

Micah chuckled. "Very appropriate."

"Uh-oh," she teased, nodding to the glass of wine in his hand. "I see my sisters corralled you into joining them for cocktail hour."

"Yeah, sort of—they said you'd be joining us."

Beryl raised her eyebrows. "Did they? And I was hoping to get more work out of them."

"You guys deserve a break," Micah said sympathetically. "I don't envy the task you're facing." He paused. "Anyway, my mom thought you might need some sustenance." He nodded toward an apple crisp on the counter. "She said it's from a recipe your mom gave her years ago and she hopes she's done it justice."

"I'm sure she has," Beryl said. "It looks yummy. Please tell her, 'Thank you.' "

Rumer nodded. "It looks like a picture."

Isak looked up from filling a big pot with water. "Thanks, Micah—that was very thoughtful." She put the pot on the stove top and lit the burner. "Can you stay for dinner?"

Micah frowned and shook his head. "No, no, I couldn't . . . I mean I can't. I meant to come earlier—not at dinnertime—but Charlotte and I took Harp for a walk and it got late."

Beryl looked at the wine bottles, trying to decide if she wanted any. "Who's Harp?" she asked curiously, looking to see what color Micah had in his glass.

"Harper is my parents' Lab."

Isak eyed him thoughtfully. "Hmm, seems there was a book your dad loved to teach by an author with that name—could there be a connection?"

Micah laughed. "How'd you know?" He seemed to relax a little and took a sip of his wine.

Beryl smiled, finally pouring a glass of the Free Range Red. "I think your dad and our mom shared that odd trait of naming their pets—and in our mom's case, her children—after famous authors."

"Was your mom behind all your names?"

Beryl looked at her sisters and laughed. "She claimed to be."

Micah nodded thoughtfully. "Beryl ... Markham, right?" Beryl nodded, and he turned to Rumer. "And Rumer ... hmm—Godden?" Rumer grinned, and he looked at Isak thoughtfully. "Isak Dinesen—of course!" Then a puzzled expression crossed his face. "But her real name was Karen. ... in fact, her family called her Tanne."

Isak grinned, impressed by his knowledge. "It was Karen, but Isak is much more interesting, don't you think?" She eyed him suspiciously. "How do you know so much about all these women writers, anyway?"

"Well, you have to remember, I owned a bookstore, and they were all remarkable ladies ... and authors," Micah explained. "They lived in exotic places, flew airplanes, loved passionately—and wrote books!"

Beryl laughed. "I guess our mom had really high hopes for us." She paused. "It's funny that our mom and your dad both did that. I wonder if they got it from each other. ..."

"It's possible," Micah said. "They've known each other a lot longer than I realized. My parents remember the accident—my mom said it was ..." He stopped in midsentence and shook his head. "I'm sorry—that is probably the last thing you want to talk about now."

"Actually, I was just reading about the accident," Beryl said. She looked at her sisters. "There were some newspaper clippings in that drawer." She looked back at Micah. "Our mom never talked about it, but I'd really like to hear what your mom remembers."

Micah nodded but didn't say more.

"I never knew anything about the other driver," Isak said, looking up.

"I didn't either," Rumer added.

"His obituary is one of the clippings," Beryl said quietly. There was an awkward silence and Rumer looked up from peeling a carrot. "You really should stay for dinner, Micah. We're having lobster ravioli in a vodka sauce that looks like it's to die for; it's from that new fresh pasta place in town."

"Sounds tempting," Micah said, "but . . ."

"No buts," Isak chimed in cheerfully. "Just call your mom and tell her you're having dinner with the Graham girls—she'll understand."

Micah looked at Beryl for support, but she just laughed and shook her head. "I know, they're unrelenting. But honestly, I think you should stay, too—it would cheer us up."

"Well, when you put it that way," he said with a smile, "how can I possibly say no?" He went out on the porch to call home, and Isak and Rumer both grinned and gave her a thumbs-up.

Beryl shook her head and, in a hushed voice, whispered, "You guys are crazy, you know that? We're supposed to be getting ready for a funeral."

"Hey," Isak whispered, looking over her shoulder to see where Micah was, "we are getting ready, but that doesn't mean our lives have to come to a screeching halt. Besides, I'm sure Mum's looking down and smiling—and giving a thumbs-up too. In fact, she probably guided Micah over here."

"*His* mom guided him over here," Beryl whispered, taking down four of their mom's blue Staffordshire plates.

"If I'm staying," Micah said, coming back in the kitchen, "you have to give me a job."

"Jobs are hard to come by," Isak teased, "but you can set the table."

Micah laughed as Beryl handed him the plates.

"These are kind of fancy," he commented, admiring the plates.

"Well, dinner's always a special occasion around here," Beryl said. "Growing up, we always had candles, music, fresh flowers . . . and used special plates."

"In fact, we need some music," Rumer said, following the same train of thought. "Ber, want to pick out another album?"

"Somethin' old and classy," Isak said as she stirred the vodka sauce.

"I don't think Mum has anything but old and classy." She looked at Micah. "Want to help?" He reached for his glass and followed her into the office.

"Don't mind the mess," she said, waving her hand across the room.

"Don't worry, I've seen worse."

He peered over her shoulder as she flipped through the albums and she felt his arm touching her back. She breathed in his wonderful, clean scent—was it soap or aftershave? She couldn't tell, but she could feel her heart pounding. "See anything you like?"

"They're all great; it's all the same stuff I grew up on. How about that one?" he asked.

She pulled the album out of the box, slid it from its sleeve, and carefully placed it on the turntable. "This was one of my mom's favorites," she said, gently setting the needle on the spinning disc. The record crackled to life and was followed by the unmistakable, melancholy voice of Billie Holiday singing "I'm a Fool to Want You."

Micah took a sip from his glass. "My dad used to always listen to these old songs."

Beryl nodded. "I know what you mean. We were listening to Frank Sinatra before you came and it brought back so many memories of dancing around the kitchen with my mom." She shook her head. "It must've been so hard for her to carry on without my dad, but she never let on; she just tried to fill our lives and our home with happy memories." She paused, suddenly realizing she was telling him something he already knew. "My sisters told me about your wife, Micah—I'm so sorry."

"Thanks," he said, pressing his lips together in a sad smile. "It's been hard. I met Beth when we were in college. We had so much in common—my mom said we were like two peas in a pod. We'd both wanted a big family, but she had trouble getting—and staying—pregnant. She had two miscarriages before Charlotte, so when she was diagnosed with cancer, she didn't want to do anything to jeopardize the pregnancy. After Charlotte was born, she lived long enough to see her smile . . . and hear her laugh . . ." His voice trailed off, his eyes glistening.

"I'm so sorry," she said again, wishing she had the courage to give him a hug, but she felt foolish and awkward, so she just laid her hand gently on his arm.

He looked up. "What can you do? Death is a part of life—as you well know." He shook his head and smiled. "How'd we get on this subject anyway? I'm supposed to be cheering you up!"

Beryl laughed. "It's my fault—I brought it up."

Micah looked down at the spinning record. "Can they hear that in the kitchen?"

"Yup, my mom put speakers everywhere in the house. She liked being able to hear it no matter where she was or what she was doing."

"She was a smart lady!"

As they walked past the desk, Beryl pointed. "Those are the clippings."

Micah stopped to study them. He picked up the picture of her dad. "You have his eyes," he said with a smile.

"That's funny—everyone always said I look like my mom."

"You do, but I can see your dad too. It's funny how that happens. My brother Noah looks exactly like my dad, and I don't think I look anything like my brother, but everyone says I look like my dad too. Go figure."

Beryl nodded. "Well, look at us—somehow my parents managed to have a blonde, a brunette, and a redhead."

Micah laughed. "It's like having chocolate, yellow, and black Labrador puppies all in the same litter."

Beryl gave him a funny look. "Nice analogy!"

Micah laughed again. "Sorry."

He picked up one of the other clippings. "Why did your mom save these?"

Beryl shook her head. "I don't know. I just came across them and I haven't really had time to figure it out."

"Do you know who this is?"

"Well, it says he's a painter."

"He's a very famous painter. He's in his seventies now and I heard he lives up near North Conway, but he's a bit of a recluse. Could your mom have known him?"

Beryl shrugged uncertainly. "Well, she worked at Mac-Dowell Colony for a while after my dad died and"—she pointed to the clipping of the Old Man of the Mountain—"this caption says he was there in 1969."

"Seems to me he stayed at MacDowell more than once. His paintings are pretty valu—"

"Dinner's ready," Rumer said, popping her head in the doorway. They followed her into the kitchen where steaming plates of lobster ravioli in creamy vodka sauce and colorful salads were already on the table.

"Need a refill?" Isak asked, holding up the red wine.

"Sure," Beryl said.

They all sat down at the kitchen table with the late-day sun streaming through the windows.

"So," Beryl said, "I think I found a clue." She described the clippings and Micah elaborated on what he knew about David Gilead. Rumer and Isak listened intently and, between bites, asked questions.

Finally, Isak leaned back and took a sip from her glass. "I

don't know," she said skeptically. "What connection could she have possibly had to him? It doesn't make any sense."

"Maybe she liked his artwork," Rumer suggested hopefully.

"She worked at MacDowell," Beryl reminded them. "They probably met there and became friends."

"Do you think he's the one who gave her the ring?" Rumer asked.

Micah looked up and Beryl said, "I'll get it." She pushed back her chair and, moments later, returned with the ring and the card.

Micah studied the card. "This painting is definitely reminiscent of David Gilead's work and the signature is spot-on." He looked up with raised eyebrows. "From what he's written, it seems like they were more than friends."

Beryl shook her head. "How can that be? How could we have not known—unless we were too young and it ended before we were old enough to be aware of it?"

Isak sighed. "I guess that's possible, but I wish we had more to go on."

"Maybe there is," Rumer said. "We still have a lot of papers to go through."

Isak stood to clear the table and Beryl went to the office to get the clippings. She spread them out on the table and her sisters studied them.

"Dad looks like he's about seventeen," Isak said with a sad smile.

Rumer nodded and then pointed to the image of the artist. "Look at those eyes—talk about seeing right through someone!" Then she picked up the photo of Catherine Gilead. "I wonder if this was ripped by accident . . . or on purpose?!"

Beryl looked up and realized that Micah was standing at the sink up to his elbows in soapsuds and the dish drain was almost full. "Hey, you're not supposed to do those!"

She reached for a towel and started to dry, and he smiled. "I can't leave you with all this."

"Are you leaving?" she asked, sounding disappointed.

He nodded. "Afraid so, I have to tuck in my little pal."

"You should've brought her."

"I would've, if I'd known."

"You didn't have any apple crisp."

"My mom made two, so I'll have some later—probably with vanilla ice cream," he said with a grin.

"I'm coming to your house then."

"Where's our vanilla ice cream?" Isak teased, feigning disappointment.

Micah laughed and shrugged. "I don't know—in your freezer?" he asked hopefully. He rinsed the sink, then dried his hands. "I do have to go, though."

Beryl nodded. "I'll walk you out."

"Bye, Micah," Rumer and Isak called. "Thanks for doing the dishes, and thank your mom for the apple crisp."

"Bye! Thanks for dinner," he called back, slipping on his jacket.

Beryl pulled on her fleece and held the door for him. Then she looked back at Flannery lying on her bed with all four legs in the air. "Flan, do you need to get busy?" Flan grunted, clambered to her feet, stretched, yawned, and trotted out the door.

"She's such a character," Micah observed with a grin.

"She is, indeed," Beryl said, nodding. "She helps keep everything in perspective."

"Dogs'll do that," Micah agreed.

They stood by his car and he nodded to the two cars next to it. "I'm guessing by the New Hampshah plate," he teased, "the cool Mini Coopah is yahs."

Beryl laughed. "Yup! You sound like my sistahs."

He laughed. "I usually try not to sound like a New Englander." He opened his door and she saw the car seat in back. "A Honda wagon," she mused. "I can't remember the last time I saw one of these on the road."

"It's a vintage 1997," he said proudly. "They don't make 'em anymore. It has over two hundred fifty thousand miles on it. I've thought about trading it in, but I'm having a little trouble letting go." He paused. "It's actually Beth's car . . ." he added, his voice trailing off.

"I know what you mean," Beryl commiserated. "It'd be like letting go of this old house—it's so full of memories."

Micah nodded and started to get in the car, but then leaned against the frame, hesitating. "Ber, I . . . I'm not very good at this sort of thing," he stammered, "and I know you're going to be busy . . . but . . ." He cleared his throat and shook his head. "What I mean is—"

"Micah," Beryl interrupted with a smile, saving him, "if you get a chance tomorrow, could you call me—I know I'll probably need a break from all this."

He grinned. "I was hoping you'd say that."

She laughed. "Now, you better get going or Charlotte will be sound asleep."

He waved as he pulled away and, with Flan standing by her side, watching him go, too, Beryl waved back and smiled.

"Ber, we found more stuff!" Isak called, hearing the screen door squeak and bang shut.

Beryl found them back in their mom's office. Rumer held up a stack of white envelopes with a red ribbon around them, and Isak held up a small pile of lined notebook paper filled with their mom's long, familiar handwriting. She handed the pile to Beryl and continued to sift through the drawer's contents.

Beryl studied the top sheet. It was like all the others, but it was wrinkled and it had a stain on it—round like a cup. Beryl read silently:

I haven't written anything in a long time—but an old friend came to see me today. He told me his wife had died. I told him I was sorry. At first, I wasn't sure of his name—but, now, I know it was David. As we sat together, I could see tears in his eyes. . . .

"It's very hard to lose a loved one," I said, reaching for his hand.

He nodded as tears spilled down his cheeks.

The rest of the pages were held together with a rubber band and clipped to the top page was a blue envelope with their names written on it in their mother's hand.

PART II

For now we see in a mirror, dimly;
but then face to face: now I know in part;
but then I shall know even as also I am known.

—I Corinthians 13:12

15

Beryl pulled her leg up under her as she sat in one of the Adirondack chairs on the porch. Taking a sip of her tea, she looked at the pond reflecting the pink and orange sunset stretching across the sky and leaned back, listening to the peepers and feeling oddly content.

"Do we need the porch lights?" Isak called.

"Not yet," Beryl called back. "Candles would be nice, though."

"Got 'em," Rumer called from the kitchen. Moments later, her sisters joined her on the porch, Rumer bringing the candles, already lit, and Isak carrying glasses and a newly opened bottle of wine.

"Can the beasts come out?" she asked.

Beryl nodded and Isak held the door open. The old bulldog waddled out, plopped down at Beryl's feet, and promptly lifted her leg over her head. "Not if you're going to do that, though," Beryl warned, nudging Flan with her foot. Flannery looked up indignantly, snorted, rested her blocky head on her paws, and looked gloomy. Thoreau, meanwhile, curled up happily on Rumer's lap and purred loudly as she stroked under his chin.

"Okay," Beryl said, taking a deep breath, "are you ready?"

They nodded and, with the candles flickering in the warm evening breeze, she opened the blue envelope, slipped out the stationery, and began to read—her voice soft and clear and, to her sisters, sounding remarkably like their mom's.

> *To my beloved daughters—who are dearer to me than life itself!*
>
> *It's very odd to sit down at this old kitchen table—the scene of so many fond memories—and write a letter, knowing you probably won't read it until after my time on this lovely old earth has passed—but who knows how things will turn out?*
>
> *Perhaps the good Lord will spare me and allow me to tell you these things instead—though I don't deserve to.*
>
> *My life has been blessed, dear ones. Not only have I been given three lovely daughters to fill my days with joy and wonder, but in my lifetime, I've loved—and been loved by—two good men—yes, two!*
>
> *Your father was everything to me, and when he died, I was devastated. I didn't know how I would manage—how I would carry on and raise three little girls alone. But the Lord held me close in those dark days and gave me the strength I needed; I pray every day that you, too, will find Him to be a source of strength and guidance, no matter what trial you're facing.*
>
> *I never expected to love again, but when David came into my life, I was surprised and swept away. Ours is the story I leave behind. Try as I might,*

though, I'm afraid bits and pieces are missing—as my memory has already begun to fail. Only recently has it occurred to me that you will come across these pages one day—and then you will know me fully—and I pray you will forgive me, just as I pray God will forgive us both.

Don't be sad for me, dear ones! I've lived and loved with all my heart! And I will always love you—much more than you know!

Mum

Beryl handed the thin blue page to Rumer and waited while her sisters read it for themselves; then she pulled the rubber band from the stack of papers on her lap and took a deep breath. "Still ready?" she asked with raised eyebrows. They sipped their wine and nodded.

It's funny how one knows, deep down, when something's wrong. At first it was just little things— like trying to remember a name, or a word, or where I'd put something—but lately it feels as if long shadows, the kind that fall across the backyard late in the day, are slowly creeping across my mind. I can't bring myself to say the words, but in my heart, I'm terrified that the lovely, silken days of my life will be lost in these long finger-like shadows—that my voice will grow silent, and a strange darkness will close in around me, stealing all that is dear. It is my fervent hope and prayer, however, that—by writing down my most intimate memories—they won't be lost in the shadows forever.

As I write now, I find it so very difficult to be- lieve that I could ever forget the first time I saw him—it is as clear to me as if it happened yesterday.

It was one of those steamy August evenings when the air is so heavy all you can think about is standing in front of a fan or plunging into icy water. Unfortunately, there was no time for such frivolities; it was my second night working at MacDowell and I'd been assigned to serve dinner. I was late, and the hall was already crowded and busy. Some of the staff had unexpectedly taken off to go to a three-day concert in upstate New York, so we were very short-handed. John pointed to my tables and I hurried over to deposit steaming bowls of garlic mashed potatoes and oven-warmed platters of rare roast beef on the rustic oak table boards. It was then that I saw him, sitting near the open windows, talking with another artist and sopping up his salad dressing with one of the hot, crusty rolls we serve. The late-day sunlight fell across his face, illuminating cheerful laugh lines that crinkled around his eyes. He was roguishly handsome—his nose angled straight and narrow, his chin chiseled and square—the combination giving him the look of an aristocrat. His hair was long, parted to the side, and fell carelessly over his eyes, and the back was cut in a thick dark wedge, forming a duck's tail against his sunburned neck. As I watched him, he reached up to brush it back with one sweep of his long brown fingers—a gesture I would grow to know very well and, later on, when I was missing him most, ache to see again. Both men looked up when I set down their food and he smiled, his dark blue eyes reflecting the sunlight. Flustered and still trying to catch up, I said I'd be right back, hurried away, and returned with a blue ceramic bowl filled with grilled summer vegetables, swimming in melted butter, and a gravy boat brimming

*with rich brown mushroom gravy, which, I discov-
ered later, was a hearty meal in itself when sopped
up with those warm, buttery rolls. I set these down,
noticed their glasses were empty, and asked if they'd
like some iced tea. They both hesitated, looking perplexed, as if they hadn't realized they didn't have
anything to drink, and I thought to myself:* It's not a
hard question.

"*I forgot to bring a bottle," his companion said,
"so I guess I'll have tea."*

"*Don't be silly," the aristocrat replied in an accent that fit him perfectly but caught me completely
off guard. "I must have something on the table."*

*He started to push back his chair, but I inter-
rupted, "I'd be happy to get it for you . . ." And
then—surprised by my own impulsiveness—plowed
on, "I-I just need to know your name."*

*He looked surprised as he eased back into his
chair. "It's Gilead . . . David." I nodded, and as I
hurried over to the long table that served as a
makeshift bar, I couldn't help but think of the lyrics
to one of my favorite old hymns, "There Is a Balm
in Gilead." It didn't take long to find a bottle of
Merlot with his name scrawled in long, elegant handwriting on the luggage tag hanging around it. I
reached for one of the corkscrews lying on the table
and, because I didn't have much experience with
opening wine, I accidently screwed it in on an angle;
fortunately, I was finally able to pry it out in two
pieces—without dropping in any cork crumbs!*

*I brought the bottle back to the table and tried to
appear nonchalant as I poured, but I needn't have
worried; they were so caught up in their conversation they didn't even notice me, at least not until I*

picked up his salad plate and sent his fork clattering to the floor. He retrieved it and, with a smile, placed it gingerly on top of my pile. "Got everything now?" he teased.

"I think so," I said, laughing. When I looked up, his eyes caught mine and I hesitated, feeling the heat of my body rush to my cheeks. We both seemed caught up in that moment . . . until his friend broke the silence.

"Sorry to be a pest, but when you have a chance, do you think we could have some more of those rolls?"

"Of . . . of course," I stammered, trying to regain my composure—my heart pounding and my mind wondering what in the world had just happened.

After dinner, he didn't linger for coffee and dessert, as so many of the other artists did, and I only happened to see him through the open window as he headed down the path toward the studios. The sun was setting, silhouetting his tall, slender frame, and I noticed that his gait was uneven—then I realized he was using a cane.

The rest of that evening dragged on endlessly in the oppressive heat. When I finally arrived home, the entire house was asleep, including my poor mom, who'd dozed off with her book in her lap. I shook her gently and asked if she wanted to stay, but she said no and I hugged her and watched as her car bumped up the driveway. I turned off the lights, tiptoed up the stairs, and slipped into the girls' room. Rumer was already in a twin bed by then because little Beryl needed the crib, but she'd been very grown up about it—happy, I'm sure, to be treated like her big sister. I gently kissed their warm foreheads, whispered their prayers, and retreated to the bathroom for a quick shower. The cool water rushed over my shoulders, but the relief was only temporary as I was steaming by the time I'd dried off. I collapsed onto my bed and stared into the darkness, trying to unwind. My thoughts drifted to the Englishman . . . and I couldn't help but wonder why someone as young as he appeared to be using a cane.

Finally, I fell into a fitful sleep—tossing and turning and dreaming—reliving the night terror I longed to put behind me. But there it was, as real as ever—Tom's truck rolling, falling—until I awoke, screaming—tears streaming down my cheeks, my heart pounding. I covered my face, muffling my heartbroken sobs, and rolled onto my side to look out at the hazy moon, trying to discern what was real. A small figure appeared in the darkness beside my bed—little Isak, barely five, hair mussed, eyelashes glistening with frightened tears. "Mama?" she whispered, her tiny finger lightly touching my hand. "Why are you crying?" She climbed onto the bed and I felt her small, warm body and smelled the sweet, clean scent of her hair. I stroked her smooth cheek as she snuggled next to me and I whispered, "Don't worry, honeybee." She drifted off, immediately unburdened, but I lay awake for a long time, listening to thunder booming in the distance.

MacDowell Colony in Peterborough, New Hampshire, was the home—and idea—of the great American composer Edward MacDowell and his pianist wife, Marian. Edward had often credited the tranquil setting of the farm—purchased in 1896—as the reason for his success, but when he became gravely *ill, he expressed his desire to see the farm become a retreat for other artists, and Marian immediately set to work making his dream come true. The plan was dubbed The Peterborough Idea, and a fund, established in Edward's name, received national support; over time, thirty-two studios were built—each a private retreat in which an artist's creativity could flourish. Edward lived to see his dream realized in the summer of 1907 when the first fellows arrived and, before long, artists of all disciplines—painters, writers, poets, and composers—from all over the country were applying for the eight-week residencies offered by the prestigious MacDowell Colony.*

To me, however, MacDowell was simply an answer to a prayer for work that I found in the Help Wanted section of the Monadnock Ledger. *It was a blessing that kept me busy and kept my mind from dwelling on all that might have been. Even though Tom had life insurance, the money wouldn't last forever, so soon after he died, I began looking for work. Because I had three little ones at home, my availability was restricted; on top of that, the only sitters I could afford were my mom and Tom's mom—because they were free and because they were willing to help in any way they could; but I couldn't burden them all the time. In the beginning, they took turns watching the girls, but soon they decided they'd much rather babysit during the day than late at night, so I asked John if I could change my hours. He must've known my situation because he was always accommodating—and patient when I was late, which was often. Looking back, I can't help wondering at God's amazing providence.*

Isak shifted uneasily in her chair. "Okay, I'm sorry to interrupt here, but Dad is killed in a tragic accident, Mum's life is turned upside down—she's devastated, has to find a job, raise three little girls alone—and she's still amazed by God's providence?!" Isak's voice was incredulous and edged with anger. "How is that amazing providence?! Wouldn't it have been more providential for God to let Dad survive?" She shook her head defiantly. "I definitely wouldn't have had the same reaction—in fact, I honestly don't know how Mum kept her faith . . ." Her voice trailed off, her eyes glistening.

Rumer put her arm around her sister and Beryl swallowed, trying to think of an answer. "I don't know, Isak. I don't think Mum blamed God. Everyone faces tragedy and sadness in life, but God doesn't make bad things happen." She paused. "He promises to be with us when we're going through them, though, and I think that's where Mum's faith came from."

Isak wasn't convinced. "What about having a plan for good? I don't see the good in His plan for Mum."

Rumer nodded sympathetically. "I guess we don't always get to see the good because we don't get to see the effect a tragic event has on other people. Ber, what did Mum call it?"

Beryl smiled. "God's tapestry."

Isak rolled her eyes and took a sip of her wine. "Whatever. I still think a better plan would've been for Dad to live to see us all grow up."

Beryl looked back at the page. "Should I keep going?" They both nodded and she pulled the candle closer and found where she'd left off.

My assignments in those early days varied, from serving meals to working in the kitchen, depending on the need, so it wasn't unusual for me to not cross paths with residents for several days, especially if I was working in the kitchen. Needless to say, I didn't see the Englishman for nearly a week, but then my assignment changed to delivering lunch.

Although breakfast and dinner are served family style in Colony Hall, lunch is an entirely different affair. After breakfast, hickory picnic baskets are lined up in the kitchen and filled with sandwiches, soup, cookies, and hot coffee. Afterward they're quietly delivered to the residents' porches so that, when they're hungry at midday, they only have to go as far as their front door to find sustenance. It's a favorite tradition at MacDowell, and one that allows the artists to work through the day without interruption or human interaction. Oh, how I could've used a day like that!

On my first day delivering lunch, I was surprised to find many of the residents sitting outside, basking in the late-summer sunshine. Most were working on their projects outside, but some were just working on their tans! I couldn't blame them—it was one of those beautiful blue-sky days. The oppressive heat from the week before had pushed out to sea and the sweet summer breeze whispered of September. It was a treat for me—an aspiring writer, who had absolutely no time for writing—to have the opportunity to chat with artists and writers who were living the kind of life of which I dreamed! Everyone was welcoming and friendly and open to human interaction; as a result, lunch was late to several of the artists at the tail end of my route. I hoped no one would complain and, to this day, I think it's a wonder John never fired me! When I finally reached the most remote cabin on my route and lifted the last hickory basket from my backseat, I turned and saw him standing there, leaning on his cane.

"Thank goodness!" he said. "I was beginning to fade away to nothing."

I handed him his basket. "I'm sorry—I didn't mean to keep you waiting." His eyes sparkled mischievously and he set the basket down and reached up to push back his hair. It was then that I realized he truly depended on his cane. "Do you want me to put it on the porch for you?"

"No, no," he said, shaking his head. "I can manage—thank you, though." He leaned down to pick it up again and I noticed a long, angry scar that cut across his ankle.

"What happened to your leg?" I blurted out; then, surprised by my impertinence, blushed. "I'm sorry, that was rude."

"It's quite all right," he said with an easy smile. "It's an old injury—and a long story."

I nodded and glanced at my watch, knowing I should go, but at the same time feeling drawn to stay.

"What's your name?" he asked, leaning on his cane.

"Mia," I replied.

He smiled. "Thanks for lunch, Mia."

I nodded, loving the way he said it.

The summer days slipped by and I continued to deliver his lunch—late! And he continued to tease me about being famished. Our daily exchanges seemed innocent, but I sensed something unsaid— unacknowledged—smoldering like an underground fire waiting for a bit of oxygen to bring it to full flame; I could feel its heat when he teased me and I could see it in his eyes, and although I missed Tom desperately, those fleeting moments with David made my heart feel lighter.

I began to wonder when his residency would end, and on a rainy afternoon in late September, I found out. I parked beneath the huge old oak tree that was next to the cabin, looked up, and noticed a trail of white smoke whispering from the chimney. I peered through the windshield, hoping the down-pour would let up long enough for me to make my delivery. My wiper blades slapped back and forth noisily, and the rain pounded on the metal roof, seeping in along the windshield and leaving a clear rivulet trickling across my dusty dashboard. I looked up and saw him standing on the porch, grinning, with one of his palms up—as if asking, "Well?" I turned off the car, reached into the backseat for his basket, and, counting to three, threw open my door and ran for cover, almost slipping on the top step.

He reached out to catch me, but I managed to stay upright and he laughed. Then he looked down at my wet dress and realized I was shivering. "You're going to catch pneumonia," he said. "Come in and warm up." I carried the basket inside and set it on the table.

"It's so raw and rainy—I thought a fire would take the chill out of the air."

I walked over to it and held my hands out to soak up its warmth and then turned to warm my back. "It feels wonderful!"

He hesitated. "You really should take off those

wet things." I raised my eyebrows and he smiled impishly. "I mean . . . I have a robe."

I shook my head and laughed. "That's very tempting, but I better not."

He nodded, looking a bit relieved, and then, remembering the picnic basket, peered inside. "How about some soup? That'll warm you up."

I was starving, but I shook my head. "No, thanks—it's your lunch."

"I'm not much of a soup person."

I laughed. "Well, in that case, I'll have some."

"Good," he said, pulling out the thermos. "How 'bout half a sandwich?"

"Oh, no—I wouldn't want you to fade away to nothing," I teased.

"Ah—touché!" he said with a grin.

While he poured steaming tomato soup into two mugs, I looked around the room. It was simply furnished with mission furniture and a small matching table with four chairs for dining. The mullioned windows were tall and clear, and on a sunny day, I imagined the studio was airy and bright. The fieldstone fireplace filled the entire end wall, and above it hung a beautiful painting of the Old Man of the Mountain. Being a native of the great state of New Hampshire, I was very familiar with the iconic image and I paused, admiring the scene. Then I noticed another painting propped on an easel in the corner. It was a landscape, too—and I immediately recognized the setting, and walked over to it.

"This is beautiful!" I murmured.

He followed me, balancing one of the mugs in his hand. "Do you think so?"

*I nodded and realized he was focusing on not
spilling, so I held out my hands and he gratefully re-
linquished the mug to me. He studied the painting
critically. "I was working on it outside earlier and it
started to rain. It's not easy for me to break camp, so
it got wet—I should've known better." I nodded,
suddenly realizing how many trips he must've had
to make with only one free hand.*

*"I love the sunlight behind the trees and the way
the light and shadows stream across the canvas,
drawing your eye to the cabin . . . and I love that
old oak tree—it's so big I think it must have been
here during the Revolution."*

Rumer caught her breath and Beryl looked up in amazement.

"What?" Isak asked, looking from one to the other.

"It's the painting," Rumer said.

"What painting?"

"The one in Mum's shop," Beryl said.

Isak looked puzzled, trying to remember.

"The one over the fireplace," Beryl continued, trying to jog
her memory. "It's that exact scene—a cabin with an old oak tree
next to it."

"Are you sure?"

Rumer nodded. "It has to be! Ber, go on . . ."

Beryl traced her hand over the paper, scanning the lines,
looking for her spot.

*"I want to remember my time here," he said.
"It's been such a wonderful experience—even the
lunch lady—who's always late," he teased. "I almost put her old Plymouth Valiant in front of the
cabin."*

I cradled the mug in my hands and laughed. "Well, I'm glad you didn't—that would've ruined it."

He nodded toward the table. "I need to sit."

I glanced at my watch. "I can't stay—but I keep meaning to ask you . . . when does your residency end?"

He unwrapped the egg-salad sandwich and held out half to me, but I shook my head and took a sip of my soup. "Tomorrow," he answered with a sad smile.

"Oh," I said, suddenly feeling as if the rug had been pulled from under me.

"Mia," he said, searching my eyes. "I know we hardly know each other—in fact, I don't know anything about you—but, oddly, I feel as if I do." He paused. "It's almost as if . . . as if . . . we knew each other in another life." He shook his head. "I know that sounds crazy—I don't even believe in reincarnation. But I feel so . . . drawn to you—What is it about you? Is it your seeming zest for life? Is it how you—so easily—make me smile?" He shook his head. "I can't explain it—but I dare say, I'm going to miss you . . . and your beautiful smile." He laughed. "It's foolish for a married man to say such things to a married woman, but it's true." I was stunned by his words . . . and by his admission—it had never occurred to me that he was married. I'd never seen a ring and, at the same time, I'd never stopped wearing mine. What a pair!

I nodded slowly. "I'm sorry to hear it's ending so soon." I hesitated. "I'm going to miss delivering your lunch . . ." I smiled as I added, ". . . late!" I touched my rings and paused. "David," I said, shaking my head slowly, "I'm not married . . . any-

more." He looked surprised and I struggled to explain—the words feeling strange on my lips. *"I guess I never thought of taking off my rings . . . but, you see, my husband was killed in an accident."* As soon as I said the words, I felt hot tears stinging my eyes and, try as I might, I couldn't seem to stop them—they fell like the rain outside the window.

"Oh, Mia," he whispered, *"I had no idea—I'm so sorry."* He pulled me up into his arms, and I clung to him as I would a life raft. I don't know how long we stood there, I only remember the way it felt to be held after so long. I was weary from bearing my burden alone.

Finally, I pulled away—the reality of the world tugging me back. *"I'm sorry,"* I said, shaking my head and trying to muster a smile. *"I really should go. I have three little girls at home."*

"You do?!" His voice sounded incredulous, and he shook his head and laughed. *"Mia, I've learned more about you in the last eight minutes than I have in the last eight weeks!"*

I laughed, too, and he cupped his chin, thinking. *"Well, I don't want to lose track of you . . . what if I were to write?"*

"I'm sure you have more important things to do . . . Besides, what would your wife say?"

He didn't answer as he looked around for a pencil and paper, and I jotted down my name and address.

He looked at the paper and smiled. *"I will write to you, Mrs. Mia Graham."*

I nodded and laughed, but I honestly thought I would never hear from David Gilead again.

Beryl looked at her sisters. "Can you believe Mum never told us this?"

They both shook their heads. "It's crazy!" Rumer said.

"If it wasn't her handwriting," Isak added, "I wouldn't believe it."

"Should I keep going?"

Just then, Isak's phone rang. "It's Meghan," she said with a smile, getting up and going inside.

Beryl yawned. "I *must* be getting old, because lately wine just makes me very drowsy."

Rumer nodded. "I know what you mean." Then her phone rang too. She looked at the screen and sighed. "It's Will, Ber; I better take it too."

Beryl nodded as her sister went out into the yard. She stood and stretched too. "C'mon, Flan," she said, gently nudging the dog with her toe. "I guess story time is over."

Flan opened one droopy eye and then promptly closed it again. But after another encouraging toe nudge, she pulled herself up and tromped groggily down the steps.

❦ 16 ❧

From the bottom of the stairs, Micah could hear Harper's tail thumping on the hardwood floor, and when he reached the landing, he peeked around the door. The ceramic sleepy moon nightlight from his childhood softly illuminated the small bedroom that had also once been his, and Harper looked up, her tail still drumming on the floor as she wriggled onto her back expectantly. Micah knelt down to scratch her belly and whispered, "You're silly, you know that?" The soft kindness in his voice made her tail thump harder. Finally, he sat on the edge of the bed and looked around. After he'd asked his parents if he and Charlotte could move back home until he got his bearings again, his mom had immediately begun transforming his old room into one that was perfect for a little girl; and she'd claimed, after raising two boys, she'd loved every minute! Ocean blue walls had been painted a warm, sunny yellow; the windows had been cleaned to a sparkle, and the faded John Deere curtains had been washed, pressed, and tucked away; in their place were hung crisp new gingham curtains that were held open with playful Winnie-the-Pooh pull-backs; on the bed was a matching quilt and sham; other furnishings included a small white bureau and mirror, a child's refurbished wooden desk, and, in the corner, a small rocking chair that his dad had given a fresh coat of green paint—and sitting in the chair was Winnie himself.

Micah listened to Charlotte's soft breathing and lightly brushed back her wispy blond curls. He gazed at her sweet face—her nose sprinkled with freckles—and, for the millionth time, decided she looked just like her mother. "Good night, Char," he whispered. "I love you."

He leaned down to gently kiss her forehead, and she murmured sleepily, "To the moon and back."

Micah smiled and felt oddly at peace. This old house, with his parents downstairs, made him feel safe—just as he had when he was a boy—and it was a welcome respite from a world that left him feeling abandoned and broken.

"C'mon, Harp, let's go," Micah whispered and the happy-go-lucky Lab scrambled up to follow him down the stairs. Micah let her out the front door and then settled in a chair across from his mom.

Maddie peered at him over her glasses. "Sleeping?"

Micah nodded. "You really made that room so nice, Mom. I hope you know how much I appreciate it."

"It was my pleasure, hon. Charlotte's such a love and we enjoy having her—and you—here. It brings life back into this old house"—she eyed her husband—"and she definitely puts a sparkle in your dad's eyes."

Asa looked up from his book. "I always have a sparkle," he protested, sounding wounded.

"I know," Maddie teased. "But ever since that little girl marched up your front walk carrying her little pink suitcase and climbed into your lap, you sparkle all the time."

His dad grinned, knowing she was right. "What can I say? She's my little honey." He closed his book and stretched. "But you're my big honey," he teased, kissing the top of her head. His mom shook her head, and Micah laughed and wondered if he'd ever be able to let go of his past and fall in love again—if he'd ever have an easygoing, loving relationship like his parents had.

Asa opened the front door and Harper bounded over to Micah, wagging her tail. She leaned against him happily and then tried to push her hind end onto his lap.

"I think she likes you," his mom said with a laugh; then she looked up at her husband.

"Why don't you tell Micah your idea?"

Micah looked up at his dad, puzzled, and waited, scratching Harper's haunches.

Asa hesitated. "Well, I don't know if it's a good idea and I don't know if Beryl and her sisters already have plans—but I was thinking of offering to make a box or an urn out of wood. I have some nice oak."

"Dad, I think that's a great idea," Micah said with an approving nod.

Beryl woke with a start, disoriented, and glanced around the dark room. Gazing through the open window at the predawn sky, she suddenly remembered, with a sinking heart, why she was there. "Oh, Mum," she whispered, tears springing to her eyes. Sleep, she realized, offered only a temporary respite from the world and its troubles; inevitably, one had to wake up— only to be mercilessly slammed back into heart-wrenching reality. She laid still, her heart aching to relive one last treasured moment with her mom.

Listening to the familiar creaks and moans of the old house, she stared at a small crack in the ceiling and recalled the poignant scene in Thornton Wilder's beloved play, *Our Town*, when Emily is given the chance to return to life and witness a day from her childhood; it's not a birthday or holiday—it's an uneventful day like any other, and as the lovely voices from Emily's past come to life, she suddenly and sorrowfully realizes how fleeting and precious life is—and how we humans, tragically, don't seem to notice the loveliness of everyday moments while we are living them. A breeze whispered through the pines outside the window and Beryl, lying in her childhood bed, could almost hear her mom's voice calling up the stairs. . . .

"C'mon, girls, get moving or you're going to miss the bus!" The squeaky oven drawer clunks open and pots clank noisily against one another as one is yanked from underneath the pile of lids. "You're not going to have time for breakfast," warns her mom's exasperated voice. "Mum, where's my blue blouse?" Isak hollers impatiently. "It's still in the laundry, dear. You'll have to wear something else." The teakettle begins to sing softly. "Did you iron my skirt, Ma?" "It's hanging in your closet, Ru. Please hurry, and don't forget your homework!" The kettle whistles impatiently now and when it's finally lifted from the burner, it squawks with little bursts of steam. "Blueberry, are you up yet?" "Yes, Mum, I'm up," she calls back . . .

Beryl's reverie was suddenly interrupted by a cardinal calling—tentatively at first, then with more conviction. Not to be outdone, Mr. Grosbeak answered, adding a string of notes for good measure. Beryl glanced at the bedside clock: It was 4:30. She smiled; her mom always said the songbirds woke at 4:30—without fail; she'd said you could set your clock by it! And, oh, how many summer mornings had they cuddled in soft blankets on porch chairs and blinked at the gray sky, waiting in the cool misty air, just to hear that first sleepy chirp blossom into a chorus? As she listened now, a cheerful chickadee chimed in, and a bluebird, landing in the pine, cleared his throat and squeaked his bright, cheery greeting. Before long, there was a symphony coming from the trees, serenading the dawn. Beryl smiled and, as she brushed away her tears, an overwhelming sense of peace swept over her. . . . *"I'm right here, Berry, dear . . . I'm right here with you!"*

Beryl gulped down the last of her lukewarm tea and placed the empty teacup in the sink where Rumer was washing the breakfast dishes.

"Is the coffeepot empty?" Rumer asked, nodding at it.

Beryl swirled the ancient percolator and pulled off its top. "Yup." She unplugged it, gingerly lifted out the hot grounds, and dumped them in the garbage.

"Aren't you supposed to put those on the compost?" Rumer asked, eyeing her.

Beryl looked up in surprise and realized she was teasing. Rumer smiled and turned to look out the window at the mountain of rich, dark earth covered with tall, lush weeds. Mia had always been so conscientious about maintaining the compost pile: vegetable skins, banana peels, apple and cucumber peels, egg shells, coffee grounds—anything remotely biodegradable had gone into a pail, which, once full, had been carried out and deposited on the pile; then Mia had faithfully turned the pile with a pitchfork. *Who will benefit from all Mum's labor?* Rumer wondered sadly. . . . *Some family who just won't give a damn— that's who!*

Isak came into the kitchen carrying the boxes she'd been re-assembling with tape. "Are you two almost done with your room?" Not waiting for an answer, she continued, "Because I think we should start making some trips to the thrift store. There's going to be a lot and we don't want to overwhelm them."

"Maybe if we take a little every day, they won't know it's all coming from the same horde," Beryl suggested.

Isak nodded in agreement. "Well, I think we should try and take a load this morning if we can get one together." She paused, looking troubled. "Another problem, though, is we're not going to fit very much into either of our cars."

Beryl dried the last of the dishes and Rumer leaned against the counter, drying her hands. "I wonder if that old trailer is still in the garage."

Beryl groaned. "Now, that's a scary thought. None of us was ever very good at backing up that trailer—can you imagine trying to maneuver it in town? Besides, the Mini doesn't have a hitch, and I'm sure that Mustang doesn't either." She looked at Isak and teased, "How come you didn't rent a big SUV this time?"

"I didn't think of it," she said regretfully. "Don't you know anyone who has a truck?"

"Well, I know Will and Ru ..." she started to say, but Rumer just rolled her eyes. "Hey!" she added brightly. "Micah has a station wagon—and he did say he was going to call today."

"He did?!" Rumer and Isak both asked in surprised unison.

"Yup," Beryl replied with a grin.

"All right, well, let's start filling boxes and hopefully he'll call soon," Isak began. "If not, Ber, you'll have to call him."

They carried the empty boxes up the stairs. "This is so depressing," Rumer groaned.

"At least you two are working in the same room," Isak replied. "I'm all by myself."

"That's payback for having your own room when we were growing up," Beryl teased.

Isak shook her head and continued down the hall. "We need to start on Mum's room when we're finished with these," she called over her shoulder.

"That'll be even more depressing," Rumer lamented.

Beryl dropped her boxes on the floor and put her arm around her sister's shoulder. "We'll get through it, Ru."

"I know, but I just keep wishing we didn't have to sell the house at all."

"I wish that, too, but what else can we do? You're in Montana, Isak's in California—and it's too big for me. It'll be okay—I think you'll find that you won't miss it as much as you think. With time, material things—once we let go—have a way of not having the significance we've pinned to them."

"I hope you're right," Rumer said as she folded faded shorts, jeans, T-shirts, and blouses, and tucked them neatly into boxes.

"In fact," Beryl went on, "once we take this stuff to the thrift store, you probably won't ever think of it again."

Rumer raised her eyebrows doubtfully.

The morning slipped by—punctuated by numerous beeping from Rumer's phone, signaling texts from Rand. The first one reported that Norman had thrown up on the carpet—GROSS! And, as a result, he'd missed the bus—which made DAD even MADDER! The second one said that he'd gotten a C+ on a math test :-). The third text revealed he'd forgotten his lunch and had no money. STARVING! :-(

"I thought kids weren't supposed to use their phones in school," Beryl said.

"They're not," Rumer replied as she tediously pressed buttons two and three times in an effort to respond to him on her outdated flip phone, which was held together with artist's tape.

"C-plus on a math test—what's up with that?"

"That's good!" Rumer replied with a smile, obviously pleased by the report.

"What's he going to do about lunch?"

Rumer was concentrating on her phone and answered slowly as she typed, "I . . . hope . . . he . . . can . . . borrow . . . some . . . money . . ."

Beryl left her sister to her archaic texting and carried a heavy box out into the hall. She dropped it with a thud, arched her aching back, and decided to check on Isak. Peering into the room at the end of the hall, she asked, "How's it going?"

"Almost done!" Isak said, looking up as she sealed a box with tape. Several piles of boxes were already stacked around the room, and the closet and bureau drawers were open and empty. "I just need to vacuum."

"You're such a go-getter!" Beryl teased.

"Right," Isak replied with a hint of sarcasm. "I just want to go-get it over with. This is definitely not fun."

"Did you find anything worth keeping?"

Isak nodded and lifted the lid off a box on the bed. "I found this Steiff toy." She held up a small, bristly beaver. "But he's missing his tag—probably because I cut it off when I was little. And I found my Bible and some other books Mum gave me through the years." She glanced through the titles: "*Out of Africa* and *Shadows on the Grass*—of course—"

"That's funny," Beryl interrupted, "I found *West with the Night* too."

Isak smiled and continued, "It's an eclectic collection . . . *Catcher in the Rye, Siddhartha, The Fountainhead, Jane Eyre, Dandelion Wine, East of Eden, The Great Gatsby* . . . Oh, I also found *Where the Wild Things Are*—I think it might be a first edition."

"It would say on the copyright page."

Isak opened the book and scanned the page; her face lit up. "First edition—1963—didn't it win the Caldecott, though? It doesn't have a sticker."

"It wouldn't if it's a first edition—it hadn't won yet."

"It was a birthday present—and it's signed by Mum and Dad."

"You're lucky—I don't have any books like that. Unfortunately, their inscription probably brings down its value."

"Not for me—besides, I'd never sell it." Then, suddenly realizing her younger sister couldn't possibly have any gifts from their dad, she asked, "Do you want it, Ber? I'd give it to you."

"Don't be silly, it's yours—besides, you're going to be a grandma someday and you'll have someone to read it to."

Isak groaned. "Don't remind me!"

Beryl slipped her hands in her pockets and leaned against the door. "Aren't you looking forward to being a grandma?"

Isak sat on the bed and sighed. "I am—someday. I'm just not looking forward to being old enough to be one."

"Mum loved being a grandma."

"I know she did—too bad we were so far away." She shook

her head sadly. "I really regret not living closer. I wish I hadn't been so selfish."

Beryl frowned. "You weren't selfish. You just had a life of your own—Mum understood that." She sat on the bed next to Isak, slipped the famous children's book from her hands, and slowly turned the pages.

Isak looked at the pictures too. "I was a lot like Max," she said with a chuckle. "Bossy, unruly, imprudent . . ."

Beryl laughed. "You still are! But Mum *always* had supper waiting for you." Isak's face was shadowed with pain, and Beryl could see the unguarded grief in her sister's eyes. It was the same look she'd seen in her sister's eyes the day their beloved golden retriever, Hemingway, had been hit by a car— and Isak, older and wiser at age ten, had been the one to find him lying by the side of the road.

"I miss her so much, Ber," she whispered, her eyes filling with tears.

Beryl put her arms around her. "I know . . . I know—I miss her too."

Just then, Rumer appeared in the doorway. "Hey! Is this a private party or can anyone . . . ?"

"You can . . ." they said, wiping their eyes and motioning for her to join them.

Rumer sat down next to Isak and Beryl explained, "We were just missing Mum . . . and Isak finally admitted she was a lot like Max." She smoothed her hand over the book's cover and Rumer realized she was talking about the wayward character in the children's book.

"Well, I won't argue with that," she teased. "She still is!"

"Thanks a lot, you two," Isak sniffled. "I love that you both feel the same way about me."

Rumer paused. "Anyway, I came to see if you guys are ready for lunch."

"Yup," Beryl said with a nod. "Speaking of which, did Rand resolve his problem?"

"His teacher gave him a pass to buy a hot lunch, thank goodness."

A soft beep came from Beryl's pocket, but she didn't seem to hear it, and Isak and Rumer both looked at her curiously. "What?" she asked innocently.

"No wonder you don't get your messages," Rumer said. "You don't hear your phone."

"I thought it was one of yours," she said, feeling foolish, and pulled her phone from her pocket. Sure enough, the tiny screen indicated she had two new messages. Isak eyed the old phone and groaned. "I totally know what I'm getting you guys for Christmas!"

Rumer shook her head. "As much as I'd love an iPhone, the monthly charge is twice as much as a regular phone—so don't get one for me!"

"Ru, you do realize you'll be able to afford an extra ten dollars a month by then?"

Rumer shook her head doubtfully. "I'll believe it when I see it."

Beryl was smiling to herself and they both looked over her shoulders trying to see the screen. "Micah wants to know if we'd like a pizza for lunch," she said quietly.

Isak nodded. "Sure! And ask him if we can use his car too."

Beryl started typing slowly, pressing buttons multiple times, and Isak just shook her head. "You guys really need to come out of the Dark Ages."

"I don't think two or three years ago can be considered Dark Ages," Beryl said, concentrating on her phone.

"In this day and age it is!"

Beryl's phone beeped again and she immediately clicked on the message. "Any preferences?"

"Pizza Barn," Rumer suggested hopefully.

"I don't think they're open on Mondays."

"Grappelli's, then—how 'bout Hawaiian?"

"Fine with me," Isak said with a shrug. "Can you ask him to grab a bottle of Diet Coke too? Or, on second thought, a six-pack of Corona with a lime would be even better."

Beryl shook her head. "Let's not make it complicated."

"Fine," Isak said with a resigned sigh. She stood up and carefully slipped her books back into her box.

"Hey!" Rumer said, eyeing the dog-eared copy of *The Fountainhead*. "Is that mine?"

"I don't think so," Isak said, opening the cover. But on the title page it was inscribed: *For Rumer, on the occasion of your eighteenth birthday! Lots of Love, Mum.* Sorry, I guess it is!" she said, smiling and handing it to her sister.

While they waited for Micah, they started carrying filled boxes down the narrow stairs and stacking them by the door. Beryl found paper plates and napkins in the pantry, and was pouring iced tea when Flannery pulled herself up from her bed, plodded over to the door, and pressed her flat nose against the screen. Moments later, Micah appeared, holding a large pizza box; trailing up the stairs behind him was Charlotte, happily clutching a fistful of droopy dandelions that she'd gathered on her way from the car.

"Come on in," Beryl called.

Micah pulled open the door and held it for Charlotte, who had finally reached the top step; but before he realized it, Flannery had pushed past him and headed straight over to greet the newest little arrival. Surprised, Charlotte stopped in her tracks and eyed the homely face uncertainly, but, ever-uninhibited, Flannery marched right up to her, sniffing and wiggling happily. Charlotte tentatively held out her hand and Flan gave it a sloppy, wet kiss, making Charlotte giggle.

"This is Flannery," Micah explained, squatting down next to

her. Charlotte nodded and gently rested her hand on Flan's big head.

Beryl appeared at the door and smiled. "Did you find a new friend, Flan?"

Micah looked up and grinned. "Charlotte loves dogs."

"Well, then, it's a match made in heaven because Flan loves kids—they're more her size."

Smiling, Charlotte walked through the door with Flan at her heels, but then the little girl stopped short to give Beryl the bouquet, and the old dog, who had her head down, sniffing, bumped right into her and Beryl had to reach out to steady her. "Watch where you're goin', Flan," she scolded gently. "These are beautiful, Charlotte—thank you! Do you want to help me put them in water?" Charlotte nodded and they went right over to the sink where Beryl lifted her up onto the counter. She rinsed out an old dusty Mason jar that was on the windowsill, filled it with fresh water, and Charlotte carefully arranged each stem, trying to encourage them with her finger to lift their heavy heads, but they just continued to droop. Beryl saw the dismay on her face and quietly reassured her, "Don't worry, Char, they'll perk up." She looked up and saw Micah, still holding the pizza box, watching them. He smiled and she laughed shyly. "You can put that down, you know."

Just then, Rumer and Isak came down the stairs and dropped two more heavy boxes onto the pile. "Hey, Micah!" they both said.

"Hey! Looks like you're making progress."

"We are—but did Beryl tell you? We need a way to transport all these boxes to the thrift store."

"She did tell me, and Charlotte and I, and our old station wagon, are at your service."

Isak and Rumer looked up and realized Charlotte was sitting on the kitchen counter. "Hey, girlfriend!" they both said.

Charlotte turned shyly away and Beryl put her arm around

her. "Charlotte brought us this beautiful bouquet," she said. The little girl looked up in surprise and pointed to Beryl. Beryl looked puzzled. "They're just for me?" Charlotte nodded, and Isak and Rumer both laughed. "You don't need to be afraid of those two crazy ladies," Beryl said. "They're just my big sisters." But Charlotte wasn't convinced and eyed them skeptically.

"She'll warm up," Micah said with a laugh. "Usually, I can't get a word in edgewise."

Beryl leaned closer and whispered in her ear, "Ready for some pizza?"

Charlotte grinned and nodded.

❧ 18 ❧

Micah looked into his rearview mirror as they turned out of the driveway and realized that Charlotte was already sound asleep. Beryl glanced over her shoulder. "Somebody's tired," she said with a smile. "She was so good helping you carry those small boxes across the yard."

Micah nodded. "She loves to help—she's just like her mom." He shook his head sadly, remembering. "Beth was always ready to help; she'd do anything for anyone. And now, whenever I'm working on a project, Charlotte's right there, ready to help too. It doesn't matter what it is—raking leaves, shoveling snow, building a birdhouse—she even has her own pint-size rake, shovel, and hammer. She's too funny!" He paused and glanced at Beryl. "This will probably sound crazy, but sometimes I think Beth is guiding her, helping her look after me."

Beryl smiled. "I don't think it's crazy, Micah," she said softly. "Ever since my mom died, it feels like she's closer than ever."

Micah nodded slowly. "I know what you mean. Sometimes,

out of the blue, I'm filled with this funny, comforting warmth that I can't explain." He paused. "And other times, when I'm trying to make a decision, I'll have a sudden strong conviction when, previously, I was pretty uncertain. It's almost like—if we're receptive—we can truly sense the presence of someone's spirit." He paused. "I also think little kids sense it the most. They're open to anything, so they naturally—and without question—can feel a loved one's presence."

"I agree," Beryl said. "Little kids are amazing."

Micah nodded and they were quiet for a while. Finally, Beryl broke the silence. "I can't thank you enough for doing all this, Micah."

"It's my pleasure," he replied with a slow smile. "Oh, by the way, my dad mentioned that he was thinking of making a box for your mom's ashes. He didn't know what you had planned, but he said the urns they sell are kind of impersonal and he thought it would be nice to have something special. He said he has a nice piece of oak . . ."

"He would do that?!" Beryl asked in surprise.

Micah nodded.

"Well, we actually haven't picked anything out yet. I guess we've just been avoiding thinking about it, but if your dad has time, that would be wonderful."

"Okay, I'll tell him. Actually, you can tell him because I was thinking that, after we drop this stuff off, we can swing past my parents' house, drop Charlotte off, and borrow my dad's lawn mower. Then while you're getting another load ready, I can mow the lawn." He smiled. "Charlotte thinks you live on a dandelion farm!"

Beryl laughed and shook her head. "You know, you—and your parents—are really going above and beyond, Micah. I'd love to thank your dad in person, and if you just let us borrow the mower, I'm sure one of us can mow."

"Don't be silly. You already have plenty to do and I'm happy to help. Besides, my dad's mower can be a cramp—you have to know just where to kick it."

Beryl laughed. "Well, you'll just have to stay for supper again, which reminds me, can we stop at the store on our way back? Isak handed me a list when we were leaving."

"Sure, but I don't think anything can top last night's supper; that ravioli was amazing."

Beryl pulled the slip of paper from her pocket. "Let's see—angel hair, asparagus, tomatoes—which we already have—olive oil, butter, garlic, fresh basil, fresh spinach, strawberries, sliced almonds, more wine—with a smiley face next to it—and vanilla ice cream—sounds like another pasta dish is in our future."

"Sounds like you're part Italian," Micah said with a grin.

"How'd you know? My mom used to tell us we had olive oil running through our veins. Her maiden name was Gentile, and pasta was always on the menu in our house. She used to make the most amazing gravy."

"Gravy?" Micah asked, looking puzzled.

Beryl smiled. "Spaghetti sauce."

"Oh!"

"It's an all-day event, though. I wish I had time. Maybe someday, when things settle down, I'll make it for you."

Micah pulled into the parking lot of the thrift store and smiled. "I'm going to hold you to that."

"Okay," Beryl laughed. "It's the least I can do!"

The ladies who were manning the thrift store that afternoon tried valiantly to hide their dismay when they saw all the boxes coming through their front door at closing time, and Mrs. Harrison—who Micah and Beryl had both had for kindergarten, and who looked the same as she had back then—didn't seem to recognize them, but mustered a bright smile and asked them if they'd like a receipt.

"No, no thank you," Beryl replied. "That's not necessary."

"Well, thank you very much, then," Mrs. Harrison said cheerily.

"Until what time are you open?" Beryl asked.

"We're open until four—but we're closed on Tuesdays."

Beryl's face dropped. "Oh, okay," she replied. "Well, thank you. Maybe we'll see you on Wednesday."

Mrs. Harrison squinted, studying Beryl's face. "Aren't you one of Mia Graham's daughters?" Beryl nodded and the gray-haired lady smiled sadly. "I'm so sorry to hear about your mother, dear—she was a sweet, sweet lady."

Beryl nodded again. "Thank you," she said quietly.

As they got back in the car, tears spilled down Beryl's cheeks. "I'm so not ready for this," she whispered.

Micah reached his arm around her. "Nobody's ever ready, Ber—all you can do is take one day at a time."

Beryl nodded and wiped her eyes. "I'm sorry, I seem to cry at the drop of a hat these days."

"Don't be sorry. I know how it is," Micah commiserated.

"I know you do," Beryl said, wiping her eyes. "We're quite a pair, aren't we?"

"We are," he whispered, pulling her closer.

Ten minutes later, they turned into the driveway of one of the most beautifully restored Victorians in town, and Micah gently unhooked Charlotte's car seat and lifted her out.

"Hi," Maddie Coleman called as she came out onto the porch, drying her hands with a dish towel.

"Hi, Mrs. Coleman," Beryl said with a wave.

"Is Dad here?" Micah asked as he handed Charlotte, still sound asleep, to his mom.

Maddie nodded. "He's puttering around out back somewhere."

"I was hoping to borrow your mower."

"I'm sure you can."

Micah raised his eyebrows questioningly. "Also, do you think you can look after Charlotte again tonight?"

"I think I can manage that, hon," she said, winking at Beryl.

"Thanks," he said with a grin, kissing her cheek.

Beryl followed Micah around the house and they found Asa cleaning out bluebird houses. Nosing along beside him was Harper, who bounded over happily when she saw them. Beryl also noticed four little Bantam hens and a rooster pecking around at Mr. Coleman's feet; they seemed completely uninhibited by the big black dog racing around the yard. Asa looked up and smiled. "Where's my little helper?"

"Asleep," Micah said, scratching Harper's head. "Dad, I was wondering if I could borrow the mower to mow Beryl's mom's place?"

"Sure, but you'll have to get gas."

As Micah walked toward the shed, a bluebird landed on one of the houses. "Guess he knows you're getting his house ready for him," Micah observed with a smile.

"There've been a couple of pairs around, so I thought I'd better get out here. The problem is the damn wrens fill all the houses with sticks as soon as I empty them—just to keep out other tenants."

Beryl shook her head. "It's too bad some birds are like that. My mom had a bluebird house and she had the same pair come every year."

Asa nodded. "They'll do that; sometimes they even have more than one brood in a season. Speaking of which, would you like some fresh eggs?" He motioned to a basket full of brown speckled eggs on the steps. "These little ladies bless us with more than we can ever possibly eat."

"Yes, I'd love some."

He retrieved an empty egg carton from the garage, filled it, and handed it to Beryl. "Thanks!" she said. "Oh! And Micah was telling me about your idea, Mr. Coleman—are you sure you have time to do something like that?"

"I would be honored," he said solemnly.

"Well, it's very thoughtful. We would certainly appreciate it."

"Good!" he said with a smile. "I have some beautiful wood that came from an old oak tree that fell down over at MacDowell Colony. They said it crushed one of the cabins—and when they were milling it into boards, they hit several bullets that they think are from the Revolution."

Beryl stared in wonder. "That sounds perfect," she said. "Thank you."

She saw Micah pushing the lawn mower toward the car with one hand while carrying the gas can with the other. "I guess I better help! Thank you, Mr. Coleman."

"Good luck with that pesky mower!" he called.

As they drove back to the house, Beryl was quiet and Micah looked over. "A penny for your thoughts . . ."

She smiled. "My mom used to say that." She paused, reflecting on the news his dad had shared—news that wouldn't mean anything to anyone else. "Did your dad tell you where the oak came from?"

"No."

"It's from an old oak tree that was on the MacDowell property."

Micah looked puzzled. "I'm sure there're lots of oak trees on that property."

"He said this one crushed one of the cabins."

"That's too bad."

"Well, the odd thing is, we found a memoir, of sorts, that my mom wrote and we started reading it, and in it she mentions an old oak tree that was beside one of the cabins. She said it was old enough to have seen the Revolutionary War."

"I wonder if it's the same one."

"Your dad said it had bullets in it," Beryl said. "It's unbelievable if it is. I was actually hoping you'd have a chance to look at the memoir before supper—since you know so much about David Gilead," Beryl said as they pulled into the driveway.

"I'd like to," Micah replied. "I still can't believe your mom knew him."

"Well, we didn't get very far. I wanted to keep reading it last night, but it got late and my sisters' phones kept ringing. Later, though, we're going to read more—so you should stay . . ."

"I'd like to."

∽ 19 ∽

Suppertime had always been an event at the Graham house and, from a very young age, the girls understood it was a time for family fellowship and renewal—a time to catch up after a long day apart—and from preparation to cleanup, everyone pitched in, unless someone was mercilessly buried in homework. And now, although Mia was dearly missed, her girls were determined to keep the tradition.

"Finally!" Isak said when Beryl came in with two green bags over her shoulders and a bottle of wine tucked under each arm.

"Did you get lost?" Rumer teased. "We were going to start on Mum's room, but we decided we couldn't do it without you."

"You could do it without me."

"No, we couldn't—there's too much jewelry and too many sentimental things. We need to agree on what should be donated, and the rest will have to be divided up somehow," Isak said, leaving little room for dispute.

"Well, there's no hurry—the thrift store is closed tomorrow," Beryl reported, unpacking the bags.

"Shh-ugar!" Isak said with a frown. "That'll set us back."

"It doesn't have to," Rumer offered. "We need to get more boxes anyway."

"Oh, you should've reminded me," Beryl said. "We were just at the store."

Outside the window, the lawn mower sputtered to life, and Isak and Rumer looked up in surprise.

Beryl explained loudly, "Micah offered to mow."

"That's great!" Isak said. "It needs it!"

"I know, Charlotte thinks we live on a dandelion farm."

"She's such a honey," Isak said.

"So is Micah . . ." Rumer added with a grin.

"Yeah, Ber, he definitely has potential—and he obviously likes you; otherwise, he wouldn't be helping so much."

"Maybe he's just being a good neighbor," Beryl countered, but Isak and Rumer both shook their heads.

The mower started to move away from the house and the sweet scent of freshly mown grass drifted in the windows. Beryl told them about the box Mr. Coleman had offered to make, from the fallen oak, and they agreed it was a wonderful gesture—and very serendipitous if it was the same tree!

"Okay," Beryl said, changing the subject. "So, what's on the menu?"

Isak glanced at the clock above the kitchen sink and realized it was after five. She reached into the drawer for a bottle opener, and answered, "Angel hair with asparagus and tomato." Then she held the bottles out at arm's length and squinted. "Red or white?"

"Red," Rumer said.

"None for me yet," Beryl answered. "I'm waiting for Micah— and besides, I really could use a cup of tea."

Isak opened the red while Rumer set out glasses and Beryl filled the kettle with fresh water.

"Can you fill the pasta pot too?" Isak asked.

Beryl pulled the heavy pot from under the counter.

Rumer took a sip from her glass. "Do you have a job for me?"

Isak slid out three cutting boards, explained the recipe, and they all set to work rinsing, trimming, and chopping vegetables, and when Micah was finally far enough away from the house so they could hear, Beryl slipped Ol' Blue Eyes on the turntable again.

Isak took a sip of her wine and, holding a wooden spoon to her lips, joined in as Frank sang "Someone to Watch over Me." Rumer and Beryl both grinned, held up their own utensil microphones, and sang along dramatically.

They were so caught up in the song, they didn't notice when the mower grew quiet or when Micah pulled open the screen and leaned against the door frame, but when the song ended, he started to clap. "You guys should take it on the road!" he teased. They looked up in embarrassment and laughed.

"Dinner smells good!" he said, dropping into one of the chairs. Flannery moseyed over to say hello and he scratched her behind her ears and then took off his glasses to wipe them with his shirt.

"Thanks for mowing," Beryl said.

"Yeah, thanks, Micah!" Isak and Rumer chimed in.

"Want somethin' to drink?"

"Water'd be great."

"Lemon?"

"Please."

Beryl filled a tall glass with ice, squeezed lemon over it, filled it with cold water, and dropped the lemon in.

"Let me know when you're ready for something stronger," Isak said with a wink.

Beryl rolled her eyes and then slid the manuscript in front of him. She wasn't sure why she was eager for him to read it when they didn't even know what was in it, but she knew he was genuinely interested . . . and she really wanted him to have a reason to stay.

"Why don't you take this out on the porch where it's quiet," she said. "Then you don't have to listen to us sing."

Micah looked wounded. "But I love your singing."

Beryl laughed and shrugged. "Suit yourself."

Twenty minutes later, Rumer scooped fresh spinach, strawberries, and almonds tossed in sweet homemade vinaigrette onto the four blue Staffordshire plates that were lined up on the kitchen counter; and Beryl, using a pasta spoon, followed, heaping a bed of fresh angel hair next to the salad. Isak was right behind her, ladling generous portions of buttery garlic, asparagus, and tomatoes on top.

Micah looked up from his reading and watched them. "You guys really have this supper thing down to a science."

Isak filled wineglasses and lit candles. "Yup, it's taken years, but we finally have a system . . . and it usually includes some form of pasta because pasta, as our mother used to say, is Mother Nature's answer to Prozac."

Micah laughed and quickly gathered up the papers as Beryl and Rumer carried steaming plates to the table.

"Ber, did you feed Flan?" Rumer asked, eyeing the string of drool hanging from the dog's jowls.

Beryl made a funny face.

"How 'bout Thoreau?"

This time she just shook her head. "I forgot, but I'll do it now."

"You know what they say," Rumer teased, "your memory is the first to go."

"That's not funny," Beryl said, frowning as she measured kibble into Flan's bowl.

"I'm just kidding," Rumer said, standing next to her, out of earshot of the others.

"Well, I'm not," Beryl shot back. "I'm really worried about it."

"You shouldn't be," Rumer consoled, dumping cat food into Thoreau's bowl. "You worry too much."

"You're one to talk."

Rumer ignored her. "Maybe you should start eating more berries—they're supposed to be great for your memory, especially blueberries."

Beryl set Flan's bowl down and gave her some fresh water too. "Maybe," she mumbled.

"C'mon, you two," Isak called impatiently.

Rumer and Beryl eased into their seats and Beryl said, "You know, we really should say grace—we didn't say it last night and I think Mum would be disappointed."

Isak took a sip of her wine. "Go to it."

They bowed their heads and Beryl quietly said the prayer Mia had taught them when they were little and, when she finished, a comforting peace seemed to settle over the table.

⤳ 20 ⤳

"Did you get to the part where he promised to write to her?" Beryl asked, turning to Micah, who was sitting across from her on the porch, cradling a bowl of apple crisp and vanilla ice cream.

He nodded, licking his spoon. "Yup, I'm where he's trying to convince her to model for him."

They all looked at him with raised eyebrows and he realized they hadn't gotten that far. "Hmm . . . I guess you didn't read that part yet, but she did say no—at least so far . . ." he added, as if the additional information might save him.

Beryl laughed. "You've just piqued our interest even more!"

Micah took a bite of his apple crisp. "This is very good."

"Which?" Isak teased, taking a sip of her drink. "The apple crisp or the story?"

"Both," he said with a grin.

Beryl smiled, scanned the page, and began to read. . . .

After David left, I was surprised by how much I missed the sweet anticipation of seeing him standing on the porch, waiting for me—and how much I missed being teased about being late. Work became mundane again, and an older woman moved into his cabin; her name was Jean and she was writing a novel—her third. Unlike David, she kept to herself and rarely ventured outside, but I could hear her busily tapping away on her typewriter when I dropped off her lunch. The autumn leaves swirled around my car as I made my daily rounds, but in my mind the grayness of the bare limbs was only a depressing harbinger of the cold, snowy winter to come.

Life was busy. Between working, being Mum to three little women—all with wonderfully different personalities—and single-handedly running our household, I was exhausted by the end of the day, and was even known to fall asleep on the clean laundry spread out on the bed, waiting to be folded. Looking back, my weariness was a blessing, though, as my nightmares, for the most part, subsided.

Every day after work and picking up the girls, I pulled up in front of our rusty, snowplow-battered mailbox, my heart full of hope, only to be disappointed. What was I hoping for? David was married and I was foolish to give him a second thought; at the same time, I couldn't forget the way it felt to be held in his arms. The weeks went by and I decided I was never going to hear from him again when—on what would have been Tom's and my sixth wedding anniversary—a tissue paper–thin envelope was tucked between the bills. I stared at the elegant handwriting and my heart skipped a beat. I wanted to tear it open right then and there and devour its contents; but at the same time, I wanted to sit qui-

etly and savor every word. The girls were restless in the backseat, anxious to get home, so I tucked the envelope back between the bills and turned down the driveway.

Twenty minutes later, with the little women in my charge all sitting on blankets, watching Sesame Street and contentedly munching on Cheerios, I slipped outside with a steaming mug of Darjeeling tea. Cuddled into my new cozy L.L. Bean jacket that my parents had given me for my birthday, I sat in one of the Adirondack chairs, centered my mug on the wide-board arm of the chair, and slowly unfolded the crisp, white paper.

Beryl looked up, and with a broad smile, pointed down at the arm of her chair and the mug of tea.

"You go, girl!" Isak said with an approving nod.

Beryl laughed and continued.

I read his words slowly, savoring each one. He opened by saying he was sorry for not writing sooner (for which he was immediately forgiven!) and went on to say he was coming from London to New York for an opening in December and was hoping we could meet for dinner. My mind raced—did he mean dinner in New Hampshire or in New York? I continued to read and he talked about going to see the Christmas tree together, which clarified that he meant New York. He also said he'd applied for another residency at MacDowell and he asked if I'd still be his lunch lady. I laughed out loud—of course I'd be his lunch lady! My heart grew lighter as I read—now I had something to look forward to as I trudged through the long New England winter. Not

*that I didn't look forward to all the things the girls
and I would do together—from celebrating Christmas to sledding in the falling snow—I looked forward to every minute! But this was something for
me—something special—even if it was just a friendship. He closed by saying he missed my smile, which
made me smile, and he said that he'd call when he
reached New York. It was signed: Always, David.*

*I ran my fingers lightly over his words, rereading
them carefully, then wrapped my hands around my
warm mug and gazed out at the gray November
clouds hanging over the windswept amber fields. I
already knew—even though I'd love to—that I
couldn't, in good conscience, justify running off to
New York City to have dinner with a married man.*

*If he wanted to see me, he'd just have to come to
New Hampshire.*

"Jeez-Louise!" Isak said, shaking her head in disbelief. "This
happened on their anniversary? On the first anniversary of the
accident?!"

Beryl shrugged. "Maybe it was God's way of getting Mum
through the day—it would've been awful otherwise."

"Oh, right!" Isak said, her voice laced with sarcasm. "So
now God's plan is to bring a married man into Mum's life to
help her get through the difficult anniversary of the loss of her
husband—that makes sense!"

"Hey," Rumer interjected. "You never know—everything
happens for a reason."

"Yeah, I believe that one too," Isak said skeptically, standing
up to stretch her legs. "Does anyone need a refill?" she said,
picking up her glass. Rumer shook her head; she still had some
tea in her mug, and Micah had just downed a large glass of milk
with his apple crisp.

"I'm all set," Beryl said, nodding to her mug. "But you go ahead—we'll wait."

When Isak returned, Beryl continued.

> *"Mum! Isak changed the channel," I heard a small voice shout. I groaned—so much for my moment of peace and quiet! I folded the letter, slid it back in its envelope, picked up my mug, and hurried inside to find Isak with her hand over the TV knob, and* All My Children *on the screen; Rumer was practically in tears, trying to pull her hand away and turn the knob back; and Beryl, blissfully unaware of the ruckus in which her big sisters were engaged, sat in the middle of the blanket happily feeding Hemingway—one Cheerio at a time.*

"Hemingway was such a great dog," Isak said sadly. Rumer nodded and caught Beryl's eye; they each knew what the other was thinking—having often reflected on the effect their beloved pet's death had had on Isak—and ultimately deciding it had been his tragic death and her discovery of his lifeless body that had triggered her guarded reluctance to show emotion.

Rumer quickly changed the subject. "Even at the tender age of five, Isak," she teased, "you preferred soap operas over cartoons."

Isak laughed, knowing she was right.

> *In the weeks that followed, I must've changed my mind a hundred times—I would go to New York. I'd make up an excuse and leave the girls with my parents—it wasn't too much to ask—dinner, the tree, the bustle and bright lights of the city, seeing David—it all seemed so exciting—how could I say no? After all I'd been through, I deserved to go!*

This was my argument as I lay in bed late at night; but in the morning, as I braided hair, made oatmeal, washed dishes, and cleaned up after little people, I knew I wouldn't go—but, believe me, in my mind, it was an ongoing battle!

Thankfully, on the night David called, the weather forecast usurped all further argument. It was early December and I'd just tucked the girls into bed, when the phone rang. No one ever called that late, so my heart was pounding when I picked up the receiver. I could hardly believe my ears—on the other end was the unmistakable voice I'd been longing to hear! I could hardly catch my breath as I excitedly peppered him with questions. His answers were measured and calm. Yes, he'd been granted another residency; yes, he'd be coming to MacDowell late that spring; yes, he was in New York—it was beautiful in the snow—and . . . he couldn't wait to see me.

I was silent. Oh, how I wanted to see him! Finally, I stammered, "David, I-I can't come. The snowstorm you're having in New York is headed our way. We're expecting eighteen to twenty-four inches in the next couple of days and I hate traveling in the snow. I can't just think about myself, I have to think about the girls." I could hear the disappointment in his voice as he spoke and I asked him if he might be able to venture north instead.

He was quiet, then answered softly, "If it's supposed to be that bad, Mia, I don't think it would be wise for me to come either. If something happened, I'd have trouble explaining . . ."

"Yes, of course," I said quickly. "I completely understand."

I should have known right then and there—I could hear the alarm bells going off in my head; I could feel the sting of his words at the mention of having to consider someone else; and I could feel a heavy, dull ache in my heart because there was someone else—but, for some reason, I ignored all the signs. I just didn't care.

"I'm sorry," I said softly.

"Me too," he said.

I went to bed that night feeling confused and sad, and lay awake for a long time, second-guessing my decision. The next morning, however, the girls and I woke up to a good old-fashioned blizzard, and I couldn't help but wonder if God's hand had played a part in saving me from my own weakness.

"There!" Isak declared, her voice unexpectedly loud. "That makes more sense," she blurted. "God working to foil their plans—that's more like it!"

Rumer eyed her. "Isak, aren't you the one who said Mum should've 'lived a little'?"

"I did—but I didn't mean this. . . ."

Then Rumer caught Beryl's eye and they both wondered at Isak's sudden, strong sense of moral indignation.

My mother, whose family hailed from southern Italy, always said it takes fortitude and endurance to be a New Englander—an observation that's especially true when the power goes out, as it did that weekend. It was the first time the girls had experienced life with no electricity or running water—which meant no TV, flushing toilets, or heat—and the novelty of pioneer life wore off quickly. I brought in armloads of firewood and we huddled near the woodstove, playing *Candy Land*, roasting hot dogs, making s'mores, and trying to keep warm; and later in the day, as the house grew dark, I rooted around in the drawers, looking for candles. I found Tom's old Coleman lantern at the bottom of a jumbled closet and a down sleeping bag from his Boy Scout days. With Isak and Rumer curled up in the sleeping bag and Beryl sound asleep under a wool blanket, I pulled out a worn copy of one of my favorite books and began to read out loud; the girls were immediately captivated by the lyrical story of Mary Lennox and the hidden garden she discovered.

I read until they fell asleep; then I added more wood to the stove and heated up water for tea. With my hands wrapped around the warm mug, I gazed at my three little sleepyheads—their faces softly lit by Tom's lantern—and I was amazed by how much they looked like him. Listening to the wind howl around the house and the snow rattle against the windows, I remembered how much he'd loved snowstorms. He would've called this an adventure and he would've kept the porch swept off, brought in more firewood than we could possibly use, regaled the girls with Boy Scout stories, and made it fun for all of us—especially me. As I sat there, remembering him, a warm peace filled my heart . . . it was almost as if he was near.

The winter that followed on the heels of that blizzard was the harshest I'd ever known—but we hearty New England girls survived! I'd never shoveled more snow or brought in more firewood than I did that year. My dad, a true New Englander whose roots could be traced back to the Revolution, always said, "Hard work builds character"—and there was *plenty of character building going on during those cold months! There was also plenty of time to think— and even though David's letters were warm and funny and caring—my new-found fortitude triggered a surprising resolve to keep our relationship platonic.*

The long, snowy winter finally eased and, as the days grew warmer, the girls and I spent more and more time outside. Rumer—my blossoming horticulturist, inspired by The Secret Garden*—loved to help in the yard and kept careful watch as each flower—from snowdrop and crocus to black-eyed Susan and lily—and, later on, to chrysanthemum and aster—enjoyed its proud moment in the sun. Our winter reading choice had had a profoundly different effect on Isak, however; she was deeply saddened and frightened by the realization that a young girl could lose both of her parents, as Mary had. For months afterward, tears welled up in her eyes in the evening at bedtime. "Mum, please don't die," she'd whisper. "I just couldn't live without you." Oh, how my heart ached for my little girl—I knew all too well the paralyzing fear that could grip a heart. "Don't worry, honeybee," I'd say softly, brushing back her strawberry-blond wisps of hair. "I'll be around for a very, very long time. I won't leave you alone—I promise."*

Isak bit her lip stoically, trying to fight back her tears, and Rumer put her arm around her. "I don't know how Mum did it," Isak murmured, her voice barely audible. "It must've been so hard." She wiped her eyes and stood up. "I'm sorry, I think I've had enough for one night."

Micah looked at his watch and nodded. "I should go anyway." He stood and stretched. "Thank you for dinner."

"You're welcome," Rumer said with a smile.

Beryl got up to walk him to his car. "We didn't even get to where you are in the story."

"That's all right," Micah said. "I like listening to you read—you sound just like your mom and it makes it seem like she's reading it."

Beryl laughed. "That's funny, Rumer and Isak said the same thing. Every night I ask them if they want to read and they say no—they like listening to me."

Micah folded down the handle of the mower, lifted it into the back of his Honda, and braced it with the gas can.

"Thanks again for mowing. I hope you didn't hit any of Flannery's land mines."

Micah laughed. "Nope, I scouted those out with a shovel first."

"I didn't even think of that. I'm sorry, I should've come out and taken care of it."

"Not a problem," he said, shutting the trunk and leaning against the car.

"I know you probably have better things to do tomorrow—but is there any chance we'll see you?"

"Actually, I'm starting a new job."

"You are? I thought you worked for a publisher."

"I do—in a warehouse—but it's only part-time. I'm also going to be tutoring some high-school kids in English. My dad used to do it, but he's retired now, so they were looking for someone to take his place."

"That's great, Micah—so many people today can't find any work these days."

"Well, it's only temporary. They're looking for an English teacher, too, so I have to get my act together and get in my résumé. Right now, I can only be a full-time sub because I don't have an education degree—but I have plenty of credits and a degree in English, so I'm going to take some courses over the summer and hope they don't have too many other applicants. My dad always told me to get a degree in education, but at the time, I wasn't interested in teaching."

"It's hard to know, when you're eighteen or nineteen, what you want to do for the rest of your life."

He nodded. "Or predict what the job market will be like."

"True!" Beryl said. "Speaking of jobs—when this week is over, I'm going to start looking for someone to help out in the shop—so, maybe when you're tutoring you could keep an eye out for a student who seems hardworking."

"I will," he said with a smile. "By the way, tutoring is only in the morning, so I could still come by for story hour."

Beryl laughed. "How about dinner too?"

He shook his head. "I wish I could, but I think I better have dinner with my family once in a while. Besides, I don't want to wear out my welcome."

"You could never wear out your welcome."

"Really?" he teased.

"Really," she said with a grin.

He stepped toward her but hesitated, shaking his head and smiling. "I should go."

She nodded. "Okay, well—don't be a stranger."

He laughed. "Don't worry, I won't be."

∼∽ 21 ∽∼

"Have you guys seen Thoreau?" Beryl asked as she filled the teakettle with fresh water. "He's been curled up on my bed the last couple of mornings, but today he was a no-show."

Rumer looked out the kitchen window. "I think he's found the old Nepeta cataria patch."

Beryl frowned and followed her gaze. The proud, old cat—usually poised and well-mannered—was rolling deliriously around in a bed of green leaves. "Oh, my goodness—the catnip! I forgot that was out there!"

Isak poured a cup of coffee and looked out too. "Do you remember Emily—the orange tiger we had when we were little? She used to fall asleep in it!" She sighed. "Too bad they don't make catnip for people. I could use a little euphoria now and then."

Rumer slid her mug in front of Isak to be filled too. "So, what's for breakfast?"

"Micah's dad gave us a dozen fresh eggs yesterday," Beryl offered.

"Scrambled or fried?" Isak asked, filling Rumer's mug and pulling out the oven drawer with a loud clank.

"Fried," Beryl said. "We had scrambled yesterday."

"Sunday," Rumer corrected, opening the fridge.

"Was it Sunday?! This week is a blur. What'd we have yesterday, then?"

"Apple crisp," Isak said matter-of-factly, dropping butter into the pan.

"Oh, yeah," Beryl said as she filled Flan's bowl with kibble.

Rumer pulled three slices of bread out of the bread bag, and Beryl found an unopened jar of their mom's raspberry jam in the pantry. "Does jam go bad?" she asked, popping open the lid and peering inside.

Isak eyed it skeptically and handed her a spoon. "Here, try it, and we'll see."

"Thanks," Beryl said, making a face. She dipped the spoon in and licked it. "Mmmm-mmmm good!" She smacked her lips with an approving nod. "There are also three jars of Mum's bread-and-butter pickles in there."

"Nothing tastes like summer more than Mum's pickles," Rumer said with a grin. "I wonder if I can get one through airport security."

"Just wrap it in a towel and put it in your checked bag," Isak said. "It'll be fine."

"Are you sure about that?" Beryl asked skeptically. "I'm pretty sure they scan luggage, too . . . Otherwise, anyone can wrap a bomb in a towel."

Isak shrugged, and Beryl said, "I'll just mail one to each of you."

As they sat around the kitchen table, planning the day, Isak said, "First thing we need to do is get more boxes. Then we need to start on Mum's room. By the way, I'm having second thoughts about the church taking care of the reception. It's nice of them to offer, but we really don't have any idea what they're going to make, and I don't want to have just cheese and crackers and store-bought cookies. I think it might be better to have it catered."

Beryl shook her head. "They'll do a good job—they always do. Besides, everyone at church loved Mum."

"How do they know how many people to plan for?"

Beryl shrugged. "I don't know, Mum lived here all her life—she knew everyone. I'm sure they're expecting a good turnout."

Isak shook her head, still unconvinced. "Maybe we could subsidize what they make with a caterer; then we could have some waitresses passing trays too."

Rumer groaned. "I think that's overkill. I can't imagine Mum would have wanted all the fuss."

Isak nodded. "I know, I never take anything from those trays either—especially when they keep passing the same thing—but lots of people like having food brought to them."

Rumer raised her eyebrows in surprise. "That's not what I meant . . ." She paused. "Isak, please tell me you aren't one of those people who ignore the waitresses when they come around with trays of hors d'oeuvres."

But Isak missed her sister's warning look and unwittingly kept talking. "Honestly, Ru, between hospital events and all the parties we go to, I get tired of being interrupted all the time—so, on second thought, maybe it is a bad idea."

"You *are* one of those people!" Rumer exclaimed.

Isak looked puzzled. "What people?"

"A snob!"

"What are you talking about?"

"Do you have any idea what I've been doing for the last two years to help make ends meet?"

Isak hesitated, trying to remember. "I'm sorry, I don't think you told me—"

"I *did* tell you," Rumer interrupted. "You weren't listening! Isak, I work for a caterer—I'm the waitress you ignore because you're tired of being interrupted. I'm the one who carries around the trays of appetizers that don't have very much variety because that's what the hostess paid for, and I serve snooty people who treat me like I'm second class—or worse—ignore me!" Her voice grew angrier as she spoke. "That's when I want to accidently spill a whole tray of shrimp cocktail all over their Anne Klein white linen sundresses or Armani sports coats. Believe me, Isak, I'd be much happier not interrupting lame conversations with the same old sesame chicken and mango sauce—but if I don't do what I'm told, I won't be working." She paused. "I hope you, at least, know not to plop your shrimp tail back on the tray!"

Isak swallowed uncomfortably. She did know that much— but she *didn't* know what to say.

"I definitely didn't go to school for this," Rumer went on. "And it's definitely not how I want to spend my life—but we need the money! Some of the people we serve are so incredibly clueless, they don't even consider that waiters and waitresses have greater aspirations than serving them stupid stuffed mushroom caps!"

"I'm sorry, Ru, I guess I never thought about it that way. I promise, I will never turn down another pig in a blanket again."

"You joke, Isak, but you're not funny. It just proves you don't get it."

"I'm sorry, Ru—I *do* get it. I was just teasing."

"Yeah, whatever."

They were both quiet, each lost in thought. Finally, Beryl broke the silence. "Good eggs," she said, dipping her toast into a pool of egg yolk.

"Thanks," Isak replied, standing up to clear. Beryl looked up and realized her sister still had a big puddle of yolk in the middle of her plate, but before she could say anything, Isak had dropped it in the sink and turned on the water.

Beryl looked dismayed. "What'd you do that for—the yolk is the best part!"

Isak shrugged indifferently. "I didn't have any toast left."

"You have to plan ahead and save some toast."

"It's no big deal, not everyone loves egg yolk like you do."

"You could've given it to Flan—she loves egg yolk."

"Sorry, Ber, get over it," she said dismissively.

Her words stung and Beryl pushed back her chair, dropped her dish in the sink, and said, "You know what? Rumer's right—the way you treat people does reflect the kind of person you are." Then she grabbed her keys and her purse and walked out, letting the screen door slam behind her, hoping it would punctuate how she felt: She was sick of Isak's moods—*and* her indifference. Maybe if she wasn't so self-centered, she'd realize that other people were hurting too.

"Guess I'm just pissin' everyone off today," Isak said as she rinsed soap off the plates and stood them up in the dish drain.

"I guess so," Rumer replied as she reached for a dish towel.

Two hours later, Beryl pulled into the driveway with a sack of chocolate croissants on her front seat and a stack of flattened egg boxes in her trunk. She got out, wearily pushed her hand through her hair, and walked around to open her trunk. As she did, she heard a voice call, "I hope you left Ms. Cranky Crankenheimer back in town!" She looked up at her mom's bedroom window, saw Isak smiling and, in spite of herself, burst out laughing. She hadn't heard that name in years.

Ms. Cranky Crankenheimer was a fictitious character Mia had created when they were little, and when one of them was getting ready to dissolve into a fit, she'd say, "Oh, dear, is Ms. Cranky Crankenheimer here again?" Then whoever was about to have the meltdown would stomp her foot and shout, "I'm *not* cranky!" and Mia would make a funny face, and the frustrated child—try as she might—would burst out laughing. Sometimes the unfortunate child's siblings would sense a pending storm and in a singsong voice warn: "Mum, you-know-who is here." And Mia would reply, "Oh, no—not again!" And this alone could diffuse a meltdown before it had even begun.

Now, Beryl dropped the boxes on the kitchen table and turned to see Isak standing at the bottom of the stairs, looking sheepish. "I'm sorry, Ber. I didn't mean to be so . . . insensitive. You know how redheads can be."

"I know . . ." Beryl said with a forgiving smile. "I'm sorry I got mad over a dumb egg yolk."

"It's okay; everyone has their shortcomings," Isak teased. "I'm insensitive—you're overly protective of egg yolks—there are worse things." She gave her little sister a long hug. "Oh, Ber, I know you're hurting, too—probably more than anyone—but we'll get through this."

"I know," Beryl whispered, her eyes filling with tears.

Rumer appeared at the bottom of the stairs. "Are you two crying again?" she asked. "Every time I leave you alone, you turn into puddles."

Beryl and Isak laughed and wiped their eyes.

"Sooo . . . I have good news . . ." Rumer said.

"What?!" they asked in unison.

"Will just called and said they're flying in on Thursday!"

"Oh, Ru, that's great," Isak said. "Do you need money?"

"Nope, he said it's all set, and our neighbor's going to take care of Norman."

"Too bad they couldn't bring Norman," Beryl said.

"I know, I wish they could. He's been so good for Rand, especially after the move. But he'll be fine. Norm's in love with Pam's yellow Lab, Rosie, so he probably won't even notice we're gone."

"I love that name—Nahm," Isak said, pronouncing it the same way Cliff Clavin did on *Cheers*. "It's so perfect for a big, old Lab. How'd you ever come up with it?"

"Will named him. He thought we should keep the family tradition going, so he named him after Norman Maclean."

Isak laughed. "Oh, my goodness, that's even better!"

Beryl nodded. "Well, it's great they're coming; it'll be so good to see them. I haven't seen Rand since you moved."

"It's been longer for me," Isak said. "He's probably all grown up."

Rumer smiled. "He is all grown up," she said wistfully. "You won't know him."

"Are those chocolate croissants?" Isak interrupted, spotting the sack on the table.

"Yup," Beryl answered.

She grinned. "Well, let's pop 'em in the oven."

"For lunch?"

"Why not? Chocolate is almost as good as catnip," she said, "and I could use a fresh cup of coffee."

"Sounds good to me," Rumer agreed.

While the croissants heated and the coffee perked, the egg boxes were reassembled and brought upstairs. Beryl dropped two on the floor and, seeing the piles of clothes on her mom's bed, groaned.

"I couldn't agree more!" Isak said, coming in behind her with two more boxes. "You need to go through some of her clothes and see if there's anything you want. It's all too small for me."

Beryl started to look through one of the piles. "I don't know—I think I'd feel funny wearing Mum's clothes now. It's not the same as borrowing them." She looked at Rumer. "Did you pick out anything?"

"I did," she said, motioning to a small pile. "I can understand how you feel about wearing her clothes now, but I think she'd be happy if she knew we kept some of her things."

Beryl nodded and started sifting through a pile of neatly folded T-shirts that seemed to be from every vacation they'd ever taken. The top one had a comical picture of a birdwatcher looking through a pair of binoculars; underneath the picture it said, The Birdwatcher's General Store, Cape Cod; the next one was from Maine and it posed the question, "Got Lobstah?" Next was one from Pennsylvania that bore a rendering of Abraham Lincoln. Beryl held it up. "Remember when we drove all the way to Gettysburg with Gram and Poppy because Poppy said he'd always wanted to see the battlefields?"

Isak nodded. "I'll always remember that—it was the only time I'd ever seen him cry."

"I remember that too," Rumer added. "It was at Pickett's Charge. And then we stopped at that restaurant where everyone sat at long tables with red and white tablecloths and they served the food family-style."

"That was in Lancaster," Isak said. "Remember that really cute Amish boy who was driving the buggy?"

"Yeah, Poppy was going to follow him for you, but Mum said no."

"We went on some fun trips," Rumer said wistfully. "I wish we could take Rand on trips like that."

"You will," Isak assured her.

"I don't know how Mum did it," Beryl said as she pulled three more shirts from the bottom of the pile and suddenly realized what they were. "I also don't know how she sent us all to college without taking out any loans." She tossed a maroon T-shirt to Rumer and a light blue one to Isak; then, grinning, slipped off her blouse and pulled on the royal blue T-shirt Mia had proudly worn for a week after her youngest daughter had been accepted to Wellesley.

"Yup, there's that too," Rumer agreed.

"I don't know either," Isak said, pulling a Barnard shirt over her head while Rumer pulled on her mom's old RISD T-shirt.

Beryl picked a shirt up off the floor as Isak looked at it over her shoulder. "Bermuda? Where'd that come from?"

"From Bermuda, silly," Beryl answered, and Isak rolled her eyes.

"Maybe she got it at the thrift store," Rumer suggested.

This time, Beryl rolled her eyes. "Right, that's something I'd buy at a thrift store—someone's old vacation T-shirt."

"Well, where'd Mum and Dad go on their honeymoon?" Rumer asked.

"They went to the Poconos," Beryl reminded her, "like everyone else in their generation."

Just then, a faint beeping came from the kitchen and Beryl remembered the warming croissants.

"Okay," Isak said, licking chocolate off her fingers and taking a sip of her coffee. "You guys are sure about the clothes? Those boxes are the only ones you're keeping?" she asked, pointing to two boxes stacked in the corner of the room.

Rumer nodded. "Ber, did you decide on that jacket from Bean?"

"Yup, it's in great condition and it's very retro. I'm going to keep it unless you want it."

"Nope, I'm gonna take the snow boots."

"Well, we're set, then," Beryl confirmed, taping closed the last box of clothes and setting it on the floor.

"Okay, then—on to knickknacks and jewelry."

Rumer slumped gloomily onto the bed. "I wish we had more time. I feel like we're rushing through this. We haven't had any time to even digest what's happened."

"I know," Isak said. "But when else can we do it? I don't know when I can get out here again, and we can't very well have a realtor showing the house when it's full of stuff."

Rumer leaned back on the bed and closed her eyes. "Why don't we just pack up the jewelry and Beryl can keep it until we can get together again. It's not that urgent."

"If that's what you want to do, it's fine with me. Ber?"

"Fine with me," Beryl said with a nod as she climbed a small stepladder to reach the shelf in her mom's closet. She pulled down a cardboard box and handed it to Isak, who dropped it on the bed and opened it.

"Oh, no," she said softly.

"What?" Rumer asked, opening her eyes.

Isak pulled three neatly wrapped Christmas gifts out of the box, complete with ribbons and tags.

Beryl climbed down from the ladder. "Oh, no," Beryl repeated sadly. "Those must be the gifts Mum bought in Boston that day." Isak held out the presents as Beryl continued, "She was so proud of herself because she'd started her Christmas shopping early, but she was worried that she wouldn't remember where she'd put them when Christmas got here, so I told her I'd remind her—but then she tucked them away without telling me where and, as Christmas approached, she couldn't find them. She was so upset and she kept telling me she'd wrapped them and put them in a safe spot. We looked everywhere—I even looked in all the places she'd hidden our presents when we were little. Finally, she ended up buying different gifts, but on Christmas morning she was still upset about it and kept saying, 'I know I got you something else, but I just can't find it anywhere *and* I can't even remember what it is.' I told her it was okay, but it didn't seem to help."

"Should we open them?" Isak asked.

Beryl nodded. "Unless you want to wait till Christmas . . ."

"No, let's open them now," Rumer said, looking at Isak. "Age order—you go first."

"You don't need to rub it in," Isak said. She hesitated. "These are the last presents we'll ever open from Mum," she said, her voice choked with emotion.

"Unless we find more somewhere . . ." Beryl said, trying to lighten the mood, ". . . which *is* possible!"

"True!" Isak agreed with a nod. She carefully unwrapped her gift and pulled away the tissue, revealing a beautiful silk scarf. "Oh my," she whispered, "look at this color!"

Beryl nodded, remembering her mom's words. "Mum said it was the color of the September sky."

"It's gorgeous," Isak said, slipping it around her neck.

"It's the same color as your eyes," Rumer remarked. "In fact, it makes them look even bluer."

"And it matches your T-shirt!" Beryl teased.

Isak laughed and looked at Rumer. "Your turn, hapless middle child!"

Rumer slipped the paper off her gift with the same quiet reverence. Then she slowly lifted the lid of a small jewelry box and laughed. "Mum always knew I loved turquoise!" she exclaimed, lifting out two silver hoops with gorgeous turquoise stones hanging from them.

Beryl nodded. "We were at one of those outdoor vendors in Quincy Market and Mum saw those earrings with onyx stones and asked the designer if she had them with turquoise. The lady looked and looked. She was just about to give up when she found those in the last box she opened. Mum was triumphant and said it was meant to be!"

Rumer put them on. "How do I look?"

"You look maahvelous!" Isak said in her best Billy Crystal impression.

Rumer laughed and looked at Beryl. "Your turn! What's the backstory for your gift?"

Beryl shook her head and lightly touched the ribbon. "I only know where she bought it—The Bookend—Micah's store." She told them about the display of books and their chance encounter with Micah, then shook her head sadly. "Mum didn't remember him."

"She didn't?!" Rumer said in surprise. "But he worked for her all those years. . . ."

"I know, but she hadn't seen him in a long time and, by then, she was having trouble remembering people she saw *all* the time."

They were quiet—lost in their own thoughts—until Isak finally asked, "Well, are you going to open it?"

Beryl pressed her lips together and gently pulled on the ribbon. Then she carefully slid a thin book from the wrapping. "You open gifts just like Mum," Isak teased, "like you're planning to use the paper again."

"I might . . ." Beryl teased back, "on *your* next Christmas present." She turned the book over and held it up for her sisters to see. It was a copy of Anne Morrow Lindbergh's *Gift from the Sea.* She smiled. "Mum must've seen me looking through it when we were shopping."

Isak looked puzzled. "Doesn't Mum have that book?"

Beryl nodded. "Somewhere. I always wanted to read it, but I never found the time." She opened the thin volume and quickly scanned the flyleaf. "Did you know she was an aviator too?"

Isak laughed. "Well, I guess we're all lucky, lucky, lucky she didn't name one of us Lindbergh!"

Beryl laughed. "Well, you know, my middle name *is* Anne."

"That's true," Rumer said. "Do you think . . . ?"

"I wouldn't put it past her," Beryl answered with a grin.

"Mum certainly was one of a kind," Isak said.

"She certainly was!" Beryl said, embracing her gift as if it were a long-lost friend.

22

"Are we waiting for Micah?" Isak asked as she wrapped up the leftover chicken and put it in the fridge.

"We are," Beryl answered, downing the last of her Pinot Grigio and washing her glass. "He just texted me and said he's on his way."

"You heard your phone?!" Rumer teased, drying the glass.

"Yup," Beryl answered proudly.

"I guess it depends on who's texting . . ."

Beryl suppressed a smile and looked around the kitchen to see if there was anything else to wash. "Isak, are you having more?" she asked, nodding to her glass.

Isak took a deep breath and looked decidedly undecided. "Hmm—that's a good question. I would, but I think I'm going to have coffee tonight so I can stay awake."

Rumer handed the empty glass to Beryl, who washed it and handed it back to her. "Is that it?" she asked, glancing over her shoulder.

"That's it," Isak said, nudging her aside to fill the perk pot with cold water. "Do you guys want coffee?"

"I will," Rumer said.

"Me too," Beryl said, drying her hands. She moved toward the stairs. "I'm just gonna freshen up."

Isak stopped measuring coffee and looked up. "You don't need to freshen up for us."

"I'm not," Beryl assured her.

"You should've said something," Rumer chimed. "We would've cleaned up the kitchen."

"Not a problem," Beryl called as she ran up the stairs.

Isak and Rumer both looked at each other and Rumer laughed. "I can hear Mum now . . ."

Isak nodded, "Yup, she'd say, 'And the plot thickens . . .' "

They heard a car pull up, and when Micah knocked on the door, Flannery hurried over and pressed her nose against the screen, her tail wagging.

"Come on in!" Isak called.

He pulled open the screen and Flan's whole hind end started to wiggle. He knelt down in front of her and looked into her somber eyes. "Hello there, Miss O'Connor." Almost immediately, the old dog flopped onto her side and rolled onto her back with her legs straight up in the air.

"Wow! You really have a way with women!" Isak teased.

Micah laughed and Beryl appeared at the bottom of the stairs. "Oh, my goodness, Flan, could you be any less lady-like?" The homely dog gazed at her; then her eyes rolled back in her head in shameless pleasure. Beryl shook her head. "She hasn't had many men in her life."

Rumer laughed. "Well, it looks like she's fallen for the first one to pay attention!"

Micah stood up and Flannery's eyes opened in dismay. "Sorry, ole girl," he said. "I know you'd probably like me to keep doing that, but my knees won't like it very much."

"What's wrong with your knees?" Beryl asked, getting out four mugs.

"They ache sometimes—I can always tell when it's going to rain. I think it's from all those years of running cross-country."

"I know what you mean. I used to love running, but I did something to one of my knees last fall and now I'm resigned to walking. I guess I should have it looked at, but I just haven't had the time." She paused. "Coffee or tea . . . or we also have the usual—wine, iced tea, milk, water . . . ?"

"Coffee sounds good, thanks." He looked around and noticed their shirts. "You should've told me it was college night," he said. "I would've worn my Bowdoin shirt."

Beryl laughed. "We found these in our mom's bureau."

"Did you go to Bowdoin?" Isak asked, setting out cream and sugar.

Micah nodded.

"One of my friends went there—Sarah Riley?"

Micah shook his head. "Her name's not familiar."

"Well, she'd be older than you. She still lives in Maine. We lost touch for a while, but thanks to Facebook, we reconnected."

Micah nodded. "It's amazing how small Facebook makes the world."

"Are you on Facebook?" Beryl asked in surprise.

"I am, but I'm afraid I don't check it very often."

"See!" Rumer said, nudging her sister.

"Beryl is the last remaining holdout," Isak explained, putting spoons next to the sugar.

Micah laughed. "Well, I probably wouldn't be on it either, but when my business started to go downhill, I was willing to try anything, so I started a page for the store—and for myself, hoping it would bring people in—but as it turned out, it wasn't enough." He looked at Beryl. "You should at least start one for Tranquility," he suggested. "It's free publicity."

"Maybe," Beryl said, considering his suggestion; then she added, "Are we reading on the porch?"

"Yup!" Rumer said, taking her mug and a pillow from the couch. Micah held the door open and the parade trooped out, including Flan, who immediately plopped down at his feet. Even Thoreau, who'd been acting aloof all day, appeared and seemed ready to rekindle old friendships.

"Okay, where were we?" Beryl murmured, scanning the page.

"We were where Mum promised she'd never leave," Isak said.

> It was still early May—and tulip time—when I pulled up in front of the cabin and saw all the colorful blooms lining the walkway. Sitting on the bottom step with his cane across his knees was David! He stood up slowly, smiling and shaking his head— as if he couldn't believe it was me. And I climbed out of the car, tears stinging my eyes—I couldn't believe it was him! I stood in front of him and we didn't say a word—we just took each other in—trying to find our way back to where we'd left off.
>
> "I brought your lunch," I said.
>
> He looked at his watch. "It's about time!"
>
> "I know," I laughed.
>
> "How've you been?"
>
> "Okay."
>
> He nodded. "Me as well—better now."
>
> "When'd you get here?"
>
> "Evening before last."
>
> "I was off yesterday."
>
> "I know! Some lunatic kid pulled in here like a bat out of hell—even the chipmunks ducked for cover!"
>
> I laughed, picturing the chipmunks diving under the tulips.

"I thought you might've found another job."

I shook my head.

He smiled. "It's so good to see you."

I nodded. "It's good to see you."

"How are the little ones?"

"They're fine—busy."

He laughed. "Aren't all women?"

I nodded and tried to think of something to say. "How's your painting?"

"Good—I've been taking a break from landscapes. I'm trying to teach myself how to paint people. There's an open studio near our flat in London—and they have models twice a week." He hesitated. "In fact, I was going to ask you—I mean, I was wondering . . . if you might be interested . . . in modeling."

I felt my face blush and looked away. "N-no," I stammered. "I don't think I'd be comfortable doing that."

"Clothed, of course—I meant clothed."

I shook my head. "Even clothed, I don't think . . ." I stopped in midsentence and eyed him. "They model without their clothes?"

He laughed. "Of course . . . ."

"You mean naked?"

He nodded.

"Well, no—definitely not."

"I'd pay you . . . and, again, I meant clothed . . . I wouldn't expect you to do it for free—or naked—unless, of course, you wanted to . . ." His eyes sparkled mischievously and I felt my cheeks heating up again.

I hesitated. "I'm sorry, David, I just don't think I'd be comfortable doing that—even clothed."

He nodded. "I understand."

I reached into my backseat for his basket.

"Can you stay?"

I glanced at my watch, flustered by the conversation. "I wish I could, but my littlest one has an earache and I don't want to burden my mom any longer than I have to."

He looked a bit deflated. "Well, maybe tomorrow then . . ."

"Yes, maybe . . ."

Almost forty years have passed since that day, but our conversation is still as clear in my mind as if it happened yesterday—and I'm convinced it's because of the conflicted feeling I had. I'd missed David so much, and I'd looked forward to seeing him for so long. At the same time, I was confused and afraid! I was completely drawn to him—and even though I knew he was married and I'd resolved to keep our relationship platonic, when he stood in front of me, I could feel my resolve melting like an old-fashioned New England thaw.

In the days that followed, I delivered his lunch—on time—and lingered! I was amazed that no one ever asked me where I was or what kept me. Some days, when I hadn't had time for breakfast, he shared his lunch with me; other days, we forgot all about lunch and just sat on the porch and talked. I learned that he'd just turned thirty-one on May 2nd—two days after his arrival at MacDowell—the day I'd declined to stay! I learned he was an only child, that his parents were poor, and that he'd lived in London all his life. He said his mum was a cleaning lady (and a sweetheart!) who worked long hours and multiple jobs; but when I asked about his father, a shadow fell across his face and he said that he'd passed away a long time ago. I also learned that he hadn't finished high school, never went to university, as he called it, married when he was eighteen, and although he and his wife of thirteen years slept under the same roof, for all intents and purposes, they lived separate lives. He seemed reluctant to elaborate and I didn't press him.

He asked as many questions of me as I did him, if not more! And I told him everything—I had no secrets, no shadows, nor crosses to bear. I told him Tom had been my life—my soul mate—and I missed him desperately. I said I was still close to his parents and they still treated me like a daughter; my parents were alive and well and supported me in every way they could; and, finally, I told him all about the little women in my life who kept me sane—and drove me crazy! I regaled him with their antics and idiosyncrasies, and he laughed and always wanted to hear more—and the little women, as I fondly referred to them, made sure I always had plenty of material!

The days turned into weeks and I found myself thinking about him all the time. I couldn't wait to get to the cabin at lunchtime. One day, he showed me a painting he was working on—a still life, because no one was willing to model for him! I don't know if he was still trying, but he showed me a large sketchbook full of drawings from his life class—the curves and shapes of the different anatomies were wonderful. He explained that sometimes the sessions were timed, as a warm-up, and only lasted for thirty

*seconds or a minute before the model changed posi-
tion. Other sessions were as long as an hour with
breaks for the model every twenty minutes. The
thirty-second drawings were fluid and beautiful,
capturing the essence of the person—and looking as
if he'd never lifted his charcoal off the paper. The
drawings from the longer sessions were much more
detailed and striking.*

*He talked about the models: Charlie—a large,
bald man in his late fifties with a torso like a barrel;
and Diamond—a full-figured woman in her thirties
whose breasts curved down to a round potbelly, and
whose thighs were thick but shapely; and Pip—a
tall, muscular, African man in his twenties. I asked
David if he preferred one model over another, fully
expecting him to say he preferred drawing women,
but he said it was the act of drawing that captivated
him—the subject didn't matter; for most artists, he
added, observing naked figures wasn't a sexual experience. That gave me a lot to think about! Could
he look at me without being aroused? Would he ad-
mire my slender shape—or decide it wasn't shapely
enough? I wasn't as well-endowed as some women,
but I couldn't believe that a man—who found
women attractive—wouldn't be aroused at all.*

"Sorry—but can I just say something here?" Rumer asked.
They all looked up.

"Okay, well, I took numerous life-drawing classes in college—and I can assure you I saw plenty of aroused boys when
the model was a woman—and even a couple when it wasn't!
So, I think David was either a saint or he wasn't being entirely
honest."

"Well, you have to remember you were in class with eigh-teen- and nineteen-year-old boys," Beryl said. "They'd take every chance they could get to see a naked woman; David was thirty-one and married, so he'd been there, done that."

Isak shook her head. "Been there, done that?! Are men ever done? I think Rumer's right. It sounds like he still wanted her to model, and by saying he didn't think of it as sexual, he might be able to convince her."

Beryl frowned. "You make him sound so... predatory. I don't get that impression at all." She looked at Micah. "What do you think?"

Micah laughed and shook his head. "Oh, you shouldn't ask me—I find the mere conversation arousing!"

They all laughed and Isak exclaimed triumphantly, "See! I told you!"

The month of May flew by, and as Memorial Day approached, John asked if I could work the dinner shift—just for the weekend because we would be shorthanded. He said he would take care of breakfast and lunch. I asked my parents and they agreed to take the girls overnight—and I was thrilled because I would get to take them to watch their grandfathers—who were both WWII veter-ans—march in the Memorial Day parade.

When I delivered David's lunch on Thursday, I told him about the change. "It's only for the week-end," I said. "I'll still see you at dinner." I didn't stay that day because I'd promised to take the girls to the beach. He said he understood, but I could tell he was disappointed. It was so nice to be off the next morning and not have to get everyone up, dressed, fed, and out of the house at the crack of dawn. Isak was the worst when we had to get up early—I think

*ole Cranky Crankenheimer crept into her room at
night. I was up early, though, hoping to make a dent
in the mountain of laundry that was taking over our
laundry room. The house was quiet and while the
teakettle clicked and sputtered, I looked outside. It
was cloudy and cool, and I knew the girls would be
disappointed because they'd asked if we could go to
the beach again.*

*It's funny, though, try as I might, I can't really
remember much else about that day. We may have
gone for a hike instead, if the rain held, but I can't
be sure. The only thing I remember is that it was
raining when I dropped the girls off at my parents',
because I had to run back and forth to the car and,
when I got to work, I was wet and chilled.*

*Some days—now—writing is a struggle. It al-
most seems as if I'm losing bits and pieces of memory
along the way. In fact, I keep picturing pieces of my
brain breaking off and falling into a dark void—
never to be retrieved again! It sounds crazy, I know,
but I keep having these moments of nothingness—
when my mind is completely blank and I feel overwhelmed with a sense of . . .*

Beryl looked up. "It looks like she couldn't think of the
word she wanted. . . ." She tried to read her mom's handwriting.
"On the next line she wrote the word *urgency*—but it's mis-
spelled—which is so unlike her." Isak, Rumer, and Micah nodded, sadly realizing the loss and helplessness their mother
would have felt.

"She must've been beside herself," Isak said quietly.

"And she never said anything," Rumer added. "She kept it
all inside."

Micah smiled sadly. "She was protecting you."

Beryl turned the page. "There's a small notation scribbled at the top of the next page. It simply says, *'Today is better . . .'* "

> *We were so busy that night that I hardly had a chance to say hello to David. He was sitting with a large group of artists and they were having a rousing discussion. I asked one of the other waitresses what they were talking about and she said they were talking about Kent State. I nodded as if I knew all the details—but, in reality, I didn't. I'd only heard that there'd been some kind of confrontation between students and policemen . . . and it had ended tragically. As much as I wanted to keep up on the news, I barely had time to keep up with my life!*
>
> *The evening slipped by and the residents finally started to leave. I was wiping down a table in the corner when David came over. "Hey," he said with a smile.*
>
> *"Hey," I replied, looking up.*
>
> *He pushed back his hair. "Do you have to head home right away?"*
>
> *I straightened up and started to answer, "Yes, I . . ." But then I suddenly realized I didn't have to head home—the girls were sleeping at my parents.*
>
> *"Want to come by for a beer?" he asked.*
>
> *"Oh, I don't know—it might be late," I said. "We still have the kitchen to clean up, and then we have to set up for breakfast."*
>
> *"I'll still be up," he said. "I'm a bit of a night owl."*
>
> *I nodded. "Okay, maybe . . ."*
>
> *An hour and a half later, I parked under the oak*

tree and rolled up my windows. Although the rain
had stopped, it felt like it might start again at any
minute. The porch light was on and I saw David
leaning against the railing with a beer in his hand.

"You came!" he called happily.

"Against my better judgment," I called back. I
opened the car door and, just as I did, the skies
opened up and it started to pour! I ran, laughing.
"See what I mean!" I said, almost slipping on the
steps. He laughed, too, catching me with his free
hand. I looked up, and he gently brushed the raindrops from my cheek—his touch sweeping through
me, arousing a sensation I thought I'd never feel
again. He searched my eyes—and then shook his
head as if trying to fight some inner turmoil.

"What's the matter?" I asked.

He shook his head and turned away. "Nothing . . ."

I looked at his back as he leaned on his cane. "It
must be something," I said softly.

"It's nothing," he said, turning to me and smiling. "Are you ready for that beer?"

I nodded.

"I'm afraid I only have Bass."

"Anything," I replied.

"I finished my still life. Would you like to see it?"

"I'd love to," I said, following him inside. He'd
set up his props on a table near the window.

"I borrowed that blue and white bowl from the
kitchen," he said. "I hope they haven't missed it."

I laughed. "Actually, I think someone was looking for it today."

"Well, I'll bring it back tomorrow."

He handed a frosty bottle to me and I thanked

him and took a sip. "Mmmm—this tastes good. I can't remember the last time I had one."

He nodded, turning the easel toward me.

"Oh, my! It's beautiful! I've always considered still lifes to be . . . well, boring, but I love the way the light from the window falls across the bowl and the way you've painted shadows in the folds of the cloth. And the apples make me think of autumn—it looks as if someone is getting ready to make a pie."

He smiled and nodded thoughtfully. "I'm learning how to do that with people, too—you should let me show you sometime."

"Ahh . . . now I see where this is going."

"Not at all," he protested, looking into my eyes. "Mia, you're beautiful—I would love to draw you."

I nodded slowly, my heart pounding. "Okay," I said softly, hardly believing I was actually agreeing.

His face lit up. "You will?!"

I took another sip and laughed. "You better hurry up before I change my mind."

"Okay, give me a minute to think. Would you like to lie down or sit?"

"Sit."

"Clothes or robe?"

"Clothes. And I don't want to be paid."

"Agreed," David said, setting a stool in the middle of the room and moving a lamp next to it. He maneuvered his easel closer and looked around for his pad.

"Okay if I freshen up?"

"Of course—down the hall, first door on the right."

I went to the bathroom and quietly closed the

door behind me. I stood in front of the mirror and tried to come to terms with my reflection. It had been quite some time since I'd given any thought to my appearance. I was busy—I had no time—and who was looking anyway? As long as I was showered, dressed, and moving in the morning, that was all that mattered. But now . . . someone was looking. I unbuttoned the top button of my blouse—and then one more, and ran my fingers through my hair, trying to get it to lie flat. Then I rebuttoned the lower button and turned my head to one side, wondering—for the first time in my life—if I might actually have a good side. I felt self-conscious and nervous . . . and then I noticed a soft terry-cloth robe hanging on the back of the door. I paused and bit my lip, trying to decide.

David looked up when he realized I was standing in the doorway. "You look comfortable," he said with a slow smile.

"I couldn't resist—I love the color—and it's so soft," I said, moving toward the stool.

"Well, I'm glad you couldn't resist," he said quietly, adjusting the light.

I sat on the stool, and he asked me to turn toward him. He stepped back and looked; then he stepped forward, turned the light away slightly, and lifted my chin. He adjusted the neck of the robe and hesitated. "Would it be okay if I open this a little?" he asked.

I nodded and he slowly slid the robe off my shoulder.

"Are you comfortable?"

"To be honest, I am a little warm."

"Well," he teased, "there's a way to fix that . . ."

"A fan?" I asked.

He laughed. "Okay, I'll be quick." He moved to his easel and began to draw, and although I couldn't see him looking, I could feel his gaze.

Ten minutes passed and a cool breeze drifted through the window. "Would you like to see it?" he asked.

I nodded and walked over to where he stood. I couldn't believe my eyes—with a few sweeps of his pencil he'd captured my likeness and made me look confident . . . and beautiful.

"That's amazing!" I said. "I can't even draw a stick figure—but you, in a few short minutes, have made me look the way I've only dreamed of looking."

"That is how you look."

I shook my head. "I don't think so."

He looked in my eyes and said, "Mia, I can't draw what I don't see." He paused. "Are you up for another?"

I nodded, feeling more at ease.

"On the couch?"

"Okay," I agreed, taking a sip of my beer. He moved the lamp closer and I sat down, trying to keep the robe around me.

"Do you want to lie down?"

"Do you want me to lie down?"

"I want you to be comfortable."

I leaned back awkwardly, trying to stay covered. "How's this?"

"Good," he said, rubbing his chin thoughtfully and eyeing the robe, which had somehow wrapped itself more tightly around me. "What do you think *about loosening the robe a bit—so I can see a little more of you?"*

"Okay," I said. "You do it."

He shook his head slowly. "No . . . you do it."

I looked down—and slowly pulled one end of the belt until it came undone. I looked up to watch his face as I pushed the robe away, but his solemn expression didn't change. I leaned back on the cushions and felt his eyes taking in my body as he began to draw.

I lay there for a long time, watching him. He seemed completely caught up in the moment, focusing intently on the different curves and shapes of my body. "Lay your hand here," he said, putting his hand on his lower abdomen.

"On you . . . or me?" I asked.

"Whichever you'd prefer," he said with a slow smile, still trying to focus.

"I think you should show me. . . ."

"I just showed you."

"I mean on me . . ."

He took a deep breath. "If I come over there and show you . . . I may not leave."

"You better stay there, then." I laughed.

He nodded and kept drawing.

Beryl looked up. "Can you believe this is our mother?!"

Isak shook her head. "Yeah—no!"

Rumer grinned. "I can believe it."

Micah laughed. "She really had a wild side!"

Beryl glanced through the next few pages. "Well, that looks like the end of this section—she didn't use chapters. Should we stop?"

Micah sat forward. "I'd like to stay, but I should get going.

You don't have to stop on my account; I can always catch up later."

Beryl looked at her sisters.

"We can stop," Rumer said. "I need to call Will anyway."

"Fine with me," Isak agreed. "I need to call my kids, too, before it gets too late."

"Okay, well, tomorrow's Wednesday, and if we're going to finish before everyone starts arriving, we'll have to have a marathon session tomorrow night—although..." she said, thumbing through a number of blank pages on the bottom of the pile, "it might not be as long as it looks."

"Marathon it is," Rumer said with a nod.

Micah stood up and stretched, and Beryl handed the papers to Rumer and got up to walk him to his car.

"Good night, Micah!" they called.

"Good night," he called back with a grin.

"I forgot to ask you," Beryl said, falling in step beside him with Flannery at their heels, "how did tutoring go?"

"Good! There were four boys and two girls—and one of the boys has autism. His name is Henry and my mom said she's known him since he was little. His grandfather was Mr. Wyeth, the history teacher."

"I had Mr. Wyeth—he was great, everyone loved him!"

"I know, silly," Micah said. "I sat behind you."

"You did?"

"Gee, I can tell I made a big impression on you."

"I'm just teasing; I remember. I always borrowed your pen."

"And never gave it back—I went through more pens that year! Anyway, my mom said Henry's on the cross-country and track teams—in fact, he's their best runner—and he's very neat and organized—perhaps it's characteristic of autism. So, when I mentioned that you were looking for someone to help in the shop, she said he'd be great at making sure the shelves are stocked and everything's in its place—he's very particular about stuff like that."

"Does he have any negatives?"

Micah shook his head. "None that I know of. He has a service dog named Honey that's always by his side—I don't know if he'd need to bring her, but she's a beautiful yellow Lab, very well behaved and mellow."

"Hmm . . . Henry and Honey—I'll have to think about that. Are you tutoring tomorrow?"

"I am—in the morning. I saw all the boxes, though. Do you want help after lunch?"

"Are you sure you don't have something better to do?"

"I'm sure," he said. "Oh, and before I forget to ask, tell me again what time the service is?"

"Eleven," Beryl said with a lump suddenly forming in her throat. "I don't even want to think about it," she said, her voice full of sadness.

Micah put his arm around her shoulder. "It'll be okay, Ber—you need to think of it as a celebration of her life."

"I know, but I just keep thinking that all the people she loves will be together in one place and she won't even get to enjoy it."

"She'll be there in spirit," he said softly, "*and* she'll be smiling."

Beryl looked up at him. "How come you always know the right thing to say?"

He shook his head. "I don't always," he said, resting his chin on the top of her head. "I say the wrong thing all the time." He kissed her forehead lightly and whispered, "I should go."

"You're right," she said.

"I *should* go?"

"No—you're right about saying the wrong thing."

He gave her a puzzled look.

"You're supposed to say, 'I should stay . . .' "

He shook his head and laughed. "Believe me, I've been thinking about it . . ."

She smiled. "Well, as long as you're thinking about it. I'll see you tomorrow, then."

"Tomorrow, then," he said with a grin. "Tomorrow, ole girl," he said, squatting to scratch Flannery's head.

23

Beryl looked at the clock—it was 5 a.m. She groaned. It couldn't have been the cat landing on the bed that woke her—Thoreau was sound asleep; and it couldn't have been the birds singing—they'd already been up for half an hour. Someone was singing, though—and the out-of-place sound had roused her from her slumber. She looked over at the twin bed against the wall and saw the lump that was Rumer. "Ru," she called softly. No answer. Finally, she pushed off her covers, swung her legs over the side of the bed, and shuffled sleepily into the hall. The singing was coming from her mom's room, and when she pushed open the door, she saw Isak sitting on the opposite side of the bed with her ear buds on. Beryl leaned against the door and listened as her sister softly sang the melancholy, lonely song, "Desperado."

"Hey," she said when it ended.

Isak looked up, startled, and then looked away. "Hey," she said, pulling the ear buds out of her ears. "Did I wake you?"

"No," Beryl lied.

"I did so."

"It's okay, I wanted to get up." She walked around the bed and sat next to her. "How come you're up so early?"

"I couldn't sleep," Isak said, trying to brush away the tears on her cheeks before her sister saw them.

But Beryl *did* see them. "Hey," she said softly, "what's the matter?"

Isak shook her head, feeling her eyes filling with more tears. "Nothing," she whispered, her voice tight with emotion.

"Something," Beryl said, refusing to be put off. "Tell me . . ."

Isak shook her head again.

"Is it Mum?"

"No . . . well, partly . . ."

"And—what else?"

Isak nodded and bit her lip. "It's just . . . I think . . ." She cupped her hand over her mouth as she tried to fight back her tears. "Oh, Ber, I just keep having this terrible feeling that Matt's cheating on me."

"Oh, no!" Beryl caught her breath. "Why? Why do you think that?"

"I don't know," she said, hot tears spilling down her cheeks. She shook her head. "I wouldn't blame him . . ." She looked up and laughed. "Well, I would *blame* him."

Beryl nodded.

"Sometimes I'm such a bitch, ya know—and, honestly, recently our love life sucks—so I wouldn't blame him if he went somewhere else—but, damnit, he better not be!"

"Well, what makes you think he is?"

"I don't know. He works long hours—he's always at the hospital, or so he says. We never see each other—and when we do, it's like we're total strangers. Everything is different now that the kids are gone—we have nothing to talk about, nothing in common. At least, before, we had the kids and their activities—they needed us." She shook her head sadly. "I don't know for sure, but I've heard him talking a lot to a colleague—a

young woman doctor—I know who she is—single and pretty—
and their conversations are always so cheerful and friendly."
She fiddled with her phone, flipping through the songs without
really seeing them.

"And this whole thing with Mum—I just can't believe she
was capable of having an affair with a married man. It's like the
one person on earth who I absolutely trusted and revered—
who could do no wrong—has let me down."

"Isak, Mum was only human—just like the rest of us. Look
at her life—she was only twenty-six when Dad died, and there
she was—with three little girls—all by herself. Do you think
she would've ever met someone who'd be willing to step into
Dad's shoes and take on that kind of responsibility? Do you
think she even wanted to take the chance of bringing someone
new into our lives? There are all kinds of risks involved in that.
She did the best she could. Besides, we haven't even finished
reading the story—we don't know what happened, we don't
even know what the circumstances were . . . But I think you
should give her the benefit of the doubt, and I think you should
give Matt the same benefit. You need to talk to him—not shut
him out."

Isak wiped her eyes. "I know. I shouldn't jump to conclu-
sions—but for some reason, I always do."

"I do it too."

"No, you don't."

Rumer appeared in the doorway. "Oh, my goodness!" she
said, rubbing her eyes. "Are you two crying again?" She shook
her head. "I'm gonna have to keep you separated!"

"Like that's ever gonna happen!" Beryl said, laughing and
putting her arm around her sister.

Suddenly, Isak remembered the treasure she'd tucked in her
pocket. "You guys have to see what I found!" She reached into
the pocket of her jeans. "I was packing up Mum's jewelry because you said you wanted to go through it later and I found

this." She held up a small, round yellow and red tag. "It's the tag I cut off my Steiff toy when I was little—Mum saved it!"

"That is *so* Mum!" Beryl said, looking at the tag.

Isak handed it to Rumer and she read the name. "His name is *Nagy?!* What kind of name is that for a beaver? They should've named him The Beav . . . or Theo."

Isak rolled her eyes. "Steiff is German, silly, not American."

"Well, there's the problem right there," Rumer said, handing the tag back to her. "Did you find anything else?"

Isak looked around. "I found this box," she said, reaching for a small, flat box on the bed. "The only thing in it, though, is a faded blue pillowcase wrapped in tissue paper." She opened the box and lightly touched the pillowcase. "Oh, and I also found our old Canasta game," she said, closing the box. "Remember how we used to play it for hours on snow days?"

Beryl laughed. "Yeah, we sat around in our pj's all day long, drank cocoa, ate cinnamon toast, and played Canasta. Those were the good ole days!"

"Mum made the best cinnamon toast," Rumer said wistfully. "I wish we could go back and relive one of those days."

They all sat on the bed, remembering—until Beryl said what they were all thinking, "We should play Canasta today, for old time's sake!"

"We should," Isak agreed. "This afternoon, though. I don't know about you guys, but I need to go somewhere and log back into the world. Being off the proverbial grid is driving me crazy!"

Beryl nodded. "How about the diner? I think they have Wi-Fi and we could have breakfast."

An hour later, they were sitting in a booth at the Peterborough Diner, looking over menus while Isak checked her e-mail. "Crap," she murmured, half to herself. "I have a hundred and sixty-four new e-mails."

"Wow! I had no idea you were so popular!" Beryl said, closing her menu.

A waitress bustled over to the table. "Can I get you ladies some coffee?"

They all nodded and Isak eyed Beryl. "You're having coffee?"

"I love diner coffee. And the coffee you made last night was so good—what'd you do to it?"

"I sprinkled cinnamon on it."

"Well, it tasted like Christmas!"

The waitress brought over three mugs of steaming coffee and a bowl of creamers. "Ready to order?"

Beryl and Rumer both nodded, but Isak shook her head as she quickly opened her menu. "You two go—I just need a sec."

Beryl ordered blueberry pancakes with sausage, and Rumer ordered French toast with bacon. "Real maple syrup, please," Beryl added.

"That'll be a dollar fifty more," the waitress warned.

"That's okay," Beryl said. There was no way she was contaminating her pancakes with the icky fake stuff.

Isak could feel the pressure of the waitress's eyes. "And—I'll—have . . ." she said slowly, ". . . the . . . uhm . . . I'll have blueberry pancakes, too—with bacon and real syrup."

"That'll be a dol—"

"I know," Isak interrupted. "A dollar fifty more."

"Any OJ with that?"

"No, thanks," she said, closing her menu. The waitress took the menus and hurried away as Isak grumbled, "You'd think that a diner in the heart of maple syrup country would *only* offer the real thing—and not charge extra! What is this country coming to?"

Rumer, who was sitting next to her, eyed her laptop. "Is that the new MacBook Pro?"

Isak nodded and Rumer peered over her shoulder. "Wow! Look at that display," she teased. "My retinas have never been happier!"

Isak rolled her eyes and poked her with her elbow.

"Ouch," Rumer said, grinning at Beryl.

Isak looked up. "So, Ber, want to set up your Facebook page?"

"No . . . I don't think so," Beryl said, sipping her coffee.

"C'mon, Ber," Rumer cajoled. "You only have to post what you want, and you can set it up so that only your friends—and your sisters—can see it. Don't forget, Micah's on . . ."

"Oh, okay," she said reluctantly.

Isak pulled up the Facebook Web site, clicked on *Register,* and typed in her sister's name. "Password?"

Beryl eyed her suspiciously. "I'll do it."

Isak sighed and turned the laptop to face her.

Five minutes later, with her mouth full of pancakes, Isak asked, "Wannausethanicepicherathathreeaus?"

"What?!" Beryl asked.

Rumer interpreted, "She said, 'Do you want to use that nice picture of the three of us—for your profile picture?'"

"Sure," Beryl answered with an indifferent shrug.

Isak swallowed. "Okay, so now you're gonna friend Rumer and me."

"K," Beryl agreed halfheartedly—more interested in her pancakes than in "friending" the people she was already sitting with.

"There!" Isak said triumphantly. She turned the laptop so Beryl could see her new page and Beryl nodded, trying to show the appropriate amount of enthusiasm.

When they finished breakfast, Isak clicked on the friend request icon. "Look!" she said, "You already have thirteen friend requests—and one of them is Micah!"

"Where? Lemme see," Beryl asked, her eyes lighting up. Isak showed her the requests. "What do I do?"

"You either accept or decline. You want to decline him, right?"

"No!"

Isak laughed. "Then click 'Accept,' silly."

For the first time, Beryl looked at her homepage with interest. "Who's James Dixon?"

"Did he send you a friend request?" Isak asked, elbowing Rumer.

Beryl nodded.

"That's Jimmy Dixon," Rumer said. "Click on his picture."

Beryl clicked on his profile and her eyes grew wide. "No way!" she exclaimed, trying not to laugh. "He still has that gap between his teeth. How come he never got that fixed?"

"I don't know, but I told you it's fun to see how people have changed—or not," Rumer said with a grin.

Before they left, Beryl had six posts on her wall from old high-school classmates saying how sorry they were to hear about her mom.

❧ 24 ❧

"Read 'em and weep," Beryl said, laying down her last meld.

"Again?!" Isak said, slapping down a fistful of mismatched cards. "I'm done!"

"Me too," sighed Rumer, dropping her cards on the table. "*And* I'm hungry—what are we having for dinner?"

"We just had lunch," Beryl said, glancing at the clock.

"I know, I was just wondering."

"Well, Micah should be here soon and we can stop at the store after we drop off the boxes. What do you feel like having?"

"We should try to keep it simple," Isak reminded them, "since we want to finish the story tonight. We also need to think about what we're going to feed everyone over the weekend—we should probably go food shopping tomorrow."

Rumer nodded, remembering Rand's appetite. "We could have wraps tonight; we have leftover chicken and lettuce and all the fixings," Rumer said. "We just need the wraps."

"That sounds good," Beryl agreed.

"I know a good dip too," Isak added, gathering up the cards. "I just need cream cheese, a can of chili, a can of chopped mild chili peppers, a package of shredded Mexican cheese, and some tortilla chips. And," she added with a grin, "if you get a can of frozen limeade and some tequila, we could have margaritas with it."

"I'm in!" Rumer said.

"Okay," Beryl agreed, getting up to jot everything down.

As she pushed back from the table, there was a light knock on the screen door and Flannery, who'd been dozing under the table, let out a startled bark and scrambled to get up. Then she waddled over to press her nose against the screen, her hind end wagging. Beryl looked out and saw a small figure standing on the porch.

"Hi, Charlotte," Beryl said, pushing the door open as Flan wiggled out.

"Hi," Charlotte replied softly, putting her hand on Flan's head.

"Where's your dad?"

Charlotte pointed and Beryl looked over and saw Micah walking toward the house with a round plastic container in his hands.

"What did you guys bring?" she asked in surprise.

"Cookies," Charlotte said with a shy smile.

"Chocolate-chip cookies?!"

Charlotte nodded and grinned, showing both dimples.

"Those are my favorite! How did you know?"

Charlotte shrugged, still grinning.

"Did you help?"

She nodded again as Micah reached the bottom step. "Did you say hello, Char?" he asked.

She nodded. "I helped stir," she said, finding her voice and her confidence—now that her backup had arrived.

"You did?!"

She nodded again and Micah handed the cookies to Beryl. "Hi!" he said.

"Hi! You didn't have to do this!"

"I didn't," he said, "the bakers did."

"Well, thank you, Charlotte," Beryl said, kneeling down to give her a hug.

"You're welcome," she said softly.

Beryl stood up again. "And please thank your mom—and give her a hug too."

"I will," he said. "And be forewarned—this is just the beginning of the food that's coming your way. My mom said to tell you *not* to go food shopping. She and some of the ladies have been cooking up a storm and they're bringing everything over tomorrow. She asked me if I knew when your family was arriving, but I said I wasn't sure."

"Tomorrow," Beryl confirmed.

"That's perfect, then."

"They really don't have to do that, though—we were planning to go to the store."

"They want to do it," Micah assured her.

"Are you sure?"

He nodded and Beryl lifted the lid off the container. "Mmmm, look at these!" she said, smiling at Charlotte. "Can I share these with Rumer and Isak?"

Charlotte looked up at Micah and he nodded, and she turned back to Beryl and, clinging to Micah's pant leg, nodded too.

"I don't have to," Beryl said. "If you think I should eat them all myself . . ."

Charlotte looked up at Micah again and he shook his head and mouthed the word *nooo!* Charlotte looked back at Beryl and shook her head too.

"Okay," Beryl replied. "It probably wouldn't be good if I ate them all! Besides, Isak and Rumer will be very happy too. Should we show them?"

Charlotte nodded, reached for Beryl's hand, and followed

her into the kitchen. "You guys," Beryl said, "look what Charlotte brought us!"

Isak peered curiously in the container. "All right! Thanks, Charlotte!"

"Wow!" Rumer said with a big smile. "May I have one?" Charlotte nodded and Rumer picked out a cookie and took a bite. "Oh, my goodness," she said, "this is the best chocolate-chip cookie I've ever had!"

Micah smiled and said, "Char, why don't you tell them the secret ingredient?"

Charlotte gave him a puzzled look and he knelt down and whispered in her ear, and her face lit up. "Vanilla pudding," she said shyly with a dimpled grin.

Beryl offered the container to everyone. "Would anyone like a glass of milk?" Charlotte raised her hand, then three more hands went up too. "Okay, a round of milk coming up! Char, want to help?"

Micah watched his little girl laughing with Beryl as they poured milk into glasses and, for the first time since Beth died, he wondered if maybe there was room for someone else in their lives.

25

"Who wants a margarita?" Isak called as she slid her Mexican dip into the microwave. Three hands went up, but this time Charlotte's wasn't one of them.

After Micah and Beryl had dropped the boxes off at the thrift store, they'd brought Charlotte back to his parents' house, where Beryl had the chance to thank—and hug—his mom. While they were there, she also noticed a sour cream coffee cake cooling on a rack and two trays of lasagna under construction. "These probably won't be as good as your mom's," Maddie had said with a smile, "but they'll taste pretty good to a hungry crowd."

"I can't thank you enough, Mrs. Coleman," Beryl had said.

"You're welcome, hon," Maddie had replied. "I'm not the only one cooking though, so I hope you have room in your fridge."

"What's the ratio of tequila to limeade?" Rumer asked, filling their old blender with ice.

"Oh, I don't know—I usually just dump and taste," Isak said, pulling the white strip of plastic off the limeade can and lifting off the top.

"Dump and taste—hmm, I'd like to see those directions in a cookbook."

Isak laughed. "Well, sometimes I use a shot glass, but I don't think Mum has one."

"Yes, she does," Beryl called from the porch.

"Where?"

"In the cabinet, behind the glasses."

Rumer moved the glasses and found an old, tall shot glass in the back corner.

Meanwhile, Isak half-dumped, half-measured the ingredients and turned the blender on high while Rumer ran a lime around the rims of four goblets and then spun the rims in a small saucer of salt. Isak tasted the frosty mixture, added a little more tequila, blended it again, smacked her lips approvingly, and poured. Then she pulled the hot, cheesy dip from the microwave and brought it out on the porch with a big bowl of chips. Rumer followed with two glasses. "It's all right, Ber," she teased, handing her sister and Micah each a glass. "We'll just serve you."

"That's the way it should be," Beryl said with a grin. She reached for a chip. "We're not going to need wraps tonight. This dip could be dinner!" she said, taking a bite. "Mmmm, and I'm going to need the recipe!"

"It's so easy," Isak said, lighting the candles on the porch as Rumer brought out two more glasses and they all settled into chairs within easy reach of the dip.

Beryl took a sip, licked her lips, and looked around. "Ready?" They all nodded . . .

I continued to watch his eyes and I was amazed
by his focus—it truly seemed that he really only saw

curves and shapes... shadows and light. If he was aroused, I couldn't tell—his jeans were loose-fitting and unrevealing, and I wondered if I was enjoying looking at him more than he was enjoying looking at me. I continued to watch him until he finally asked, "Want to see?" I nodded, pulled the robe around me, and walked over to stand beside him.

"Oh, David," I said quietly. "I don't know what to say. It's exquisite." I couldn't believe it was me— lying there looking so seductive—but it was!

"Do you really like it?" he asked, searching my eyes.

"I love it!"

He looked away. "Oh, Mia, if you only knew..."

I stepped forward, standing between his legs as he sat on his stool. "Knew what?" I asked, touching his thighs. He gently held my face in his hands, and I closed my eyes and felt his lips brush lightly against my lashes and my cheeks, slowly searching until his warm mouth found mine.

When we pulled apart, he had tears in his eyes. "What's the matter?" I asked, my heart pounding.

"Mia, don't you know?!" he said, shaking his head. "I'm in love with you. I want you so much my whole body aches... but I'm married—married to a woman I don't love—and who doesn't love me. And nothing on this earth can change that. In the eyes of God, I will always be married." He brushed back a tear. "What do I do?"

I looked down and slowly pulled one end of the soft terry-cloth belt and watched his face as it came undone. He reached out and gently pushed back the robe, his eyes taking me in as if it was the first time he'd ever seen me.

"I wanted your hand here," he said, pressing my hand against my abdomen and sending a rush of heat through my body. I nodded and he slowly stood, shifting his weight to his good leg and moving my hands to his hips. He pulled me against him and I felt how aroused he was ... and he kissed me again—tasting, teasing—and slid his hands inside the robe.

In the years that followed, I've replayed the memory of that night over and over—savoring each moment, feeling his gentle touch, seeing his body in the candlelight, watching our bodies become inter-twined ... and aching to relive those moments again. Sadly, that's how life is—the moments are fleeting—in the next breath, they are just memories. And, at the end of our lives, we are left with only that—a collection of memories to warm our hearts, to give us direction, and to offer us a safe haven when the storms of life are overwhelming. But some don't even have that.

I stayed with David the following night, too, and as I lay beside him in the darkness, feeling the warmth of his body against mine, he opened up about his past.

His father, he said, had been an abusive drunk whose rage was most often directed at his mother. He couldn't remember a time when it hadn't been that way—and he couldn't forget the pain and fear he saw in his mother's cheerful eyes whenever his fa-ther came home. Finally, one night when he was six-teen, his father came in, looking for dinner, and when it wasn't ready, he began shouting at her. He started to push her around the kitchen; then he slapped her so hard she crumpled to the floor. David saw everything, ran to her, and, in a protective rage, turned and swung at his father with all his might. He landed a punch to his father's jaw that broke his hand and sent his father reeling, but when he regained his feet, he seethed, "Get the hell out of this house!" But David defiantly refused and his father pushed him toward the open door, causing him to stumble and fall backward down the stairs. His father stormed down after him, kicking him as he stepped over his body. "That'll teach ya, ya son of a bitch!" David had writhed in pain—his ankle folded unnaturally under him.

His father never came home again—and two weeks later, they found his body floating in the Thames. There was no evidence of foul play, and the police were never able to determine if he had committed suicide or accidently drowned.

David was laid up for months. He dropped out of school and, when he was finally able to get around, he looked for work so he could help his mum pay the bills; but his ankle was never quite right, and no one was interested in hiring a cripple. One day, he saw a Help Wanted sign in the window of a pub in Piccadilly Circus. He leaned his cane in a crook outside and went in—trying his best not to limp. He convinced the owner that he knew how to bartend—after all, he thought, how hard could it be to serve pints of ale and shots of whiskey? The owner was skeptical—but desperate—and hired him on the spot.

It wasn't long before the pretty blonde he'd seen hanging around the pub driving the busboys crazy came over and introduced herself. Catherine Walker—five years his senior—was the pub owner's daughter and she'd set her sights on the slender, young man with the solemn dark eyes who tucked a cane under the bar when he worked. Catherine was a good listener, and young David Gilead was lonely. After the pub closed one night, they had a few pints at the bar and he walked her back to her one-bedroom flat on Regent Street.

A month later, Catherine pretended to weep as she revealed to him that she was pregnant, and the next day, her father informed David that he would be marrying his daughter. David never believed he was the father—he knew, for a fact, that Catherine had been with several of the pub's patrons, but when he suggested the possibility, her father's face had turned a menacing shade of red. "My daughter was raised in the Catholic Church—and she was as innocent as a lamb before you came along, you bastard. She will not be disgraced! If you ever want to work in this godforsaken town again, you'll heed my warning!" A month later, Catherine and David were married in a small, quiet ceremony in St. James's Church. And two months after that, she miscarried.

In his free time, David began to attend life drawing sessions. He had a natural eye for composition, and he quickly learned the importance of light and shadow. The most rewarding discovery, however, was the peace it gave him. One day, an art buyer happened to stop by the studio where the sessions were held. David was cleaning up his area when the gentleman stood in front of his drawing and, out of the blue, offered him more money than he was able to make in a month of bartending. David was on his way—and Catherine would never let him go . . .

* * *

The weeks flew by and, before we knew it, David's residency was over again. He had filled his pad with drawings and on the day he left, he gave them to me. Neither of us could bear the thought of someone new living in our cabin—as we had come to think of it—but someone did. I was told he was a composer, but he was never outside and he never said hello. I don't know how he could have possibly composed anything uplifting, so I decided his compositions must be morose and depressing. It was difficult for me to stop at the cabin—so full of wonderful memories—and not go inside, but I clung to the promise that David would be back the following spring and the cabin would be ours again.

For twelve years, David returned to that little cabin in the woods—a place I'd come to cherish— and would love to visit once more in my life. After that last year, both of our lives changed. The girls were getting older—sixteen, fifteen, and thirteen—I had a house full of teenage girls! It was the exact scenario Tom had worried about, but I know he would've loved every minute! I'd also set aside enough money, along with the last of Tom's insurance money, and money from my silent partner— who encouraged me to follow my dreams—to buy a downtown storefront and turn it into a tea shop—a thankful tribute to the endless cups of tea that kept me going all those years!

Although we missed the privacy and opportunity the cabin had given us, we found other ways to be together. It was always important to David that we keep our relationship a secret, and although my heart silently ached because he never publically acknowledged his love for me—I didn't say anything. If it was the only way I could be a part of his life, I was willing to endure the heartache, but I secretly hoped that we would both live longer than Catherine and a day would come when we could love openly—without shame or guilt.

I wish I'd begun writing these memories down sooner. Sometimes, now, I have flashes when I see clearly in my mind—a smile, a place, or a moment when our bodies were lost in lovemaking—but when I try to assemble these into any kind of order, it seems impossible. I know some of the images in my mind are from photographs—and I've often thought that seeing the photographs again would help me remember—but I can't, for the life of me, remember where I've put them.

Some days now, I sit down to write and I become very tired and find it difficult to remember the words I want to use—it's almost as if the door in my mind is closing and behind it are all the things I've ever known. Sometimes, when I feel this way, I lie down and I feel the cool breeze whispering through the open window, rustling the curtains. I hear a cardinal chirping his midday chirp . . . and the way the sunlight filters into my room reminds me of my childhood—and staying home from school when I didn't feel well. I remember the melancholy feeling I had, thinking of my classmates running around the schoolyard at recess without me. Oddly, it feels the same way now. I know the world and all its excitement is going on out there—but instead of being a part of it, I lie here—alone and quiet . . . listening . . . and wondering if the world will notice when I'm gone.

I've been trying to remember our trip to . . . ? Oh, if I could only find those photographs! I can still see David standing next to the mast of that beautiful sailboat—tan and handsome—his thick dark hair, peppered with gray, blowing in the cool breeze as he looked out to sea. To think he was mine for the asking!

When I woke up this morning, it felt like Christmas because I suddenly remembered, with vivid clarity, a weekend trip we'd taken to North Conway. After years of traveling back and forth from London to New York—and countless trips to New Hampshire—David had finally decided to build a second home in the States. He and Catherine rarely saw each other anymore—the only proof of their marriage was a slip of paper. The girls were all in college by then and David had been after me to take a ride up to the mountains to see the construction site. I'd agreed, but on the morning he was to arrive, I'd run to the store to pick up a few things. On my way back, the car started to bump along and I couldn't figure out why. Finally, I pulled over and discovered I had a flat tire! I panicked—David was on his way and I wasn't there. What would he think? I'd never in my life changed a flat tire before. I didn't even know where to begin! I suddenly regretted all the days my dad had wanted to teach me but I'd put him off. Why hadn't I ever taken the time? I opened the trunk and looked at the spare tire. I must've looked pretty helpless because the first pickup truck that came along pulled alongside and the young man asked me if I needed help. I nodded and he immediately hopped out. He had the tire changed in no time, but when I tried to pay him, he refused. I said, "Well, I can't thank you enough," and I asked him his name. He said his name was Colin; then he said it was the least he could do. I didn't know what he meant, but before I could ask him, he was gone.

By the time I got home, David's dark green Land Rover—an accessory he'd purchased to go along with his future life as a country gentleman—was already parked in the driveway. He'd stayed in my bed on numerous occasions by then, so he knew the way, and I found him dozing on the porch. When he heard me, he opened one eye and teased, "Here you are—late again!" I laughed and went inside to quickly pack our picnic; when I came back out, carrying an old hickory basket from MacDowell, he eyed it suspiciously and said, "Excuse me, ma'am, but does that basket belong to you?" I laughed and told him it did indeed!

On our way to the house site, we stopped in North Conway for a bottle of wine and then drove up the long, winding driveway that led to a clearing that was on top of the world! The views were stunning and the air was so clear we could see for miles in every direction. We stood together, breathing in the crisp autumn air and taking in the majesty of the mountains and the dazzling display of crimson, orange foliage against a cobalt blue sky.

David showed me around the property and described the gardens he was planning—from shrubs to ornamental grass and from flowering perennials to fruit trees, he hoped to have a little of everything—including an English rose garden—in memory of his mother—and a tea garden for me! The post-and-beam-style house was still being framed, but you could tell it was going to be expansive and stately. When we went inside, he explained each room, from kitchen and dining room to library and great room. There was a massive stone chimney in the center of the house with two fireplaces—one in the kitchen and one in the dining room; and there was a second chimney in the back of the house with another fireplace in the great room. We went up the unfinished stairs to the second floor, which had plywood flooring but no walls yet, and he showed me where his studio would be—on the northern end of the house, of course. On the other end, there were several bedrooms, including a large master bedroom with two walk-in closets and a bathroom that was as big as my bedroom at home. He pushed back his hair and pulled me toward him, and I said I hoped his new home would be blessed with love and happiness—and his hearth would always be warm. We sipped our wine; then he reached for my glass . . . and, uninhibited by the openness of our surroundings, we made love under a canopy of endless blue sky.

As I reread this last passage now, I'm no longer able to recall that day with the same clarity I had when I wrote it . . . and I can't help but wonder if I was dreaming? The days all seem to run together now. . . . I sometimes picture a gnarled, ancient oak tree in the backyard of my childhood. My dad is pushing me higher and higher on the swing . . . and the tips of my shoes touch one of the low-hanging branches. "Higher, Daddy," I shout, laughing. "I want to touch heaven!"

I haven't written anything in a long time—but an old friend came to see me today. He told me his wife had died. I told him I was sorry. At first, I wasn't sure of his name—but, now, I know it was David. As we sat together, I could see tears in his eyes. . . .
"It's very hard to lose a loved one," I said, reaching for his hand.
He nodded as tears spilled down his cheeks.

Beryl looked up, her eyes glistening. "That's it," she said softly, "she didn't write any more."

PART III

O, Lord, thou has searched me and known me!

—Psalm 139:1

❦ 26 ❦

Thunder rumbled across the skies in the early hours of Thursday morning, sending Beryl and Isak scrambling for the windows. Within seconds, the floodgates of heaven opened and a deluge of rain poured from the clouds. Beryl hurried downstairs to close the kitchen windows too. She looked at Flan sleeping soundly. "In case you're wondering," she said softly, "you're going to have to wait until this passes to go out." But Flan just kept snoring and Beryl shook her head. "Oh, to be a dog!"

"Maybe in your next life," Isak teased, coming down the stairs, still wearing her Barnard T-shirt and yoga pants.

"Maybe," Beryl smiled. "Seriously, though—look at her. There are definitely no worries in that world."

Isak filled the coffeepot with cold water. "Well, I wouldn't mind switching places with her—just for today. I can't even begin to get my mind around all the things we have to do. In fact, I need to make a list." She sprinkled cinnamon over the ground coffee, pressed down the lid, and plugged the pot in. Within seconds, it sputtered to life, perking cheerfully. "There's something comforting about that sound," she said. "Especially Mum's old pot—it has a song all its own."

"Why don't you take it home with you?" Beryl suggested.

"Oh, I don't know. It'd be nice to have it, but our Keurig is so convenient and easy, I don't think I'd ever use it."

"You could use it when you're missing Mum—or when you don't have to rush out—or when you and Matt have a cup of coffee together."

"That never happens."

Beryl sat down across from her. "Well, that's what needs to happen. You guys need to find your way back to each other—you need to make a new, smaller nest for just the two of you and stop dwelling on the empty one. Time marches on, Isak. You can't go back to the way things used to be. This whole week has been proof of that."

"It's hard to live in the moment, Ber. Even Mum struggled with that."

"I know—against everything she believed in and taught us, she fell for a married man and pinned all her hopes on some future day when they could be together—free from guilt and remorse and secrecy. But, tragically, when that day finally came, it was too late."

Rumer appeared in the doorway. "Do I smell coffee?"

Isak looked up. "I don't think it's ready yet." Then she turned back to Beryl. "Did you find out when Catherine died?"

Beryl nodded. "Micah looked it up when he got home—three years ago—right around when Mum went into the nursing home."

Isak nodded. "David must have known what was happening to Mum."

"He must've—Micah said he's still alive."

"How old is he?"

"He must be around seventy-six or seventy-seven." Then a

shadow fell across Beryl's face. "Oh, no, I wonder if he knows she died."

Isak shook her head. "He may not, but it's definitely not up to us to contact him. We aren't even supposed to know about him."

Beryl frowned. "Don't you think Mum would want him to know?"

"I don't know, Ber," Rumer said slowly, joining in. "I kind of agree with Isak. It's not really our place."

"And what place is that exactly?" Beryl's voice was suddenly choked with emotion. "She loved him—and he loved her. Besides, his wife is gone . . . it doesn't matter anymore."

"He's also famous," Isak said dismissively, "and I think we should leave him alone."

Beryl bit her lip, and as she got up to put the kettle on, she brushed away her tears.

Isak looked back at the blank notepad in front of her. "Do you guys know if it's supposed to rain all day?"

"I don't know," Rumer replied. "I can't remember the last time I saw the weather, but if it is, it's not going to be a very good day for flying."

"Or driving," Isak added. "Matt called last night and said he and Tommy are getting in to New York around three, picking up Meghan and all her stuff, and heading north. What time are Will and Rand getting in?"

"Four-ish."

"Great! We'll *all* get to deal with rush-hour traffic."

Rumer glanced at the clock. "Will offered to rent a car, but I said we'd pick them up. If it's a problem, I'll try to reach him."

"Nope, we'll pick them up." She looked at Beryl. "I know you said someone's bringing food today, Ber, but I think we should still go shopping. We definitely need drinks—soda, juice, milk, beer, ice. We also need to get cold cuts, rolls, snacks . . . I don't know about Rand, but Tommy never stops eating."

"Rand doesn't either!"

Isak laughed. "Well, trust me, the bigger he gets, the worse it'll get."

Beryl was leaning against the counter, waiting for the water to boil. "I think we should wait."

Isak shook her head. "I want to go early because I'd also like to clean the bathrooms and the kitchen today—and figure out where everyone's sleeping."

"The house doesn't have to be spotless," Beryl said. "It is what it is."

"It won't be spotless, that's for sure," Isak retorted, looking at Rumer. "We should probably leave around two—just to be safe—especially if it's raining." She started to jot notes on her paper but continued to talk. "Ber, you're going to stay here and work on your eulogy, right?"

Beryl nodded.

"We should also get some pictures of Mum together for the service. Maybe you could start on that if you have time."

"I have to check on the shop too."

Isak looked up. "Are there any more croissants?"

"I don't think so," Beryl said, pouring hot water over her tea leaves. She put a slice of bread in the toaster. "Anyone want a piece of cinnamon toast?"

"I will," Rumer said, getting up to pour a cup of coffee. "Isak, do you want coffee?"

Isak looked up. "Yes, please—to both."

Beryl put in two more slices, reached into the cabinet for the cinnamon and sugar, and when the hot toast popped up, immediately spread butter on it and then generously sprinkled the sugary mixture on top—Mia had always said, *When it comes to cinnamon toast, timing is everything*. She brought a plate over to Isak; then she and Rumer both took big bites of the warm, sweet toast—it was heavenly. "Mmm!" Rumer said, nodding her approval. Beryl smiled and looked over at Isak, whose toast sat untouched as she continued to write.

An hour later, Isak and Rumer left Beryl sitting at the old kitchen table alone, listening to the rain, and staring at the blank Word document on her laptop that she'd already titled and saved as "Mum." After ten minutes of staring at it, she got up to look out at the rain. She could see the raindrops splashing on the pond, and she pictured the frogs and peepers sitting happily on their lily pads, enjoying every drop. "Oh, Mum," she whispered with tears in her eyes. "Where do I begin?"

She sat back down and tried to picture her mom's face, but the image that kept coming to her mind was the one that always broke her heart. It was of her mom, sitting alone at the end of the hall in the nursing home, watching her go—and waving tentatively with the sweet smile that said she loved her with all her heart. Tears spilled down Beryl's cheeks. "This isn't working," she said, pushing back from the table again. As she did, she heard car doors slamming, followed by cheerful voices drawing closer to the house. She looked out and saw five hooded figures with umbrellas and trays of food climbing the porch steps.

Wiping her eyes, Beryl hurried over to open the door. "Come in! Come in!" she said.

The ladies were all laughing at their damp dilemma and shook their heads. "We can't—we have more!" One at a time, they handed her their covered casseroles and hurried back to their cars. They returned with coffee cakes, rolls, a large meat platter, deviled eggs, a big bowl of fresh fruit, and a tremendous chef's salad with three kinds of dressing.

"Oh, my goodness!" Beryl exclaimed. "Look at all this food!"

Finally, the ladies all bustled into the kitchen, leaving their umbrellas on the porch and filling the house with life, while

Flannery nosed about happily. They pushed back their hoods and Beryl realized she knew each one—they were all teachers from the elementary school and they each came forward to give her a hug.

"I'm so sorry, Beryl dear," Mrs. Williams said. "Your mom was such a lovely person."

"Oh, hon," Mrs. Conn whispered. "We loved your mom so much."

Mrs. Bayers smiled sadly and looked in Beryl's eyes. "Your mom was such a dear person. We've missed having her visit our classroom."

And Mrs. Shemeley came forward and gave her a long hug. "It's so hard to lose your mom," she said softly.

Finally, Mrs. Coleman put her arms around her. "If you need anything," she whispered, "you let us know."

Beryl nodded, tears streaming down her cheeks.

"It's okay to cry," she said gently. The ladies all smiled and nodded and began chatting at once. Beryl wiped her eyes and they each explained what they'd brought.

Mrs. Shemeley smiled. "Bill made his famous lemon chicken—and he said if you need a pie or anything, let him know."

Beryl nodded, trying to absorb everything. "Would you like a cup of tea?" she asked, suddenly remembering her manners.

"Oh, we'd love to, but we can't stay," said the chorus of voices. "Thank you, though." They pulled on their hoods and each gave her another hug as they made their way to the door. "Please give our condolences to your sisters and their families. We'll see you on Saturday. Don't forget to let us know if you need anything." And as quickly as they came, they were gone.

"Thank you," Beryl called after them.

They waved and hurried through the rain to their cars. "You're welcome!" they called back.

Beryl watched as they pulled away and then turned to make

room in the fridge. She reached for the meat platter but stopped, pulled out her phone, and slowly typed: **don't get cold cuts!** She hit Send and, within seconds, Isak had written back: **too late!** Beryl shook her head and mumbled, "Told you to wait." She pulled a slice of provolone off the tray, tore it in half, popped the bigger half in her mouth, and gave the smaller one to Flannery. "C'mon, Flan-O," she said, "let's go find the photo albums."

She went into the family room and pulled two big albums off the bookshelf. As she did, a folder that had been tucked between them fell to the floor, spilling its contents everywhere. Beryl knelt to pick them up, but then stopped and stared. Scattered across the floor were a dozen black-and-white photos of her mom sitting next to a handsome dark-haired man, whose contemplative smile and sparkling eyes would steal any woman's heart. The photos had obviously been taken aboard a sailboat, and in all of them he had his arms around her or his head against hers. Beryl looked at the folder; the year—*1986*—was scrawled on the tab, and when she opened it, she realized there were two more pictures that hadn't fallen out. The first was of the man, standing alone next to the mast, looking out to sea, and the other was of the gorgeous forty-four-foot sloop on which they'd sailed. The name *Sweet Indiscretion* was painted on its bow and, under the name, was painted its home port— Bermuda! She gazed at her mom's face and smiled—she'd never seen her look happier.

She gathered the pictures together, slipped them back into the folder, and was carrying everything to the kitchen, when she heard a loud knock on the door. Flannery bolted in front of her, trying to get to the door first and almost tripped her in the process. "Flan," she said in frustration, "could you *not* do that?!" She set everything on the table and opened the door.

An older gentleman was standing on the porch, holding the

most beautiful blue hydrangea. He had raindrops dripping from the brim of his hat. "I was beginning to think no one was home," he said. "Is this the Graham residence?"

"I'm sorry, I didn't hear you," Beryl answered.

"That's okay," he said, smiling and holding out the plant. "This is for you."

Beryl looked surprised as she took the plant from him. "Thank you."

"You're welcome," he said, tipping his hat.

She brought the tremendous, wet plant inside, set it on the counter, slid out the damp card, and stared at the words: *In memory of your beloved mum. With deepest sympathy, David.*

27

It was still raining when Isak and Rumer pulled in the driveway, and Beryl slipped into her jacket and went to help. "You're
not going to believe what I found," she shouted as they carried
bags of groceries from the car.

"What?" they asked breathlessly.

She looked at their wet hair and jackets. "You have to be
completely dry before I show you so you don't drip on them.
In the meantime," she said, opening the fridge door, "we have
plenty of food! All the teachers from the elementary school
were here, and they said to tell you how sorry they are. You
should've waited. They really outdid themselves."

"You're right, we should've," Isak said wearily, hanging her
jacket on the back of a chair.

"Where'd that come from?" Rumer asked, seeing the hydrangea.

"The florist delivered it," Beryl answered, showing them the
card.

"No way!" Rumer exclaimed.

"I guess we don't need to worry about getting in touch with him," Isak said.

"I guess we don't . . ." Beryl said, still feeling the sting of their disagreement.

"Okay, I'm dry enough," Rumer said, toweling her damp hair. "What'd you find?" Beryl pulled out the folder and spread the pictures on the table.

"Holy Sh-ugar!" Isak said softly.

"You can say that again," Rumer whispered.

They studied the photos for several minutes. Finally, Isak sighed and said, "Well, a picture is definitely worth a thousand words!"

"How the heck did she pull off a trip to Bermuda without us knowing?" Rumer asked.

"The folder says it was in 1986—so we must've all been in college."

"Unbelievable," Isak said. "I wonder if they went anywhere else." She studied the photo of the sailboat. *"Sweet Indiscretion,"* she murmured. "That's very telling," she said with a smile. "What I'd really like, though, is to find David's drawings. They must be in the house somewhere." She glanced at the clock. "Anyway, how'd you make out? Did you get anywhere with the eulogy?"

"I started it," Beryl said with a sigh, "and that's the hard part."

"Find any other pictures? Because we can't use these," Isak said with a grin. "Can you imagine?"

"That would certainly surprise everyone," Beryl said, laughing. "The reserved, little tea lady with her famous, very handsome . . . and very illicit lover." She handed them some of the family pictures she'd pulled from their old family albums, including some from Mia's childhood.

"Are you sure this isn't you?" Isak said, holding up a picture of their mom when she was twelve years old. "It looks just like you!"

Beryl laughed. "It says 1954, silly, so, no, it's not."

"These are great, Ber," Rumer said, handing them back to her. "Now we just need to get some poster board to put them on."

"I'll stop and get some on my way to the shop, and I'll make copies of the story so we each have one."

Isak nodded. "I'm going to clean the bathrooms before we leave."

They all got to work—cleaning, dusting, vacuuming, and pulling the couch out into a bed.

"Any idea where the cot might be?" Isak shouted over the vacuum.

"Mum used to keep it in the closet in the spare bedroom," Beryl called back.

Isak disappeared into the room where they'd just put fresh sheets on the double bed. When she didn't reappear, Beryl went to check on her. "Did you find it?"

"I did," she said with a smile, "and, behind it, I found this . . ." She held up a large, old-style drawing tablet. "And this!" She pointed to a large, flat package wrapped in brown paper leaning against her leg. "Let's go into Mum's room—the light's better. Call Ru!"

"Rumer, come quick!" Beryl hollered down the stairs.

Rumer switched off the vacuum and ran up the stairs. "What's the matter?" she asked, her face filled with concern.

"Come see," Isak said excitedly as she leaned the painting against the bed. Then she picked up the tablet and, after a brief hesitation, opened it up and slowly turned the pages as her sisters looked on. They were stunned by its contents. Each page was a drawing of Mia in a different pose . . . and in varying stages of undress. And as they came to the last few pages, it became clear that the artist had finally convinced his model to pose nude.

Isak whistled softly. Rumer and Beryl both nodded in agreement, and Isak glanced at her phone—it was two o'clock. "Damn! We have to go, Ru, but I want to see what's in the package too."

"We have time," Rumer insisted eagerly. "Go ahead."

Isak laid the ensconced painting on the bed and picked up the end of the dry, yellow masking tape. It practically crumbled in her hand as she pulled it away, leaving a brown stain where it had held the paper closed for many years. Isak slowly removed the paper wrap while Beryl lifted the painting by its hanging wire and leaned it against the headboard; they all gazed at it in amazement. It was a portrait of Mia sitting next to a window. She was wearing a beautiful ochre-colored robe that had delicate embroidery stitched around the collar. The robe was open, allowing the late-day sunlight to fall seductively across her body—and making the entire painting glow in an ethereal light.

28

"Do you want a coffee?" Isak asked, spying a Dunkin' Donuts in the airport terminal.

"Sure," Rumer said.

They stood in line and when they reached the counter, Rumer was about to order her usual hazelnut with cream, but at the last minute, she had a change of heart and ordered a hot cocoa with whipped cream. Isak gave her a funny look and she responded with a grin, "You only live once!"

Isak shrugged and ordered her usual, no-nonsense black.

"Anything else?" the woman behind the counter asked.

Rumer eyed the crullers.

"Nothing for me," Isak said, pulling her wallet out of her bag.

"I guess not," Rumer said, deciding to show some measure of restraint as she reached into her shoulder pouch, but Isak motioned for her to put her wallet away. "I've got it," she insisted.

Rumer shrugged. "All right, but next time it's on me."

Sipping slowly from their hot cups, they studied the flight

schedule monitor nearby and realized that Will and Rand's flight had been delayed. Finding seats near a window, they settled in to wait and Isak checked her phone. She'd received a text from Meghan around four o'clock telling her they were on their way, but that they were thinking of stopping somewhere for dinner. Isak had texted back that there were all kinds of restaurants off I-84, especially off exit 32 in Southington, but there also was plenty of food at Grammie's if they could wait. Meghan had written back that she didn't think Tommy could wait—he was starving. And Isak had sent back a smiley face and said she was looking forward to seeing them, but Meghan hadn't replied—hardly like her.

Isak tried to put it out of her mind and imagined the hugs they'd be sharing in a few short hours—and the surprise on her sisters' faces when they saw how grown up their niece and nephew had become, especially Tommy, who'd been sporting facial hair the last time she saw him. *Mum would've loved seeing everyone,* she thought sadly.

She stared at her phone, willing her daughter to write back, but the screen stayed ominously dark. "What's the matter?" Rumer asked, glancing over.

"Nothing," she said, looking up. "I just thought Meghan would respond to my last text. I always worry when I don't hear back right away."

"She probably fell asleep," Rumer reassured her. "She's been up late studying for exams and everything."

"You're right," Isak said with a sigh. "I don't think moms ever stop worrying, though. Do you think Mum ever stopped?"

They looked at each other. "No!" they both said, laughing.

"She had good reason to worry," Rumer teased, "with *you* in the house!" She licked her whipped cream and continued, "We just got Rand a phone last year. He drove us crazy until we did. Will was the holdout—he didn't want the extra expense. But I wanted him to have one so I could reach him, or he could reach me if he had a problem. So we made a deal with him that he always had to answer if it was me calling, even if he was in the middle of a video game or hanging out with his friends. But I can't tell you how many times he hasn't kept his end of the deal—and when he doesn't, I always imagine the worst, like he's been abducted or hit by a car. It drives me crazy, and I get on his case about it, but he just complains that I worry too much."

"Maybe you should take it away for a week," Isak suggested.

Rumer nodded. "I've thought of that, but then I *really* wouldn't be able to reach him."

Isak laughed. "It's a vicious cycle." She paused thoughtfully. "If you think about it, that's nothing compared to the stuff we pulled. My kids are so good compared to how I was. I don't know what Matt and I did differently, because Mum was a good parent—strict and always there for us—but when I think back to some of the crazy things we did—the parties we had and the amount of alcohol we consumed—I honestly think we're lucky to be alive."

Rumer smiled. "Remember the time we said we were sleeping over Jenny Hollister's house and the boys told their parents they were camping, and then we all met at the abandoned barn?"

"I remember," Isak said, smiling, but then looked puzzled. "Was Ber there?"

"No, she was too young."

"I was in tenth or eleventh grade," Isak reminisced with a smile, "and we got Sue Burton to buy us a case of beer."

"And Jenny's sister bought us some Boone's Farm—and then Adam Wiley showed up with a dime bag . . ."

"Adam Wiley," Isak said wistfully. "Damn, he was cute. Did you know we spent the night in the hayloft?"

Rumer laughed. "Everyone knew that!"

Isak laughed too. "Oh, well, we had some good times. But I'd absolutely kill my kids if they ever pulled something like that."

"I'm sure they've had their share of fun—fun you don't know about!"

"You're probably right," Isak said, looking at her messages again. "Okay—if Meghan's asleep, I'm texting Tommy." She sent him a quick note that asked: **how're you doin'?** Then she waited expectantly and, after ten more minutes of staring at her dark screen, she whispered, "Okay, that made it worse."

Beryl sat in front of her laptop with a pot of English tea steeping beside her. She glanced up, realized she'd forgotten all about the tea, and poured herself a cup. Then she wrapped her hands around the steaming mug and leaned back to reread what she'd just written. She made a few edits with one hand and took a sip, wishing she had a scone. Then she remembered the cookies and got up to get one. As she sat back down, there was a knock on the door.

"Come in," she called with a full mouth.

Micah pulled open the door. "Uh-oh, someone's in the cookies again," he teased.

She laughed. "Want one?"

"I never turn down a chocolate-chip cookie," he said, kneeling down to scratch Flan's belly.

"Me neither—want some tea to go with it?"

"Sure."

"Is it still raining?"

"No, just misting."

"That's good. Did you hear the thunder this morning?"

He nodded. "It woke me up, but Charlotte slept right through it."

"It woke us up, too—I thought the sky was falling!"

"We need the rain."

Beryl nodded and looked up. "Oh, my goodness, I have to show you what we found."

Isak had just settled in for the long wait for the delayed flight from the West Coast when her phone rang unexpectedly, making her heart jump. She looked at the screen. "Connecticut State Police?" she whispered to herself. She pressed Answer and felt her heart race.

"Yes, this is she," she said hesitantly.

"Yes . . . yes." Tears started to fill her eyes as she listened. "Oh, no!" she cried out, covering her mouth. "Oh, please no." She nodded her head as she listened. "Oh, please don't let this be happening."

The waiting area suddenly seemed very quiet. Rumer sat forward, trying to discern what terrible news the caller was sharing. "What is it?" she whispered, searching Isak's eyes, but Isak just shook her head.

Finally, Isak pulled herself together. "Let me speak to him." A moment passed and she blurted, "Oh, honey, what happened—are you okay? Is Meghan okay?" She listened for a long time, her eyes full of tears. "What happened to the other driver?" She paused. "Okay, I'm coming. I'm in Boston, but I'll be there as soon as I can." She paused, listening. "I see—okay— I'm not sure what we'll do then. I love you, too, honey—please tell Meghan I love her—and we will figure this out."

She stood up, in shock. "I have to go," she said.

Rumer stood too. "What happened?"

Isak covered her anguished face with her hands and started shaking uncontrollably. "Oh, Ru," she sobbed. "They were in an accident. A truck came out of nowhere and hit them head-on. Tommy said he thinks it came up the exit ramp, but he was so upset I had trouble understanding him. He said their SUV flipped and landed on its roof—crushing the driver's side. Meghan was in the passenger seat because he'd wanted to stretch out in back—and he kept saying how sorry he was—that he should've been up front. The kids are in Danbury—and the doctor thinks Meghan's wrist is broken ... and her face is bruised, so she might have a concussion."

"What about Matt?" Rumer asked hesitantly, her voice choked with fear.

Tears flowed down Isak's cheeks. "Oh, Ru," she said, shaking her head. "They Life-Starred him right to Hartford."

Rumer covered her mouth, muffling a cry.

"I have to go ..."

"I'll go with you ..."

Isak shook her head. "You can't. You—we—oh, how the heck are we going to do this? How am I going to go to both places?"

"Go to Hartford," Rumer said, taking control. "We'll manage. I'll call Beryl and tell her to go to Danbury right away, and when Will gets here, we'll come to Hartford too."

"You don't have to come," Isak started to protest, but Rumer wouldn't hear of it.

"We're coming," she said assertively, giving her sister a hug. "Now go! We'll be right along."

"Okay," Isak said, wiping her eyes. She picked up her bag and turned; as she did, an older woman put her hand gently on her arm and looked her straight in the eye.

"I'm sorry, but I couldn't help but overhear ... please know I'll be praying for you, dear."

"Thank you," Isak said with a nod.

Beryl had just finished showing Micah the photographs and was bringing him upstairs to take a look at the artwork when the phone began to ring. "Go ahead up," she said, turning around. "Go see and I'll be right up." She hurried back down the stairs, picked up the phone, and when she heard the fear in Rumer's voice, her heart stopped.

"I've been calling your cell for ten minutes," Rumer blurted in frustration.

"I'm sorry, I didn't hear it. What's the matter?"

Rumer's voice was filled with emotion as she shared what she knew. Beryl listened, tears filling her eyes. "Will and Rand are landing now—they don't know yet—but I'm renting a car and we're going to Hartford to be with Isak and Matt. Meghan and Tommy are in Danbury, in the emergency room—can you go?"

"Of course," Beryl said, wiping her eyes. "I'll leave right away."

As she hung up the phone, she turned and saw Micah standing in the doorway. "I'm going with you," he said.

29

"Concentrate!" Isak told herself as she pulled onto the highway. Although she'd driven through Connecticut countless times when she was in college, she'd always taken 91 South and picked up 84 in Hartford, so she wasn't familiar with the Mass Pike, and between the rainy conditions and the blur of her tears, she almost missed the exit for I-84.

"Oh, God," she whispered, "please don't take Matt from me." Her heart was gripped with fear as she suddenly realized it might be too late. If he was so badly injured that he had to be airlifted, he might already be gone. She imagined arriving at the hospital and the doctor solemnly taking her aside: *We did all we could—I'm so sorry* . . .

"No!" she choked as she drove through the rain, raking her hand through her hair. "Oh, God, please no . . ." A fresh wave of tears filled her eyes and she brushed them away, trying to concentrate on the road. She pictured Matt lying alone on a stretcher—bruised and bloody and broken with no loved ones at his side. "I'm coming, baby," she whispered. "I'm coming— don't you dare leave me!"

The wiper blades splashed back and forth as the miles flew by. "Think positive," she chided. She pictured his sweet, boyish grin—the one that spread across his face when he was teasing her—and his blond hair, which had just recently started showing signs of gray. She pictured him sitting on the deck in his boxers, drinking coffee from his favorite Life Is Good golfing mug, and reading the *Wall Street Journal.* And she pictured the way he'd looked the first time he'd tenderly cradled Tommy in his arms; he'd been so proud, his eyes glistening with love and amazement.

"Oh, God, don't take him from me," she commanded angrily. "I can't handle two funerals." She imagined the unending grief of her children. "Mum, don't let this happen to us. . . ."

She stared through the windshield, lost in thought—her mind, of its own accord, suddenly recalling the morning of her wedding. It was so vivid she could almost hear her mom's voice.

"Nervous?" Mia had asked when she'd come in to wake her.

Isak had nodded, wanting to bury her head under her pillow.

"Don't be nervous, hon," she'd said softly, sitting on the bed. "Matt's a good man—I wouldn't let you marry him if I didn't think so." Then she'd smiled, knowing how slim the chances were of putting the brakes on anything her oldest daughter had set her mind on doing. "I want you to promise me, though, that you'll treasure each and every moment—not just today, but every single mundane, hectic, lonely, difficult moment—because that's what life's about—it's about the journey—*your* journey—and Matt's. And when the babies that you're going to be blessed with are driving you crazy . . . and you think you can't possibly change another diaper . . . or pick up another toy—or when they're suddenly grown and it seems like they've deserted you, remember that you're just in the thick of it—the thick of your life . . . your journey! Don't ever postpone the things you want to do—every moment is precious, and in the rush of things, we sometimes forget that. Some people don't realize how blessed they are until something happens—and then it's too late. So make sure you tell Matt you love him . . . every day—and God will take care of the rest."

Isak *had* promised her mom she would, but now she suddenly realized she hadn't kept that promise at all. She couldn't remember the last time she'd told Matt she loved him. Why had it taken something tragic to realize just how much? "Please don't let it be too late," she whispered.

She pulled into a parking spot and ran inside. The receptionist looked frazzled but did her best to help. "Let's see— Matthew Taylor . . ." She flipped through the stack of new admissions, paused on one, and bit her lip. "I'll have the doctor come see you as soon as he can, Mrs. Taylor."

"Is Matt . . . is he . . . alive?"

"He's in surgery," the nurse said with a gentle smile.

Isak nodded, tears stinging her eyes, and turned to find a seat in the waiting room.

"Are you sure your mom doesn't mind coming over to let Flan out?" Beryl asked as they pulled onto the highway.

"I'm positive."

"And you told her where the food is?"

Micah nodded.

"And you're sure you don't mind driving?"

"I'm sure."

"I feel like I'm forgetting something."

"Whatever it is, we can get it down there," Micah assured her.

"I guess," she sighed resignedly. "I wish I had Tommy's cell number."

"Call Isak."

"I don't know if she's there yet and I don't want to call if she's driving."

Micah looked at the clock on the dashboard. It was almost six. "Unless something happened, she should be there by now."

Beryl stared at her phone, considering her options. "I'll call Rumer."

Without realizing it, she held her breath while she waited for her sister to answer.

"We just got here," Rumer said breathlessly. "The doctor is talking to Isak right now—can I call you back?"

Beryl nodded; she hadn't uttered a word.

She closed her phone and Micah glanced over. "Did you get her?"

"She's calling back," she said, gazing out the window at the Massachusetts landscape and noticing that the leaves were much further along than the ones in New Hampshire. She closed her eyes, squeezed back her tears, and silently prayed for her family. A moment later, she felt Micah's hand close around hers.

They were well into Connecticut when her phone finally rang. She answered it and was surprised to hear Isak's voice. Beryl could tell she'd been crying because she sounded congested and she was still very upset. "Thank you so much for doing this," she said.

"Isak, you don't have to thank me . . . How's Matt? We're going crazy . . ."

"Oh, Ber, he's not good—he has three broken ribs, a collapsed lung, a broken collarbone, a broken ankle, and possible swelling on his brain. He's still in surgery, and they said the next several hours will be critical."

"Oh, Isak—I'm so sorry. We're almost to Hartford," she said, seeing the signs for Bradley Airport. "Do you want us to stop?"

"No—no," Isak said. "I mean, I wish you could, but I need you to be there for the kids—is that okay?"

"Of course it's okay. By the way, can you give me Tommy's number?"

Isak gave her the number and then paused. "Ber?"

"Mmmm?" she said, still writing.

There was no response, but Beryl could sense her sister's agony through the phone.

"Everything's going to be okay, Isak . . ."

"I know . . ."

"We're on eighty-four and I can see the hospital. We're praying for you and Matt and the kids, and we'll be in Danbury in less than an hour."

"I-I love you, you know," Isak stammered.

"I know you do. I love you, too, sis," Beryl said softly, surprised by her sister's admission. "I'll call as soon as we get there."

30

Tommy was leaning forward in his chair with his elbows on his knees and his hands covering his face when Beryl peered into the room. "Hey," she said softly. He looked up and the distraught look on his tearstained face eased as he tried to muster a smile.

"Hey, Aunt Ber," he said, getting up and wrapping her in a bear hug.

"Oh, my goodness, Tommy Taylor . . ." she said. "When did you get so big?!"

He laughed and she laid her hand on his scruffy cheek. "You look just like your dad, you know that?" she said, searching his glistening eyes. "How're you doin'?"

"I'm okay—a little sore." He motioned to the bed. "Meggie's pretty banged up." Beryl nodded, moving closer to the bed. "She's still pretty out of it; they said the painkillers will do that. Her wrist is shattered—so I guess no tennis this summer." He brushed away a tear. "I should've been up front—then she'd be okay. She's lucky, though—the car was absolutely totaled—you can't even tell what it was." He looked over. "Have you talked to my mom?"

Beryl nodded, lightly touching Meghan's bruised cheek, and then noticed Micah standing in the hall and motioned for him to come in. "Tommy, this is Micah." The two shook hands. "Micah's an old friend. He used to work in Grammie's shop when he was in high school and he offered to come down with me."

"Thanks for coming, man," Tommy said with a nod.

Micah smiled.

"Anyway, I just talked to your mom to let her know we were here. Have you talked to her at all?"

"No, there's no service in here," he said, looking at his phone to confirm that the bars hadn't magically appeared. "I was gonna go outside and call."

"Well, your dad is out of surgery," Beryl reported, "but he's still in pretty rough shape. Your mom said the doctor sounded more optimistic, so that's a bit of bright news." She hesitated, knowing she was walking a fine line between hope and devastation. "Tommy," she said softly, "he's definitely not out of the woods, though . . . and the next twenty-four hours are critical."

Tommy nodded, trying to swallow the lump in his throat. "I want to see him," he said.

Just then a young doctor came into the room. "Hello," she said. "Are you Mrs. Taylor?"

"No," Beryl said, quickly introducing herself and explaining why her sister wasn't there. "How's Meghan doing?"

"She's going to be fine, but I'd like to speak to her mom before I leave tonight. Do you have her cell number—or maybe you could ask her to give me a call."

"Of course," Beryl said, as Tommy jotted down his mom's cell phone number on a napkin.

"Thank you, I'll check back in a bit."

Beryl sat on the bed and stroked Meghan's hand. Almost immediately, her eyelashes fluttered open. "Hey, Meggie," she whispered softly.

Meghan opened her eyes and tried to focus. "Hi, Aunt Ber . . ." she said weakly.

"Hi, sweetheart," Beryl said softly. "It's so good to see you."

Meghan nodded and promptly drifted off again.

"So, two coffees and a tea?" Micah said, feeling his pocket to make sure he had his wallet.

Beryl nodded and looked at Tommy. "Are you sure you take it black?"

Micah chuckled. "I think Tommy knows how he takes his coffee."

Beryl shook her head, still unconvinced. "Well, I think he bumped his head and is confused—or else his mother is a bad influence!"

Tommy laughed. "She *is* a bad influence." Then he looked at Micah. "Mind if I go with you?"

"Not at all."

"I could use a change of scenery—and maybe a sandwich," he added, rubbing his stomach.

"Do you want anything besides tea?" Micah asked, looking at Beryl. "Maybe a cookie?"

Beryl smiled halfheartedly. "I'm sure the hospital's cookies aren't as good as Charlotte's, but I'll split a sandwich with you if you see something."

"Okay, we'll be right back."

Ten minutes later, they returned with two coffees, one tea, and two Caesar salad wraps—one of which Tommy had completely devoured before Beryl even took her second bite.

"Ber," Micah said, taking a sip of coffee. "If Tommy wants

to see his dad, why don't I run him up there? It's only an hour, and there's no reason for him to stay here. Meghan's stable, and she's clearly not going anywhere tonight."

Beryl and Tommy both looked up. "You don't mind driving?" Beryl asked.

"Nope—and he should be there."

"If you want to, it's fine with me. Are you coming back?"

"Maybe," he teased.

"Micah," Tommy began haltingly. "Do you think we can stop at the wrecker shop so I can get our stuff? Would you have room for all of it? I have the trooper's cell number," he said, pulling a card from his pocket.

"Definitely," Micah said with a nod. "When the backseat is down, there's plenty of room. We'll do it on our way."

"Call your mom, too, and let her know you're coming," Beryl reminded.

"I will," Tommy said, giving her a hug. "Thanks, Aunt Ber."

"You're welcome, hon."

"I'll be back later," Micah said, as she hugged him too.

"I can't thank you enough," Beryl murmured into his chest and then stepped back and looked into his eyes. "Please be careful."

A moment later, she was looking out the window, wondering if she could see Micah's car from where she stood, but since he'd dropped her off before he'd parked, she wasn't even sure where it was. She watched people walking below, and after five minutes with no sign of them, she gave up and sat in the chair next to Meghan's bed and sipped her tea. She turned on the TV using the remote on the bedside table, keeping the volume low so Meghan wouldn't stir. She flipped through the channels and settled on an old classic starring Cary Grant and Debra Kerr— it had been one of her mom's favorites, and now she knew why.

⤜ 31 ⤛

It was almost dark as Micah approached exit 9, but Tommy asked him to slow down. "This is where it happened," he said, pointing to the fluid stains and debris on the side of the road, as well as the trenches in the grass. "Did you know the other driver failed a sobriety test?"

"No, I didn't. In fact, I don't think your mom knows that either."

"That reminds me," Tommy said, reaching into his pocket for his phone. "I'd better let her know we're coming."

Micah tried not to eavesdrop, but there wasn't much he could do when the conversation was occurring right beside him. He took a sip of his coffee and tried to focus on the road, but it quickly became evident that he'd been right—Isak hadn't heard the other driver was drunk—and she wasn't happy.

"How's dad?" Tommy asked, changing the subject while fiddling with a thread on his jeans. There was a long pause as he listened and Micah thought he saw him wipe his eyes. "When will they know?" He nodded. "Yeah, Meggie's going to be okay. I told Aunt Ber she probably won't be able to play any tennis this summer." Another pause, then he laughed. "Oh, did her doctor get ahold of you?" Pause. "Good. Yeah, I think she needs permission to talk to Aunt Ber. I dunno . . . can you give it over the phone?" Pause. "She's eighteen—it shouldn't be a problem. Will they let her go home with Aunt Ber?" Pause. "Do you think we're still going to have Grammie's service on Saturday?" Pause. "Yeah, I know—it's pretty impossible to postpone a funeral." Pause. "Let's see . . . uhm . . . we're almost to Waterbury . . . so, you think a half hour?" Pause. "Okay. Love you, too—see you in a bit. Love you too." He ended the call and gazed out into the darkness. "Thanks for the ride, Micah."

"No problem, Tommy. I'm happy to do it."

Tommy grew quiet and Micah glanced over to see if he'd fallen asleep. He clicked on the radio and the classic "Seven Bridges Road" drifted through the car.

"This is one of my dad's favorite Eagles songs," Tommy said wistfully. "My mom likes that really sad one . . ."

Micah frowned, trying to remember lyrics to Eagles songs. " 'Lying Eyes'?"

"No, it's about letting someone love you . . ."

" 'Desperado'?"

"Yeah, that's it," Tommy said, sitting up. "I always thought it was sort of fitting, you know, for their personalities. My dad is much more easygoing than my mom, and "Seven Bridges" is such a great song, but "Desperado"—holy cow! It's so depressing. Sometimes I wonder how my parents ever got together—they're so different from one another."

Micah smiled. "Have you ever heard the old adage 'opposites attract'?"

"Yeah," Tommy said with a laugh. "My parents are definitely proof of that."

The miles ticked by and the only sound was from the radio. Finally, Tommy said, "I haven't been out here in such a long time. Meghan and I used to come every summer and stay with Grammie for a couple of weeks. We had the best times. She'd take us mini-golfing, out for ice cream, catch frogs with us in the pond or fireflies at night. And she made the most amazing cinnamon toast.

"Aunt Ber was always around, too—she loved to go hiking. We climbed Monadnock every summer. The last time, Meghan didn't come, though. I think she must've had tennis camp or something, and Aunt Ber and I hiked Mount Washington instead. I'll never forget it because there was still snow in Tuckerman Ravine—in July! When we got to the top, it was unbelievably windy and I thought we were going to blow right off the mountain. Then we went inside and had pizza—and it was *the* best pizza I've ever had."

"Probably because you were so hungry," Micah said.

"Probably," Tommy said with a smile. "I always wanted to hike it again, but we never had the chance. Grammie developed Alzheimer's and Aunt Ber had to take care of her. I think Aunt Ber ended up missing out on a lot because of it. All of Grammie's care fell on her shoulders and she never got the chance to meet anyone or have kids of her own. She's such a great person—and she would've been a great mom. My mom's a great mom, but she's not at all like Aunt Ber. It's funny how sisters can be so different too."

Micah listened quietly, taking in every word as Tommy voiced out loud the very thoughts he'd been thinking.

"I wish I'd come out to see my grandmother one last time," he said regretfully, "even if she didn't remember me—I should've come anyway. Now she's gone."

Micah looked over. "You didn't know what was going to happen. No one knew. But through the years, you got to spend a lot of time with her—and she definitely knew you loved her. You shouldn't let all of your great memories be tarnished with regret."

Tommy nodded and rested his knee on the dashboard. "This is a pretty old Honda, Micah. How many miles are on it?"

"Almost two hundred fifty thousand."

"Wow! That's pretty impressive. Would you ever trade it in?"

"Probably not—I wouldn't get much for it—and I've begun to think it might run forever, which would make it worth keeping."

"Have you owned it since it was new?"

"Yup, it was my wife's car."

Tommy hesitated. "Was?"

"She passed away about three years ago."

"Oh . . . I'm sorry, man," Tommy said quietly.

Micah nodded. "Thanks. She left me with a beautiful little girl, too, though. Her name is Charlotte."

"How old is she?"

"Four."

"I bet she's a lot of fun."

"Yeah, she's great."

"So this car has sentimental value too."

Micah nodded. "It does—but I've begun to think it might be time to start letting go."

❦ 32 ❦

As the minutes ticked slowly by, the Graham family did what every family does in the face of tragedy—they stood watch, held each other close, and prayed. When Tommy and Micah arrived, Tommy ruffled Rand's new haircut, teased his Aunt Ru because her son was taller than she was, shook Uncle Will's hand, hugged his mom for a long time, and wept at his father's bedside. Isak had finally been able to reach Matt's mother, who lived in Newport, and gently told her the news. She'd been very upset and called Isak back within minutes to tell her she'd arranged for a friend to bring her to Hartford the following day.

Rumer had taken a break earlier to get some sandwiches and coffee, knowing everyone would have been in such a hurry, they wouldn't have stopped to eat.

Micah wasn't hungry, but Isak handed him a cup of coffee as he stood by the door, ready to leave. "I can't thank you enough, Micah," she said, giving him a hug.

He nodded. "Let me know if you need anything."

*   *   *

When Micah finally got back to Danbury, Beryl was dozing in a chair and Jay Leno's tinny voice was barely audible coming from the tiny speakers on the remote control. Micah pulled a chair up next to her and she opened her eyes. "I think visiting hours are over, miss," he whispered.

"I know," she murmured. "What are we gonna do?"

"I don't know, but if we don't get some real sleep, we're gonna be pretty useless tomorrow."

"The nurse said Meghan will be fine if we want to find a place to stay tonight, but I feel bad knowing Isak and Ru will be keeping watch all night in uncomfortable chairs."

"That's not entirely true," Micah said. "When I was leaving, Ru and Will were talking about taking Tommy and Rand to a hotel, and Isak was going to sleep on a cot in the room. So, if you want to get a room for the night, you shouldn't feel bad; we can definitely do that so you can get some rest."

Beryl glanced at Meghan, who seemed to be sleeping comfortably. She pushed the Power button on the remote and put it on the bedside table, gently kissed Meghan's forehead, and whispered, "See you in the morning, hon." Meghan didn't stir and they slipped out of the room, stopped at the nurses' station to let them know they were leaving, and asked if they could recommend an inexpensive hotel for the night. The nurse looked online and jotted down a couple of suggestions. They thanked her and walked down the quiet hall and out into the starry night. "I guess the storm's over," Beryl said. Micah nodded, putting his arm around her.

A half hour later, Beryl was brushing her teeth in the hotel bathroom, feeling awkward and nervous. She washed her face, looked at her reflection, and sighed. Then she opened the door and peered out. The room was dimly lit by a lamp near the TV, and Micah, who had laid back on one of the beds without pulling down the covers, was softly snoring. Beryl wondered if she should just leave him, but then decided *she* wouldn't want to fall asleep like that, and gently shook him. "Gonna get washed up?" she asked.

He woke with a start. "Huh? Yup." He got right up and shuffled to the bathroom.

Beryl turned the air conditioner down—it was plenty cool in the room—pulled down the comforter, slipped between the sheets, and laid her head back onto the plump hotel pillow. It felt good—What was it about hotel pillows that always made them feel so fluffy? A moment later, Micah reappeared and started to pull down the covers of the other bed.

"There's no point in messing up two beds," she said softly.

Micah looked over in surprise. "Is that an invitation?"

She smiled and he turned off the light and went around to the other side of her bed. She heard the clink of his belt as he pulled off his jeans and threw them over a chair, and then felt him slip between the sheets. She couldn't help but wonder if he'd kept on his boxers. She felt his hand close around hers, and she slid her fingers between his, locking them together. He moved closer and she felt the comforting warmth of his body through the soft cotton of his T-shirt . . . and boxers. It had been a long time since she'd felt a male body lying beside her—not since Ryan Lane, or as her sisters referred to him, the biggest loser on the planet.

Micah stared into the darkness. "It's funny how things come full circle."

"What do you mean?" Beryl asked.

"Well, way back when—a hundred years ago now—when I worked in your mom's store, I had a big crush on you, but I don't think you had any idea. And just when I was trying to work up the courage to ask you to the prom, I found out you were already going." He looked over. "I was crushed!"

Beryl laughed. "I'm sure you weren't crushed."

"I was—absolutely crushed! And now, all these years later . . ."

"Yes, a hundred, according to you," she teased.

"Yup, a hundred—probably to the day because proms are usually in May—here I am, lying beside you . . . in a bed of all places."

"Well, I think you must've gotten over your crush somewhere in the middle of all those years."

"You're right—but I never forgot about you."

Beryl laughed. "It is funny," she agreed. "And I definitely didn't know you had a crush. It just shows how clueless I was—and still am!"

"You're not clueless," he said softly.

"Oh, I'm not so sure about that."

He turned to face her, lightly kissed her forehead and her cheek, and slowly made his way to her lips. Her heart was pounding; there was no doubt she was falling in love, but at the same time, she had so many other things weighing on her heart.

Micah pulled back and leaned against his pillow. "Ber, I want this to happen—you have no idea how much—but I think we should take it slow. You have a lot going on right now, and I . . . well, I just hope you can be patient with me." He touched her cheek and she could see the tears glistening in his eyes. "I never dreamed I'd fall in love again . . ." he whispered with a smile. "And, now, I just need some time to figure out how to let go of the past."

"Micah," she said softly, "you can take all the time you need. I'm not going anywhere. And please don't think you have to push your memories of Beth from your mind. I know she's a part of you, and I would never expect you to forget her."

Micah swallowed and pulled her close; as they lay side by side, they were both overwhelmed by the wonderful possibility of actually having someone to hold and trust . . . and love.

33

At around midnight, Isak reassured Rumer—again—that she'd be fine, but after Rumer and Will reluctantly left with the boys, she'd slumped into the chair next to Matt's bed, buried her face in her hands, and cried. She still couldn't believe all that had happened; it seemed like a dream—a dream from which she couldn't wake up. She looked at Matt's face, though, and knew it wasn't a dream. His cheekbones were bruised and his face was bandaged, his left leg was in a cast, he had an intravenous drip in his arm, an oxygen tube in his nose, and his heart rate and blood pressure were checked every few minutes—an event that startled her every time the machine started up.

"I'm so sorry," she whispered, holding his hand. "I'm so sorry this happened to you." She looked at Matt's hands and thought of all the shoelaces they'd tied and all the Band-Aids they'd gently applied; she thought of all the blueberry pancakes they'd made on Sunday mornings and all the miracles they'd performed in the operating room; and she remembered, too, the pleasure they'd given her. "Please don't take him from me," she whispered. "He has so much more to do down here—he has two wonderful kids who need him, and he'll have grand-children who will run into his arms someday, and he has me—and I desperately need a second chance on getting this right."

The nurses came in several times to check on Matt and en-couraged Isak to lie down and try to rest. "No . . . no, thanks," she answered, determined to stay by his side; but finally, she drifted off with her head on his blankets.

As the early-morning sky turned from azure blue to rosy peach, Isak stirred, feeling a gentle touch on her arm. She looked up and saw Matt smile weakly. Tears filled her eyes. "Oh, my goodness—you're going to be okay," she whispered in dis-belief, squeezing his hand. His nod was almost imperceptible. "Oh, thank God," she murmured, happy tears spilling down her cheeks.

The nurse came in, saw that he was awake, and hurried out. "I'll be right back," she called over her shoulder. "I'm just going to get the doctor."

Isak turned back to him. His face was shadowed with an-guish as he struggled to speak. "The . . . kids?" he whispered hoarsely.

Isak nodded. "They're fine, baby—don't you worry. Tommy was here last night; he's sore but okay. And Meghan will be okay, too; she's in Danbury with a broken wrist and Beryl is with her."

Matt blinked, trying to understand. "You're in Hartford," she explained. "They airlifted you right from the accident, but they took the kids to Danbury by ambulance." He nodded and closed his eyes. Isak brushed back her tears and reached into her pocket for her phone.

Beryl woke up to the sound of soft breathing and looked over at Micah, sleeping peacefully next to her. She smiled, and for the briefest of moments, luxuriated in the lovely, comforting feeling of waking up next to the body of someone she loved. Then she remembered how they'd come to be in the same bed—and the feeling was swept away by reality. Her phone beeped and she reached onto the nightstand to retrieve it. Flipping it open, she saw there was a message from Isak. She clicked on it and read: **matt's awake!** She smiled and wrote right back: **that's such great news!** ☺

At the very same moment, Rumer and Tommy saw the same message—and a collective shout of joy and relief spread from Danbury to Hartford. Beryl slipped out of bed, pulled a clean blouse from her overnight bag, found her jeans, and shuffled quietly to the bathroom.

When she came out, Micah was sitting on the end of the bed in his boxers, watching a rerun of *The Rifleman.* "Hey!" she said happily, telling him the good news. Then, in an afterthought, added, "Do you want to take a quick shower? Because it's just hitting me how much we—*I* have to do. In all the commotion, I've put Mum's service on the back burner—but I just realized, it's tomorrow!"

"I know," he said, reaching for his jeans. On his way to the bathroom, he stopped and gave her a hug. "Last night was really nice," he said.

"It was," she said, gently touching his cheek.

"I'll be quick," he said, kissing her forehead and heading for the shower.

After grabbing a few muffins from the hotel's continental breakfast bar, they headed over to the hospital and found Meghan sitting up, having breakfast too. Her cheeks were pink and she looked much better. "Hi, Aunt Ber—I was beginning to wonder where everyone was. Is my dad okay?"

Beryl told her the latest news and she nodded, looking relieved. Then she introduced Micah and asked, "How're you feeling?"

Meghan shook her head. "Like I've been hit by a Mack truck!" she said. "The medicine wore off, so I ache everywhere."

Just then, the nurse came in. "How're you doing with your breakfast, hon?" she asked, eyeing the untouched food. "You have to eat something, or they're not going to let you out of here."

Meghan groaned. "Do you have anything besides cold oatmeal?"

The nurse had her stethoscope in her ears, but when she finished taking her vitals, she said, "I'll see what I can find."

Four hours later, after Meghan had eaten half a ham sandwich and a couple of stale potato chips and Isak had been called *twice* to give permission for her daughter to be released into her sister's care, they wheeled Meghan down to Micah's waiting car, and Beryl helped her into the backseat, where Micah had moved some things to make room.

"Are you okay?" she asked, and Meghan nodded, leaning back on a pillow from her dorm room.

"Did you get ahold of your mom?" Beryl asked Micah as he pulled away.

"Yup, Flan and Thoreau are fine, although . . ."

He paused and Beryl looked up. "What?! What happened?"

"Well, my mom brought Charlotte and Harper over and I guess the two dogs really hit it off. They were running around together," he explained, "and then Harper saw the pond . . . and, of course, Flan followed her." He glanced over and saw Beryl's raised eyebrows. "I guess things got a little messy."

Beryl groaned. "Oh, I'm so sorry. Your poor mom, I'm sure that's just what she needed. What did she do?"

"Well, she had a towel in her car."

"One towel isn't enough!"

"Well, she got Flannery cleaned up, and she said to tell you she's sorry if she still tracked some mud in the kitchen."

"She shouldn't be sorry! I feel terrible. Flannery is always getting into mischief."

258 / *Nan Rossiter*

"She wasn't the troublemaker—Harper was."

"Still," Beryl protested.

"Aunt Ber, you still have Flannery?" Meghan asked from the backseat.

"Unfortunately," Beryl said with a sigh.

Meghan smiled. "I love Flan! Oh, I can't wait to see her!"

Beryl turned around and gazed at her beautiful niece, now battered and bruised. "I'm so glad you're smiling, honey. She'll love seeing you . . . and she hasn't changed one bit!"

34

When they arrived at the hospital, Matt was propped up against some pillows, looking very tired. The room was full of family, including Gretchen Taylor, his mom, and her friend Margaret. Tommy and Meghan were both glad to see their grandmother, and she couldn't get over how grown up they were—even with their bumps and bruises. The nurse came in to check on Matt and announced there were too many visitors and her patient needed to get some rest. And, since it had already been decided that a large contingency was heading back to New Hampshire, the nurse's prodding moved Beryl, Rumer, Will, and Rand to finally say good-bye to Matt, while Micah said he hoped to see him again when he was feeling better; Meghan and Tommy both navigated the tubes to give him a gentle hug, and Isak smiled and said she'd be right back.

The group reconvened in the hall and Isak revealed that, with Matt's condition, she was thinking of not attending the service, but even before Rumer and Beryl could protest, Gretchen Taylor, overhearing her daughter-in-law, stepped forward and told her that she *would*, most definitely, be attending her mother's funeral. Isak, who'd felt utterly torn until that moment, was taken aback by her mother-in-law's assertiveness, but immediately saw the wisdom of her words—and later, she wondered how she'd even considered missing it.

"All right," she said resignedly. "I'll be there first thing in the morning." With that, she hugged and thanked everyone and told them all she loved them.

Rand was sound asleep when Rumer and Will finally pulled in the driveway. "Leave him," Will said as Rumer started to reach into the backseat. "He's really tired." They got out and Will looked up at the old farmhouse. "This is such a great old house. It's a shame you and your sisters have to sell it."

Rumer was surprised by her husband's sentiment. "I know, I wish we didn't," she replied.

She started to walk up the path, but Will reached for her hand and pulled her back. "Ru, before everyone gets here, I want to—well, I want you to know how sorry I am for the way things have been lately—for the way I've acted. I know it hasn't been easy for you." Rumer nodded and he went on. "I just hate this financial hole we're in, and I don't know how to get us out of it—and that makes me a little crazy."

Rumer swallowed. "I know, Will. It makes me crazy, too, but once we sell this house, some of the money will come our way and that'll help."

"If you're *able* to sell it—and if we're able to hold on that long," he said, looking up at the peeling paint and rotting sills. "The house needs a lot of work." He paused and shook his head. "That's not what I wanted to talk about, though—I wanted to talk about us." Rumer waited, and he continued, "Ru, I want to get back together."

Rumer searched his eyes. "Will, there's nothing I'd love more, but not if we're going to keep fighting all the time—and not if it isn't going to last, because we can't keep doing this to Rand." She paused. "You have to be absolutely sure."

"I am sure," he said, his eyes glistening. He looked up at the house again. "It's kind of funny, but I've been thinking about your mom a lot over this past week—how she lived her life— and how she carried on, against all odds, raising three little kids by herself. She never let life's problems get her down—right up to the very end. She had . . . gumption, and I think we could all use a little more of that," he said with a smile. "We only have one kid—and we still have each other. . . . You'd think we'd be able to manage."

Rumer laughed. "Oh, Will, you don't know the half of it. She had more gumption than you think!"

Just then, Micah and Beryl pulled in, beeping their horn, and Rand's head peered out the window. They'd stopped at the pharmacy before it closed to fill Meghan's prescriptions, and al-though Tommy had begged to stop at Kimball's, too, to grab a bite to eat, Beryl had told him to hang in there because there was plenty of food at the house and maybe they would go to Kimball's for ice cream later.

Rand climbed sleepily out of the car and Tommy snuck up behind him and playfully lifted him off the ground. "Hey!" Rand shouted, giggling and squirming. Beryl and Micah helped Meghan up to the house, and when they pulled open the screen, they found Tommy, Rand, and Flannery already had their noses in the refrigerator.

"Uncle Will and Micah, do you want a beer?"

"No, thanks," Micah said.

Will laughed. "Is that so you can have one too?"

"Sure, I'll have one with you," Tommy grinned, taking out two cold bottles with one hand and balancing the meat platter in the other. "Hey, cous, grab those deviled eggs, will ya?"

Rand, buoyed by his older cousin's attention, pulled out the eggs and asked importantly, "What about the fruit salad?"

"Sure," Tommy said. Then he remembered his manners. "Aunt Ber, is it okay if we eat this stuff?"

"Go to it!" she said, helping Meghan get comfortable. "There are rolls on the counter," she added, filling a glass with water so Meghan could take her medicine.

Micah opened the door for Flannery, who'd been let out to take care of business, and she trundled right over to Meghan and sat on her foot. "I guess I've been replaced," he observed gloomily.

"You haven't been replaced," Beryl said with a chuckle. "No one can replace *you*," she consoled, handing Meghan her pill. "She's just giving Meghan some sympathy."

Meghan smiled and reached down to scratch Flannery's head, and the old dog looked up adoringly. Micah witnessed the love and said sadly, "Nope, I've definitely been replaced."

"Flan and I go way back," Meghan said. "We're just happy to see each other."

Micah laughed. "Okay, well, I'm gonna head out, but I could use some help unloading my car."

"Oh, I forgot!" Beryl said. Immediately everyone except Meghan stopped doing what they were doing and hurried out to help. They lugged in suitcases, duffel bags, a box of college textbooks, and Meghan's desk light and laptop, which had both, except for the light bulb, miraculously survived the crash.

They set everything in the living room and then Beryl turned to Micah. "Are you sure you don't want something to eat?"

"No, no thanks. I need to get home to see my pal."

"I'll walk back out with you." She paused. "Meghan, you're supposed to eat with your medicine. Did you?"

Meghan shook her head and Beryl spied Tommy at the

counter with the rolls and meat platter. "Tommy, can you make your sister a sandwich?"

He nodded, his mouth full of deviled egg.

Rumer was back to warming up some of the casseroles and looked up. "Would you rather have some lasagna, hon? It'll just be a minute—and you can have a deviled egg to tide you over."

"That sounds good," Meghan said.

"You don't want one of my famous Dagwood sandwiches?" Tommy asked, feigning hurt.

Meghan rolled her eyes and Beryl looked at Micah. "Are you sure you don't want to stay for all the fun?"

"I wish I could," he said, "but responsibility calls." He pushed open the screen door and Thoreau scooted in. "Bye, everyone," he said.

A chorus of voices called out playfully, "Bye, Micah! Thank you!"

Beryl walked with him to his car. "Maybe you and Charlotte can meet us at Kimball's Farm for ice cream later," she suggested hopefully.

"That sounds good, if it's not too late. I'll have to see what kind of a day she's had." He opened his door. "I'm really glad Matt's going to be okay."

"So am I," Beryl said, her voice sounding relieved. "Can you imagine?" She didn't even want to finish the sentence. "Another drunk driver—it's crazy!"

Micah nodded in agreement.

"It's funny, though," Beryl continued. "My mom used to say everything happens for a reason and there's no such thing as coincidences. Serendipity, yes; coincidence, no. She always said every event was part of God's tapestry. One side—the side we see as we stumble through life—looks like a confusing mass of interwoven thread, but on the other side—the side God sees—

is a radiant, gorgeous work of art. And now, I can't help but wonder if there's a reason this happened."

"I'll have to think about that and see if I can come up with a reason for the things that have happened in my life."

Beryl nodded and smiled sadly. "I guess sometimes we never understand why things happen, or what good comes . . ."

Micah pulled her into a hug and whispered, "I guess I can think of one good thing."

❧ 35 ❧

"I'll be back tomorrow," Gretchen Taylor said, lightly touching her son's hand. "Lily's coming, too, and we'll bring something good for lunch." Lily was Matt's younger sister; she was a teacher in Providence. The thought of seeing her made Matt smile, but it ended up looking more like a cringe because it made his face hurt.

Gretchen took Isak aside and spoke quietly, "Don't worry about a thing, dear. He'll be fine. My advice comes from the heart. When my mother died unexpectedly, I was newly married and living abroad. I didn't come home for her service because I thought it was too far—and I've always regretted it. In hindsight, I know now that distance and time are simply abstract obstacles that truly don't matter. All that matters is being there for your loved ones." She gave Isak a hug and smiled at Margaret. "Of course, it always helps to have someone who'll get you where you need to be. Are you ready, Margaret?" she asked, looking at her watch. "We might still have time for dinner and a martini at the White Horse," she added, winking at Isak.

Isak gave Margaret a hug too. "Thank you for making the trip," she said.

Margaret smiled. "It was my pleasure, dear. I'm very sorry to hear about your mom, but I'm glad Matthew's going to be okay. You have a lot on your plate right now and I'll be keeping you in my prayers."

After they left, Isak sat in the chair next to the bed. "Your mom is such a classic," she said.

Matt nodded and whispered hoarsely, "I'm sorry I can't be there tomorrow. . . ."

Isak reached for his hand. "Don't think twice about it! You know me—I can handle it!" She looked at the bruises on his face and added softly, "What I wouldn't be able to handle . . . is living without you."

Matt managed a lopsided grin and squeezed her hand.

"I love you, you know. . . ." she whispered.

He nodded. "I love you too."

～ 36 ～

"My parents come here on Wednesday nights sometimes," Micah said, shifting Charlotte from one hip to the other as they waited in line for ice cream. "Kimball's has a car cruise and my dad says it's a lot of fun. I told him it would be even more fun if he restored his old Chevy pickup. I've even offered to help him, but he never seems to have the time."

"Well, maybe he will now that you're home," Beryl replied, trying to decide what flavor she wanted.

He laughed. "Well, I don't want to live at home forever. I'd like to find a place of our own, but I guess it all depends on that teaching job."

"That *would* be great. I think you'd make a wonderful teacher." The line moved up and she looked up at all the flavors. "Do you know what you're having?"

"Yup, I'm living on the wild side: vanilla and chocolate twist." He looked at Charlotte. "Char, what kind of ice cream are you having?" She gave him a classic look that said, *Da-ad! You know what I'm having!* "Hmm," he teased, "are you having black raspberry?" She shook her head emphatically, swinging her blond curls back and forth. "Are you having piña colada?" She responded with more head shaking. "I know! Vanilla . . ." Charlotte looked dismayed and then, concluding that her dad really couldn't remember, whispered in his ear. "Ohh! Chocolate!" She nodded and then buried her face shyly in his shoulder. "What should Beryl have?" Charlotte whispered in his ear again and he grinned. "Chocolate too?!" Charlotte nodded.

"Hmm, you're a woman after my own heart, Charlotte Coleman," Beryl said with a smile. Charlotte looked puzzled, not sure what that meant.

They all sat down at a picnic table with their ice-cream cones and sundaes. Tommy had also ordered a Ranchburger and fries, which he devoured in six bites.

"Oh, my goodness!" Rumer exclaimed, watching him eat. "Your mom wasn't kidding!"

He laughed and, without missing a beat, tucked into his ice cream.

Charlotte loved being with all the big kids and abandoned her father to sit between Meghan and Rand. "How's your ice cream?" Meghan asked.

"Good," Charlotte said with a chocolate grin.

"Chocolate's my favorite flavor, too," Rand explained, "but I haven't had black raspberry in, like, forever."

Micah licked his cone and watched Charlotte blossoming in the company of other kids. He was glad she'd be starting kindergarten in the fall; she was ready and he wasn't as anxious about it now that it looked like she'd be going to his elementary alma mater.

They finished their ice cream and Beryl and Micah each held one of Charlotte's hands as they walked to their cars, swinging her every few steps. "I'm glad you guys could come," Beryl said.

"Me too."

"So . . . I guess I'll see you tomorrow?" she asked.

"Yup, I'll be there."

"Will you read my eulogy if I need you to?"

"If you need me to, but I bet you'll be able to do it. Who else is speaking?"

"Tommy . . . and I'm sure he'll be fine—nothing seems to faze him."

"You'll be fine too."

Beryl looked unconvinced and gloomy.

He wrapped his arms around her and held her close. "You are an amazing woman, Beryl Graham—just like your mom, and you will do an amazing job. I'm sure of it. Just remember, she'll be listening, too, so just pretend you're talking to her."

Beryl laughed. "That'll be tough to do with all those people looking at me!"

"I'm sure you'll make her proud."

"Thanks, Micah," she said, standing on her tiptoes and kissing his cheek.

∽ 37 ∾

Beryl woke to the sound of laughter and voices coming from the kitchen. She looked at the bright sunshine streaming through the window, and with a sinking feeling remembered what day it was. "Looks like you've got yourself a blue-sky day, Mum," she whispered, feeling her stomach twist into knots. "Oh, how I wish I could just go for a long hike today. And when I got home, this would all be over."

"Who're you talking to, Aunt Ber?" Meghan asked, sitting up sleepily and rubbing her eyes. Beryl looked over in surprise, remembering that Meghan had claimed Rumer's bed last night when she'd decided to sleep in the spare bedroom with Will.

"I'm sorry, hon," Beryl said, sitting up. "Did I wake you?"

"No, I was awake. I didn't sleep very well. It's hard to get comfortable because, every time I move, my whole arm hurts."

"You should've said something. I'm sure you could've taken more pain medicine."

"To be honest, I'm trying not to take it. Doesn't it make you constipated?"

Beryl laughed. "Sometimes, but once you stop taking it,

everything gets back to normal. If you're in that much pain, you should take it."

"Maybe," Meghan said, still sounding unconvinced.

"Anyway, I was just talking to myself again!"

Meghan laughed. "I do that all the time. After all, who understands better?"

Beryl laughed too. "That's true!" She pushed off her cover. "Are you coming down for breakfast?"

Meghan nodded. "Yup, I'll be right down."

"Do you need help with anything?" Beryl asked, slipping on a robe.

"Not yet, but I'll probably need help getting dressed later."

"Okay, just let me know."

By ten o'clock, Will, Tommy, and Rand were showered, dressed, and gathered in the kitchen. Will glanced at his watch impatiently. "Ru, we need to get going," he called from the bottom of the stairs.

"Be right down," she called back. "Is Isak here yet?"

Will looked out the window again. "No, we're just going to have to meet her there."

"Dad," Rand moaned, tugging at his tie. "Can you help me with this stupid tie?"

"I'll help you," Tommy volunteered, popping the last bite of his third piece of coffee cake in his mouth. He stood behind Rand in front of the mirror by the door and deftly showed him how to tie a perfect Windsor knot. "I used to have to wear a tie to school every day when I was your age."

"No way!" Rand exclaimed.

"Way," Tommy said with a grin. "I can do it blindfolded . . . and in my sleep."

"You cannot!"

"Can!" Tommy said, ruffling Rand's hair. Rand ducked away and just about knocked over his Aunt Isak, who was coming through the door, looking tired and wearing the same clothes she'd been wearing for three days.

"Hi, guys!" she said, catching him and hurrying past them and up the stairs. Beryl, Rumer, and Meghan all stopped on the stairs. "Hi, sweetie," she said, slowing down when she reached Meghan. "How're you feeling?"

Meghan smiled. "Hi, Mom. Better, thanks. How's Dad?"

"A little better," Isak said, continuing up. "Go on without me," she called as she pulled off her clothes and left a trail behind her. "I'll be along."

They all looked at each other and Beryl said, "You guys go. I'll wait. I want to look over my eulogy again anyway."

"Oh, yeah," Tommy said, remembering the handwritten paper he'd tucked in his jeans. "Thanks for reminding me!" Beryl and Rumer looked at each other with raised eyebrows as Tommy came back into the kitchen, stuffing the paper into the pocket of his sports coat. "Don't worry," he said with a grin. "I memorized it."

"I wish I had mine memorized," Beryl murmured, looking down at her paper and feeling a rabble of butterflies taking off in her stomach.

"Okay, Ber, we'll see you there," Rumer said, giving her a quick hug.

"Unless I get lost somewhere," Beryl said with a smile.

"You'll be fine," Rumer assured her. "And if you absolutely can't do it, Micah said he would."

"You can do it, Aunt Ber," Tommy encouraged. "Just think about how much you loved her."

"Oh, my goodness, Tommy, that'll really make me cry."

"No, it won't—trust me—and I'll be right behind you."

Beryl gave him a hug. "Thank you, hon." Then she suddenly started to remember all the things she'd planned to check on when they got to the church. "Ru, do you have the poster boards with the pictures?"

"Yup, they're right here," Rumer said, holding them up.

"You guys did such a great job," Beryl said, smiling at Meghan, Tommy, and Rand.

"Thanks," they all said in unison.

"What about the stands to hold them?"

Will held them up.

"The hydrangea?"

Tommy scooped it off the counter and held it up, too, and Beryl looked at Ru. "Okay, just put everything in the fellowship hall. There should be an empty table set up in the corner with a tablecloth on it. If you don't see it, ask Reverend Peterson; he'll show you. And make sure someone has put the prayer cards in the sanctuary, and the programs too. I'm sure they've taken care of all that, but just check. And make sure Mr. O'Leary put the box Micah's dad made in the front of the sanctuary. Oh, maybe I should just come with you," she said, beginning to sound panicked.

"Ber, calm down," Rumer said reassuringly. "We'll be fine. I'm sure we can handle it."

"But we *do* need to get going," Will said impatiently.

"Okay, go. But don't go into the sanctuary until we get there. Remember, Reverend Peterson said family should wait in back."

Rumer nodded. "Got it—is Micah sitting with us?"

Beryl shook her head. "I asked him, but he said he was going to sit with his parents. Will, are your parents coming?"

"They are, but they're not sitting with us."

"Okay. Set up the display. Check cards. Check with Mr. O'Leary. Wait in back room." Rumer looked at everyone. "Got it?"

"Got it," they all answered, edging toward the door.

"Get Isak moving!" Rumer said, eyeing her.

"Got it!" Beryl said with a tearful grin. "See you in a few . . ."

"Don't start," Rumer said, pulling her sister into a hug and whispering, "because you'll get me started." She stepped back and held her sister at arm's length. "Did you remember to wear waterproof mascara?"

Beryl nodded. "You?"

"Yup," she nodded as an exasperated Will physically guided her out the door. "Have Isak bring the Preparation H—just in case," she called over her shoulder.

Beryl watched them from the porch and smiled as Will asked, "What in the world do you need Preparation H for?"

After they pulled away, it dawned on Beryl that Flan had not been underfoot during their whole extended good-bye. *Where is she?* She called her name and noticed a ball of black-and-white fur waddle around the shed. Suddenly, a strong odor drifted toward the porch. "Oh, no!" she groaned. "Flan, where are you?" she demanded. The stout little dog, completely oblivious to the significance of the day, marched out of the woods and trundled up the steps and onto the porch. She looked up at Beryl with her panting, happy, *here I am* smile, and the rank odor that emanated from her fur just about bowled Beryl over. "Oh, Flan! What am I going to do with you?"

"What is that awful smell?" Isak called from the kitchen.

Beryl shook her head in dismay. "It's Mum's way of reminding us not to take life so seriously. Fortunately, I don't think it was a direct hit—this dog is way too happy."

❧ 38 ❧

"Oh, my," Beryl murmured, trying to swallow the lump in her throat as they pulled up to the church. Isak drove slowly past, looking for a parking spot, but there were cars everywhere—on the grass, all along both sides of the road, and the parking lot was packed. Out of the corner of her eye, she saw Mr. O'Leary waving to them from behind the church and quickly pulled in. He'd saved a spot for them!

As they hurried into the back of the church, Beryl sniffed her hands and groaned. "They still smell," she said, holding her fingertips in front of Isak's nose.

Isak turned her head while pushing her sister's hand away. "That's Mum's way of helping you get through her eulogy," she said with a grin.

"Very funny," Beryl said.

When Ru saw them, her face looked relieved. "What happened?" she asked in a hushed tone. Beryl held her hand in front of her nose. "Oh, no!" Rumer whispered. "How'd that happen?"

"I'll give you one guess," Beryl said.

Reverend Peterson came over and handed them each a program. "Is this everyone now?" he asked.

Beryl looked around. "Yes." Then she looked up at the clock—it was ten after eleven. "I'm sorry we're late."

He nodded and then quickly reminded everyone that the front rows were reserved for them, and when the service was over, they should file up the center aisle to the front doors and form a receiving line in the vestibule. They all nodded and he opened the door to lead them in.

The organ was playing a somber hymn and their eyes swept the room in astonishment—the sanctuary was filled to capacity, including the balcony, and there were more people standing along the back wall. Beryl quickly scanned the crowd, looking for Micah, but she couldn't spot him. They solemnly filed into the pews, and when they were seated, Reverend Peterson began to speak.

Beryl tried to concentrate, but she suddenly felt very light-headed and queasy. She looked over at Meghan and saw tears streaming down her cheeks. Tommy put his arm around his little sister. As they stood to sing the first hymn, Beryl noticed the small wooden box in the front of the sanctuary and, realizing what it was, covered her mouth in surprise. Her eyes filled with tears as she stared at the intricately inlaid design. It was beautiful!

Through the blur of her tears, she looked back down at her hymnal and began to softly sing her mom's favorite hymn, "Here I Am, Lord," and when they reached the last verse, she wiped her eyes and felt an overwhelming sense of peace. She looked around the sanctuary and saw all of the people she knew, singing and dabbing their eyes too. She found Micah and he smiled; she saw his parents and Will's parents, the teachers from the elementary school who'd brought over the food, the ladies from the thrift store, all of her mom's friends from church, customers who frequented the shop, and several of the nurses from the nursing home. Beryl suddenly realized that every single person in this sacred place loved Mia Graham—and they'd all come to celebrate her life. All at once she knew with certainty that she would be able to share her memories of her mom . . . and if she cried, so be it.

After the second hymn, Tommy walked purposefully up to the pulpit and flashed his famous boyish grin. "He looks so much like Matt," Beryl whispered to Isak, who nodded and wiped her eyes.

Tommy looked out at everyone and then looked heavenward. "I'm impressed, Gram! You have more friends in this church than I have on Facebook!" Everyone chuckled and he continued to speak from his heart without ever pulling the wrinkled paper out of his pocket, and as he spoke, the mood in the room lifted from somber and solemn to lighthearted and loving. Tommy had everyone laughing as he shared delightful memories of his childhood and spending a couple of weeks every summer in the creaky, old New England house that had "way too many creepy hiding places for monsters." He also reminisced about trying to fall asleep in a tent in the backyard after Gram had told them "some pretty scary ghost stories," so much so that he and Meghan usually scampered to the house because it actually felt safer.

Whether playing board games or outdoor games, he described his Gram as a ruthless competitor who never showed mercy or had qualms about whacking her young opponents' croquet ball all the way to Timbuktu or sending their most forward Parcheesi piece back to Start. He said he hoped people weren't fooled by her quiet disposition, "Because a friendly game of checkers could really bring out her true colors!" Everyone laughed as they pictured petite Mia Graham smacking her croquet mallet against the ball pressed under her foot, causing the adjacent ball to speed off into the woods or, worse, the pond as her forlorn grandchildren looked on.

Tommy smiled and waited until the chuckles died down before reminiscing about his grandmother's wonderful cooking talents. He spoke wistfully of his favorite dishes—from lasagna to apple pie—until everyone's mouths were salivating. He also said that Gram could make the most amazing cinnamon toast, and he described it in such wonderful detail that everyone planned on having some as soon as they got home. "Sadly," he said, dashing their thoughts, "Gram's toast cannot be replicated. Believe me, I've tried! I don't know why, but there was just something about the way she made it—maybe it was her toaster." He smiled at his mom, cupped his hands around his mouth, and whispered, "Make sure you get the toaster." At which everyone laughed.

Tommy smiled again and shook his head. "Right up to the end, Gram was a great lady. She has given me some of my best memories . . ." He bit his lip, blinking back tears. "And I'm going to miss her very much," he said, his voice tight with emotion.

Beryl gave him a thumbs-up, took a deep breath, and waited to be introduced. Tommy stepped back, and when she came up, she gave him a hug. "You did great!" she whispered. He smiled, and she turned around and stood in front of the pulpit with her heart pounding. "Kids," she said, pulling the microphone down to her level, "even big ones, are always hard acts to follow." Everyone chuckled and she immediately started to feel at ease. She looked around at the sea of familiar faces, pausing on each one. "Thank you *all* for coming," she said in a voice that was calm and sincere. "Mum would have loved seeing each and every one of you." She looked along the back wall at the latecomers; then her eyes paused on the face of an older gentleman sitting in the last pew. He had a thick mane of snow-white hair and there was a cane leaning against the end of the pew. Their eyes met and he smiled, and Beryl bit her lip, blinking back tears; she hesitated for so long that those sitting near him turned to look. Finally, she managed to smile back and then looked away.

"My friend Micah," she began, "has assured me that Mum is looking down on us today, smiling, and I think he's right—because, from where I'm standing, I can see her sweet countenance reflected in all of your lovely faces. My dear mom has touched many lives with her kindness and friendship, her guidance and wisdom, her loyalty and love—and that is all evident today." She paused to look down at her paper.

"I've spent many hours this week staring at a blank piece of paper, trying to put my thoughts together, and trying to put her life in a nutshell. After many false starts, I finally decided to write a letter to her . . . and once I started, I couldn't stop the words from coming." She looked up and laughed. "In fact, I could hardly keep up!" Everyone chuckled and she paused. "I'd like to share it with you. . . .

"Dearest Mum, I'm writing to you today in honor of the celebration of your life! Over this past week, besides trying to figure out what I want to say today, I've also been trying to figure out how I'm going to manage without you." She paused and looked up. "And I've finally come to realize that the best way to carry on . . . is to try to live as you did.

"Mum, you were an inspiration to so many people. You lived your life with grace, courage, determination, and faith, and when life threw you a curve ball, you swung at it with all your might. In your lifetime, you faced more than your share of tragedy and heartache . . . and through it all, you never stopped smiling. No matter what, you were always ready to give a helping hand—even when you were the one who needed help.

"You had a big heart and you opened it wide to every four-legged beast that waddled, sauntered, or hopped into our lives—from Hemingway, the handsome golden retriever you rescued when we were little, to Flannery, the homely, stubborn bulldog you fell in love with after we'd moved out. There was Emily, Keats, Robert, Beston, and Thoreau—not to mention the countless other felines, bunnies, and birds that came in to warm by our fire and ended up staying for the rest of their lives. In the spring when you went for a walk, we always wondered what you'd come home with—sometimes you'd be cradling a frog that you thought would enjoy living in our pond, and other times you'd have an injured bird in the pocket of your jacket that needed a little 'TLC,' as you called it.

"Mum, you lived every day to the fullest and you tried to teach us to do the same. You always said, 'Don't postpone life!' and you underscored this favorite phrase with example. When Dad died, you had his big shoes to fill and you did it well. You took us sledding, skiing, swimming, and hiking; you tucked us in at night and read to us for hours—*The Secret Garden, Little Women, Little House in the Big Woods, Pippi Longstocking,* and *Mrs. Piggle-Wiggle* were just some of the stories you gave us to love. You taught us how to mend clothes, make a piecrust, properly brew a pot of tea, and how to patiently simmer (for hours!) the Italian gravy that has been in our family for generations. And you tried, on countless occasions, to teach us the secret to your cinnamon toast. Oh, and by the way, Tommy, I already shoddied the toaster," she teased, turning to grin at her nephew, who laughed and shook his head.

"Mum," she continued, "you loved to garden, and you could be found outside early every spring and summer morning, wearing your famous straw hat and Muck boots, pulling weeds, mulching, pruning, transplanting, and watering. In the fall, you'd be out there in your big L.L. Bean flannel shirt, planting bulbs, turning the compost pile, and getting your roses ready for winter. You knew the name of every plant—and if you didn't, you'd pull out your flower book, marred with muddy fingerprints, and promptly look up the blossom that had you puzzled. The Internet would have been a wonderful source for your inquiries, if you'd only had the chance to embrace it as you did every other source of knowledge.

"Mum, you always found ways to give back to your community—whether it was by volunteering at the elementary school and helping little ones learn to read or heading up the church fair to raise money for mission work. I never heard you say, 'No,' or 'I'm too busy.' "

Beryl paused and bit her lip. "One of the images that stays with me, though, is the sweet smile you always gave me whenever I said I had to go after visiting you in the nursing home. I'll never forget the love in your eyes, and in spite of the terrible illness that was taking you away from us, I'm thankful I never truly saw that light diminish." Tears spilled down her cheeks as she spoke, and Tommy stepped up beside her and put his hand on her shoulder. She smiled and brushed her tears away. "Mum, your life was—and will always be—one of the most radiant parts of God's tapestry, and we're all going to miss you"—Beryl looked up at all the tear-stained, smiling faces and whispered—"more than you know."

After Beryl took her seat, the rest of the service was a blur, and when it ended, she had no recollection of walking up the aisle—it almost felt as if she'd somehow floated to the back of the church to join her family in the receiving line. Everyone told her she'd done a wonderful job; many others said they couldn't have possibly gotten through such a moving reading; and still others commented on how much she reminded them of Mia. Beryl smiled, hugged, and thanked each one. Finally, Micah and his parents came through, and Beryl gave them long hugs and thanked his dad for the lovely box.

There was a lull in the line and the grandchildren took advantage of it, slipping off to see what there was to eat. In the moment of quiet, Beryl looked down the aisle of the church, waiting for the older gentleman who'd been sitting in the back pew to approach them. When the nurses from the nursing home had come through, they'd pointed to him and whispered, "That's the old fellow who used to visit your mom." Beryl had nodded and, as she looked for him now, she saw him lay his hand on the box and then slowly turn to make his way toward them. He stopped in front of Isak and Rumer, and, in an un-mistakable British accent, said how sorry he was. They both nodded in barefaced astonishment before managing to thank him. He turned away and, with tears in his eyes, smiled at Beryl. "You must be Blueberry," he said with a slow smile and a twinkle in his eyes. Beryl nodded, not knowing what to say. "You are so much like your mum," he said, taking her hands. "I almost thought you were she." He paused. "You truly captured her essence with your words."

"Thank you," Beryl said softly.

With a trembling hand, he reached up to push back his silvery hair. "Your mum was a very special lady and I miss her deeply."

Beryl nodded.

He hesitated uncertainly, searching her eyes. "There's something I've been deliberating over . . . it's something I wanted to ask you . . . but I don't know if I should and I don't want to cause any trouble. Do you have a minute?"

"Of course," Beryl said, taking his arm.

39

Puzzled by Mia Graham's youngest daughter's request, Mr. O'Leary slipped the clean, glass honey jar she'd handed him into his pocket and retreated from the church kitchen. Beryl dried her hands on a dish towel and looked out the window, silently preparing her argument. Hanging the towel on the handle of the stove, she went to find her sisters.

When she pushed open the kitchen door, she was happy to see a small crowd gathered around the photo montage the kids had put together. Then she turned to see the huge spread of refreshments that had been set out—from deviled eggs and tiny ham salad sandwiches to cream puffs, chocolate-covered strawberries, and her mom's favorite—lemon squares. As Beryl reached for one, she heard someone say her name and turned to see Mrs. Coleman standing with a neatly dressed man who appeared to be about her age.

"Beryl, I'd like you to meet someone."

"Of course," Beryl said, putting her lemon square on a napkin.

284 / Nan Rossiter

"This is Colin Davis—he's a math teacher at the high school."

Beryl reached out to shake his hand. "It's nice to meet you, Colin."

"It's nice to meet you too," he said in a soft voice. "I'm very sorry for your loss," he added.

Beryl smiled. "Thanks."

"I wanted to come," he began, carefully choosing his words, "because a long time ago I helped your mom with a flat tire . . . but I don't think she knew—in fact, I know she didn't know—who I was. But I knew who she was from a picture my mom had cut out of the paper." Colin's solemn gray eyes gazed at her with sincerity. "I can't stay," he continued. "I just wanted to tell you how sorry I am."

"Thank you," Beryl said again, looking puzzled.

He turned to Maddie. "Thank you for introducing us, Mrs. Coleman."

"It's Maddie, Colin," she said, giving him a wilting look. "You youngsters make me feel so old!"

Colin laughed and turned to go, and Beryl looked at Maddie questioningly.

"I know, you're wondering why I wanted you to meet him," Maddie said with a smile.

"His name sounds so familiar," Beryl said, taking a bite of her lemon square.

"That's because Colin is Clay Davis's grandson," she said, waiting to see a spark of recognition in her eyes, but Beryl just breathed in suddenly and the dust of confectioner's sugar made her cough. "Are you okay?" Maddie asked. Beryl nodded and swallowed, her eyes watering. "Micah said you wanted to know more about your parents' accident—and although this isn't the best time or place, when I saw Colin, I thought it might be a good chance for you to meet him.

"Colin was a baby when his father, Carl, was killed in Vietnam; his grandfather, Clay, had already lost his wife to cancer earlier that year, and he was utterly devastated when the telegram came to the mill where he worked telling him that his son had been killed." Maddie paused, searching Beryl's eyes. "Please know that I am in no way condoning Clay Davis's actions or making an excuse for him, but I think it might help you to know that, although he was very drunk the night of the accident, he wasn't a drunkard."

Beryl shook her head in disbelief. "I had no idea," she said, tears filling her eyes.

"I know, hon, and I'm so sorry. When I heard you talking about your mom's life being part of God's tapestry, I couldn't help but think about Clay's and Colin's lives too. What happened in Clay's life had a profound effect on your mom's life . . . and, in turn, on your life and your sisters' lives . . . and Colin's."

"What happened to Clay?"

Maddie shook her head sadly. "He spent the first night in jail but managed to post bail. He was ready to plead guilty—he knew he'd made a terrible mistake. But he was so distraught and despondent—not only had he lost his wife and his only son, but then he'd destroyed another family too. He told his friends that his life was cursed . . . and then, on Christmas morning, they found him hanging in his shed."

Beryl covered her mouth in horror. "Oh, no!"

Maddie nodded. "After that, Colin and his mom, Linda, moved back to Vermont to live with her parents because she didn't want Colin to grow up in a community where everyone knew his grandfather had killed someone in a drunk-driving accident—and then killed himself."

Beryl nodded as Micah appeared at her side. He took one look at her and then eyed his mom suspiciously, but Beryl managed to smile. "Thank you for telling me, Mrs. Coleman. I definitely wanted to know the truth—and I'm glad I had the chance to meet Colin. It makes it all easier . . . somehow . . . as if it wasn't so . . . senseless."

Maddie squeezed Beryl's hand. "I hope so, honey. And please call me Maddie." Then she looked around the room for her husband and spied him talking to Tom Jacobs, a local contractor, and Rumer's husband. She looked at Micah. "Are you going to the cemetery?"

Micah shook his head. "I think it's just family. . . ."

"And *you*," Beryl said, touching his arm. "I'd like you to come if you can. . . ."

Maddie smiled. "We'll pick Charlotte up—if we can pull her away from Emma."

Micah nodded. "Thanks, Mom," he said as she turned away.

"That story is almost too sad to be believable," Beryl said, shaking her head. "I have to tell Rumer and Isak—but first I need to talk to them about something else."

"Okay," Micah said, eyeing the refreshments. "I'm just going to fix a plate and then I'll be over."

"Take your time," Beryl called over her shoulder. "This might not be pretty."

Micah gave her a funny look and she just shook her head.

Beryl found her sisters standing outside the kitchen. Rumer was trying to convince Rand to keep his tie on while Isak was trying not to interfere. "I need to talk to you two for a minute," she said, pulling them away and leaving Rand free to tug off his tie.

Beryl leaned against the kitchen counter and quickly explained what she wanted. Isak stared at her as if she had grown a second head. "Are you out of your mind?" she said. "We're not doing that!"

Beryl looked at Rumer for support, but she looked uncertain too. "I don't know, Ber. It sounds a little crazy to me. Do we have to decide right this minute?"

"Yes, and I know in my heart it's what Mum would've wanted."

"How do you know?" Isak said.

"I just do—and I'm not giving in. We always do what you say, Isak, and this time we're doing what I think is right."

Isak turned to look out the window. "Okay," she said softly.

Beryl stared in disbelief. She had been preparing for a contentious debate. Instead, she whispered, "What?" in a voice that was barely audible.

Isak turned to face her. "I said, 'Okay'—as long as it's okay with Rumer."

Rumer looked as shocked as Beryl. "I guess so . . ." she agreed.

"It's settled, then," Beryl said happily. She hugged her sisters and hurried out before Isak could change her mind.

Rumer followed her through the swinging door and Will grabbed her arm. "Ru, I've been looking all over for you," he said excitedly.

"Why? What's the matter?"

"Nothing," he said, trying to suppress a grin.

She eyed him suspiciously. "Why are you smiling?"

"I have some news. Do you remember Tom Jacobs?" he asked, motioning to the gray-haired gentleman still talking to Micah's dad . . . and, now, Micah.

Rumer nodded thoughtfully and murmured half to herself, "He's Sarah's dad." Then she looked up. "Wasn't he in construction?"

"He still is," Will said. "He specializes in high-end construction and new homes, and he said he has more work than he can handle. He's looking for a site foreman." Will was absolutely beaming as he told her the news. "Ru, he offered me the job!"

"No way!" Rumer could hardly believe that the father of her childhood friend would be the one to change their lives. Would he if he knew that she and her sisters had once scared his little girl half to death with an old Ouija board?

"Way! He said he remembers my work."

"Will, that's awesome! When does he want you to start?"

"He wanted me to start on Monday, but I told him we were in Montana now and I'd have to make arrangements, so he said a week from Monday."

A shadow crossed Rumer's face. "But where are we going to move *to*? And what about the end of the school year?"

"Well, I thought we could stay at your mom's for now. And if I go out and move most of our stuff back, you and Rand could stay out there until he's done and then drive back with Norman. It would only be a couple more weeks."

"Oh, Will, that's almost too good to believe," she said, hugging him.

Isak looked out the kitchen window, mulling over her sister's request. Had she been wrong to give in so easily? Then again, maybe Beryl was right—maybe their mom would've wanted it this way. How does a family know, after a loved one is gone, what their intentions would've been? Isak sighed and her thoughts drifted to Matt. She wondered how he was doing. He'd been sound asleep when she left that morning and she was anxious to head back—even though, now, she'd have to come back up again tomorrow. She was definitely going to be racking up the miles on that rental car. Who knew when Matt would be well enough to travel? She hoped the kids wouldn't mind staying at the house while he recuperated.

* * *

Later that afternoon, in a peaceful cemetery, Mia Graham's daughters watched tearfully as their beloved mom was laid to rest beside their father. Beryl gazed through the whispering pine trees at the golden light of the setting sun and reached into her pocket to touch the cool, smooth glass of the honey jar.

40

Rumer slid the casseroles in the oven, took the salad out of the fridge, put a stack of plates on the counter, and poured two glasses of wine. She carried them out to the porch, handed one to Beryl, and sat down beside her. "It's too bad Isak had to go back to Hartford," she said.

"Especially since she has to come up again in the morning," Beryl agreed, taking a sip from her glass and watching the heated battle of croquet that was taking place in the dimly lit front yard. Meghan, who was trying to play one-handed, was lagging so far behind that she never benefited from hitting an opponent's ball and getting two extra shots, so she just fell further and further behind. Rand, on the other hand, was having a game that would make his grandmother proud. Already holding a decisive lead, he watched in surprise as his ball sailed through the last two wickets and hit the post. "I'm poison!" he announced happily. "Aunt Ber, I'm poison!"

"Good job!" she called. "Who's on your list?"

He eyed the blue ball at the previous wicket and grinned mischievously. "Tommy!"

"I wouldn't do that," Tommy warned.

Rand laughed. "You know what they say . . ." He giggled, mimicking his cousin: "Payback's a you-know-what!" He lined up his mallet so it was aimed straight at Tommy's ball. Then he sent it scooting through the dandelions to tap it and knock him out of the game. "Ah, the kiss of death is so sweet," he teased, leaning flamboyantly on his mallet. "Wouldn't you say so, cous?"

Tommy shook his head slowly and took a step toward him.

Rand laughed and began to look around for an escape route. He spied the pond and wondered if he could get to the other side before . . .

Suddenly, Tommy dropped his mallet and sprinted toward him, and Rand, caught by surprise, dropped his mallet and started to run, but it was too late. Tommy scooped him up and threw him over his shoulder, and Rand squealed helplessly, trying to escape.

"Put me down," he pleaded. "I'm gonna wet my pants!" he squealed.

Tommy swung him around onto the grass and tickled him mercilessly.

"Stop . . . stop!" Rand giggled breathlessly. Just then, Flannery trotted around the house and hurried over to investigate.

"Oh, no, it's Smelly Dog," Tommy teased. "Go ahead, Flan, give Rand a big kiss!" Flan's sloppy tongue swept across Rand's face and Rand put up his arms to protect his face, leaving his sides vulnerable. He giggled helplessly and shouted, "Uncle!"

"Wrong word," Tommy teased.

"Cousin! Cousin!" Rand shouted, and Tommy finally released him and Rand just lay there, catching his breath and looking up at the stars. "I won, Gram," he whispered with a grin.

"Supper's ready!" Rumer called from the porch, and Tommy reached out his hand to pull his cousin up.

They lined up in the kitchen, buffet style, Rand and Tommy

jostling for first, and heaping their plates with lasagna, lemon chicken, salad, and rolls.

"Is Micah coming?" Tommy asked.

"He is, but he said not to wait for him. He wanted to be home to tuck Charlotte in first."

Meghan was next, refusing help and setting her plate next to each dish to spoon some out. "Are you sure I can't help you?" Will asked with a smile.

"I'm sure, Uncle Will. I need to learn to manage myself."

He sighed. "You Graham women are all the same," he teased. "You'd think the strain of stubbornness would grow weaker with each generation, but it doesn't."

Rumer grinned, handed him a beer, and kissed him. "You wouldn't want it any other way."

"You're right," he said, pulling her into a playful hug.

Beryl watched them and laughed. "It's good to see you two happy finally."

"It's good to feel happy . . . for a change," Will said, taking a sip of his beer and kissing Rumer's forehead before pulling away to hand the sisters plates and insisting they go first.

They all sat down around the table as Beryl lit the candles. Then she sat down and said, "How about grace?" Tommy and Rand both had forks en route to their mouths but reluctantly put them back down and bowed their heads. Beryl smiled, offered a quick prayer of thanks, and said she hoped there would be many more opportunities for their family to be together.

After she said, "Amen," Rand looked up and grinned. "There will be a lot more opportunities, Aunt Ber, because we're going to be living here!"

"I know, hon—I think that's so great."

"And we're going to be here for a while too," Meghan added. "At least till Dad feels better."

"I wish I didn't have to go back to Montana to finish the school year," Rand said woefully.

"Well, you do . . . and that's that," Rumer said. "It'll be over before you know it."

"Yeah, but by then, Tommy and Meghan will be back in California."

Tommy saw the disappointment in Rand's face. "I'll tell you what, Rand, I'll stay here until you get back and we'll hike Mount Washington together."

"You will?!" Rand exclaimed, his face lighting up. Tommy nodded.

Just then, there was a light knock on the door, and Flan scrambled to get up, barking ferociously.

"C'mon in! The party's already started," Beryl called.

Micah pulled open the door and, all at once, everyone called, "Hi, Micah!"

"Hi," he said, laughing.

Beryl pushed back from the table to get another chair. "Grab a plate," she said. "What would you like to drink?"

"Whatever you're having."

"Iced tea?"

"Sounds good." He filled his plate with food and sat down next to her.

"Micah," Tommy said, "how'd you like to hike Mount Washington with us when Rand gets back from Montana?"

Micah looked questioningly at Beryl. "Is everyone going?"

"Everyone who wants to, I guess," she said with a smile.

He smiled. "I'm in."

⮜⮞ 41 ⮜⮞

Early the next morning, Isak pulled up in a Chevy Suburban. "I traded in the Mustang," she said, pouring steaming coffee into a Black Dog mug and cupping it in her hands. "It's chilly out!" she said with a shiver.

"I know," Beryl agreed. "I took Flan for a walk earlier. Why'd you trade in the car? I thought you loved it."

"Well, for one thing, it wasn't big enough for everyone—"

Beryl interrupted her, "You know it's just us going today . . . right?"

Isak looked puzzled. "No . . . how come?"

"Well, I assumed it would be just us. Don't you think it would be better for the kids? I mean, I wouldn't want to be the one to explain it to them, but . . . it's really up to you two— you're the moms."

Rumer nodded in agreement. "I definitely don't want to try to explain it to Rand right now. He's got enough on his plate. Maybe when he's older."

Isak sipped her coffee thoughtfully. "I guess you're right. I hadn't really thought about it—things have been so crazy I haven't really had time to think about anything, and I assumed we'd all be traipsing up there today."

"The kids aren't even up yet," Beryl said. "They stayed up playing Parcheesi until who knows when."

"Oh, well, it doesn't matter," Isak said with a sigh. "We need to have a bigger vehicle for trips back and forth to Boston, and when Matt gets out of the hospital, I'm sure he'd be more comfortable coming up here in a bigger car. Plus, we have all of Meghan's stuff." She paused thoughtfully. "I wonder if we could leave most of it here for the summer."

"I'm sure you could. How's Matt doing?" Beryl asked.

Isak smiled. "Every day's a little better, but the surgeon already told him he's going to need physical therapy if he's going to regain full use of his leg." Then she smiled, remembering her other news. "You guys aren't going to believe this, but his doctor is an old friend from college; his name is Jonathan Marks and they were in residency together at Columbia. It was like old home week—Jon stayed and talked to Matt for over an hour. In fact, he told Matt that Hartford Hospital and Boston Medical are both looking to have more heart surgeons on staff and he asked Matt if he'd ever consider moving back . . . and Matt's actually thinking about it!

"We talked about it after Jon left and Matt said his mom is getting older, and after seeing what you went through, Ber, taking care of Mum by yourself, he didn't want Lily to go through the same thing. He also thought it might be a good time to make a move, before he's too old. After all, Tommy only has a year left at Stanford, and it would be easier for Meghan going back and forth to Barnard."

Beryl and Rumer could hardly believe their ears. "Oh, my goodness!" Rumer said happily. "Rand will be absolutely thrilled! I've never seen him as cheerful as he's been here—it's like he's a different kid. He absolutely adores Tommy and Meghan."

"Can you imagine the fun we'd have?" Beryl said with a

smile. "Thanksgiving and Christmas . . . and Memorial Day and Labor Day picnics—it would be like old times."

"Maybe we won't have to sell the house either," Rumer added hopefully. "Maybe Will could fix it up—and we could buy you two out."

"It would be nice to not sell it," Isak agreed. "Now, Ber, you just have to bring Micah and Charlotte into the fold."

Beryl smiled. "I'm working on it . . ."

"By the way," Isak said, "Meghan said you guys didn't stay in her hospital room the other night, so . . . it's time to come clean."

"We stayed at a hotel in Danbury," she answered. "But nothing happened . . ."

"Yeah . . ." they both teased suspiciously.

"Honestly, nothing happened," Beryl insisted innocently. "There was too much going on to even think about that. By the way, do you need to shower?"

"Nope, I have a hotel room now . . . since I have no idea how long Matt's going to be in the hospital, and sleeping in his room just wasn't working." She took a sip of her coffee while cutting a piece of coffee cake. "What time are we supposed to be there?"

"Around eleven," Beryl answered.

"Do you guys want a piece?" Isak asked, and Rumer nodded and Beryl slid plates over for each of them.

"We should probably get going soon."

"Do we need to bring anything?" Isak asked.

Beryl gave her a funny look. "Yes, we do," she answered softly, "and I'd also like to bring a copy of the story."

Isak took a bite of her cake and nodded.

∽ 42 ∾

Will came down just before they left. "Don't you think this is sort of odd?" he said to Ru after Beryl and Isak had gone outside. "What should I tell the kids?"

"Just tell them we had to run an errand. It's sort of the truth."

He ran his hand through his hair. "Okay," he said skeptically, pouring a cup of coffee. "And what time do you think you'll be back?"

"We should be back by midafternoon—it's about three hours from here."

"Well, don't forget, our flight is at nine tonight and we should get there early."

"I won't forget. I'm all packed and Isak's giving us a ride. You need to make sure Rand is packed and doesn't forget anything—like the homework he still has to do."

He pulled her into a hug and grinned. "And you make sure you pay attention to which way the wind is blowing."

Rumer laughed. "Thanks for the tip!"

He walked out with her and peered in the driver's window

at Isak and Beryl. "Have a safe trip," he said cheerfully. "I hope you have your credit card to fill up this beast."

"It's already full, smarty," Isak said.

"Well, I'm sure you'll be filling it up again," he said with a grin.

Isak revved the engine. "Hey, can you make sure my two kids have their overnight bags packed?"

Will nodded.

"Thanks! You're a good brother-in-law." Will rolled his eyes and Isak looked over at Beryl. "Have everything?"

Beryl felt the lump in her jacket pocket and nodded. Then Isak looked to make sure Rumer was in, waved, and peeled out, leaving Will standing in a cloud of dust and beeping her horn all the way up the driveway.

Will shook his head and called, "Thanks for waking the kids!"

"Do you know the way?" Beryl asked as they pulled out.

"Yup," Isak answered, reaching for the directions she'd Googled that morning. "I can get us up there, but you'll have to navigate when we get to Jackson."

Beryl nodded, looking over the directions Isak had printed at the hotel. Finally, she tucked them in the door pocket and Isak turned on the radio. It was still tuned to the country station she'd been listening to on the way up, and the DJ was saying, "This one's for all the moms out there on Mother's Day . . ." Carrie Underwood's sweet voice came on, singing, "Don't Forget to Remember Me." Beryl looked at her sisters in surprise. "I forgot it was Mother's Day!"

"So did I," Isak said. "And my kids didn't even get out of bed!"

"Mine didn't either," Rumer added, "but I guess if *we* didn't remember, we shouldn't expect them to remember."

They listened to the melancholy lyrics—each lost in thought, remembering what it had been like growing up in the loving warmth of Mia's guidance.

The miles flew by, and soon the White Mountains were looming majestically all around them. "You better get out the directions," Isak said as she turned off Daniel Webster Highway. Beryl unfolded the paper and looked around to get her bearings. "We're on Route 302E," Isak said, "aka Dartmouth College Road."

"Okay, well, in a bit you're supposed to turn left onto Route 16 North—aka Pinkham Notch Road."

"What's 'in a bit'?"

"Uhm . . ." Beryl traced her finger down the page. "Twenty-nine miles."

Isak glanced at the odometer, quickly calculated, then looked in her rearview mirror and realized Rumer had fallen asleep. "Ru, we're almost there," she called. "How come you're so tired—did you have a long night or something?" she teased.

Rumer opened her eyes and grinned sleepily. "Maybe . . ." she murmured, stretching and looking out the window. "Wow! It's gorgeous up here," she observed.

"I know, it's the perfect escape for an artist," Beryl said.

"Which way?" Isak asked, slowing down.

Beryl glanced down again. "Right—through town, and then left onto Carter Notch."

Isak continued to follow the directions and stopped at the bottom of a driveway. "This must be it," she said with a nervous sigh.

Beryl nodded and looked at the clock in the dash—it was almost eleven. "Good job," she said.

Isak followed the long, winding driveway until it opened onto a meadow that wrapped around an expansive lawn and a gorgeous post-and-beam home with windows that looked out in all directions. "Wow," Beryl murmured.

"Ditto that," Isak said.

"*I* want to live here," Rumer said softly.

As Isak pulled up to the house, the older gentleman who'd been at the service came from the direction of the garden, using his cane with one hand and a fistful of weeds in the other. He smiled and waved, and then dropped the weeds into the wooden bushel that was next to the stone walkway. He slowly made his way toward them. "Welcome," he said graciously.

Isak, Rumer, and Beryl smiled warmly and politely took his outstretched hand. His eyes sparkled as he looked at Beryl. "So, you talked your sisters into this?" he said, winking at them.

Beryl smiled. "It wasn't as difficult as I expected."

"Well, I'm grateful and honored. It means so much to me, and I think it would make your mum smile." He paused. "I have some refreshments: mint iced tea, which I try to make like your mom did but, just like her cinnamon toast, it never tastes quite the same." Isak, Rumer, and Beryl all laughed and he smiled. "I also have blueberry muffins, fresh from the oven."

Beryl reached into the backseat for the envelope containing the copy of their mom's memoir, and said, "That sounds wonderful."

He led them inside, explaining and pointing out details as they went. The kitchen, where the refreshments had been set out, was bright and sunny, and when they walked in, an old orange tiger cat opened one eye and peered at them curiously from where he was curled up on a sunny armchair. "That's Alfred Lord Tennyson—also known as Al or Ally Cat. He's Thoreau's brother." He looked at Beryl. "Do you still have Thoreau?"

She put the folder onto the kitchen counter. "We do—Flannery too."

David shook his head. "Your mum loved that homely old dame." He poured iced tea into glasses. "I need to sit." He motioned for them to join him and then passed the plate of muffins around. "You have to open them up and let the butter melt inside. Your mum taught me that."

As they chatted, David asked about their families, and Mia's girls realized that even though they'd only recently learned about him, he had known of them all their lives.

When they finished their muffins and iced tea, David gave them a tour of the downstairs and showed them two more portraits he'd painted of Mia. "There's one more in here," he said, turning on a light in a small room off the kitchen. "I don't paint much anymore; I do enjoy reading, though." The room was simply furnished with a mission chair, its rich brown leather seat worn and stretched. Next to the chair was a Prairie-style floor lamp that glowed warmly over the chair, and in front of the large window that looked out over the gardens and the mountains in the distance was an oak mission desk and matching chair. The walls were lined with books, and it was evident that this was where David spent most of his time. He pointed to a pencil drawing that was hanging near the chair. "That's the last drawing I did of your mum—it was the last time she was here." He motioned to the window. "She was sitting out in the garden. She had been very quiet that day and she seemed confused about where she was. She kept asking me to take her home. It was then that I began to realize something was wrong." He walked over to the drawing, lifted it off its hook, and handed it to Beryl. "I want you to have it."

"Oh, no, I couldn't," Beryl protested.

"I insist," he said. Then he looked at Isak and Rumer too. "The paintings in the other room will be yours, too, someday."

Beryl stammered and looked at her sisters, "I . . . I don't know what to say . . . we will treasure them always."

He nodded, his eyes sparkling.

They followed him out into the backyard and Beryl looked up at the sky, recalling the words her mom had used, "A canopy of endless blue." It certainly was! He made his way down a narrow path to a stone garden dotted with ornamental grass and covered with mountain pinks. He pointed to a peak in the distance. "That's Mount Washington—it still has snow on it." Then he turned and nodded to a weathered wooden bench. "And that's where your mom was sitting when I drew her picture." He smiled wistfully. "She loved to sit out here." As he spoke, a beautiful tawny-gray mourning dove fluttered down from a nearby tree, landed on the sunny bench, and cooed softly, seeming to be uninhibited by their presence. "This is where I had in mind."

Beryl nodded, reached into her pocket, pulled out the honey jar, and looked at David. "Would you like to . . . ?"

He shook his head. "No, no—you three. I'm just happy to have a part of her here with me."

Beryl took the top off the jar and handed it to Isak. They each took a turn, sprinkling some of the jar's contents; then Rumer handed it back to Beryl. Beryl hesitated and then swung her arm out over the garden, startling the mourning dove, and releasing the last of the fine gray ash into the wind. They stood silently watching as it swirled and sparkled and drifted peacefully off into the endless blue New Hampshire sky.

43

Micah opened the car door to let Harper out and then unstrapped Charlotte from her car seat. "Sooo, how'd it go?"

"It was nice," Beryl said, watching Harper race across the yard, running circles around short-legged Flannery, who was panting happily, trying to keep up; and, once free, Charlotte ran after them. "I'm glad we did it," Beryl continued. "He gave us a drawing of my mom and said the other portraits would be ours someday too. His home is absolutely . . ."

Micah looked up in surprise. "He gave you another drawing?!" Beryl nodded and he shook his head. "Ber, do you have any idea what his artwork is worth?"

"Well, he inferred that it has some value."

Micah raised his eyebrows. "*Some* value? It's worth more than you know! Ber, his paintings are worth hundreds of thousands of dollars—and after he dies, that figure will probably increase exponentially!"

Beryl shrugged and smiled. "Well, I already told him we'd never sell them."

He laughed. "You might have to sell them—you'll go broke trying to insure them."

Beryl laughed too. "Oh, well, we'll figure it out when the time comes."

They watched Charlotte happily picking dandelions with the dogs nosing along on either side of her, and Micah leaned against his car. "I was also thinking about your mom's memoir and how you said she wanted to be a writer—like you do," he added with a grin. Beryl nodded and he continued, "Well, I think there are a lot of publishers who would be very interested in this unknown window into David Gilead's life—it's quite romantic. And if you were to write a prologue giving the back story and an epilogue explaining what happened, I think it would really get attention." He paused. "You'd probably want to wait until he's gone, though, but that doesn't mean you can't start working on it."

Beryl looked thoughtful, considering his suggestion. "You know, every now and then you come up with a pretty good idea," she mused.

He grinned. "I try."

"Well, let me finish telling you about the house, which was absolutely amazing, and the views—they were breathtaking. I know that sounds clichéd, but there's no other word for it. But what I really wanted to tell you is that he wants us to visit again, and I was hoping you could come next time."

"I'd like that," Micah said.

Just then, Charlotte ran over with a bouquet of dandelions. "For you!" she said, beaming.

"Thank you, honey," Beryl said, kneeling down to give her a hug.

Micah looked around. "Where is everyone?"

"They're packing, showering, heating up leftovers, and getting ready to leave. I'm so glad you could come over. It's going to be a shock to my system to have an empty house when they all go."

"Well, Isak and the kids'll be back, won't they?"

"Later in the week. They're going to stay in Hartford for a few days—visit Matt, do some sightseeing, maybe go up to Boston and Quincy Market, and Tommy wants to go to a Red Sox game."

Micah's face lit up. "Do you want to go too?"

"We could," Beryl said. "I can have Isak get extra tickets. Does it matter what night?"

Micah shrugged. "It doesn't matter to me—any night is fine."

"Okay, I'll tell her. We could meet them for dinner before the game."

"That sounds good," he said, following her up the steps.

The dogs charged ahead of them onto the porch, Harper just about taking out the screen door. Rand was in the kitchen, fixing his plate. He looked up in surprise when he saw Harper come bounding in. "Micah, is that your dog?"

"Well, Harper's really my parents' dog, but I can borrow her anytime."

Harper, who'd smelled the food, immediately plopped down at Rand's feet and gazed at him forlornly. "She's so cute," Rand exclaimed. "She looks just like Norman, only smaller." He scratched her head. "And you're a beggar like Norman too," he said, giving her a small piece of his roll.

"All Labs are beggars," Micah chuckled.

Just then, Rumer came into the kitchen. "Hi, Micah! Hi, Charlotte!"

"Mom, did you see Micah's dog?" Rand interrupted. "Doesn't she look like Norman? Norman's going to love having Harper and Flannery for cousins."

"She does . . . and he will," Rumer agreed before quickly changing the subject. "Are you all packed?"

"Yup," he said, sitting down at the kitchen table.

"Where's your bag?"

He pointed to a duffel by the door.

"Do you have everything?"

"Yup," he mumbled with his mouth full of lasagna.

"Homework?"

He nodded, sipping his milk.

"Okay, well, hurry up and eat, because we have to go."

He swallowed and looked perplexed. "Mom, no one else is even down here yet."

"I am," Will said, coming into the kitchen, dropping his duffel next to Rand's and then reaching for a plate. "Hey, Micah! Want a plate?" he asked, holding one out.

Micah held up his hand. "No, I'll wait—you guys are in a hurry."

Just then, Isak came in and set her suitcase by the door. "Hi, Micah. Hi, Char!"

"Hi, Isak," Micah replied while Charlotte just swung her feet and smiled.

"C'mon, guys!" Isak hollered up the stairs. "Uncle Will, Aunt Ru and Rand have a flight to catch! Tommy, you're not going to have time to eat!" She grinned. "That'll get him moving."

"I'm not very hungry, Mom," Meghan said, putting her suitcase next to her mom's.

"Well, you have to eat something to take your medicine."

"I'm not taking it," she said, plopping into the chair next to Charlotte.

Tommy finally came in, his hair wet from the shower.

"Where's your bag?" Isak asked.

"Upstairs," he said, reaching for a plate.

She took the plate away. "Go get it! You're not eating until it's down here."

He started to protest, but she just pointed at the stairs and he grumbled as he went to get it.

Twenty minutes later, the Suburban was loaded down with bags and suitcases, and hugs were being given all around. "Get in," Isak told the kids. She gave Beryl a hug. "Good thing I switched vehicles."

"I know! Good thing! Be careful and give Matt our love!"

"I will and I'll let you know about the game."

"Okay."

Micah hitched Charlotte up onto his hip and she waved as Isak climbed in the driver's seat. "Bye, honey," Isak said, waving back.

Beryl turned to Rumer and Will. "Have a safe trip! Good luck with moving."

Will gave her a hug and then turned to shake Micah's hand. "Don't let her go, man," he said with a grin. "There's nothing like a Graham girl!"

Micah grinned. "Don't worry, I won't. Have a safe trip and when you get here with your stuff, let me know; I'll help you move in."

"Will do. Thanks!" Then he gave Charlotte a gentle high five. "Be good, Char."

"I'm so glad you're moving back," Beryl murmured, giving Rumer a long hug.

"Me too."

"And have you noticed all the things—amazing things—that have happened since Mum's been in heaven?"

Rumer laughed. "You know, you're right! I told you she'd be tugging on God's heartstrings."

"Okay, you two," Will said, glancing at his watch. "You'll see each other in a month."

Beryl gave Rumer another quick hug. "Let me know when you've landed."

"Will you hear your phone? You're going to be asleep."

"I'll hear it," Beryl assured her.

"I'll repaint the shop sign when I get back."

"Okay," Beryl said with a smile.

Rumer turned to give Micah and Charlotte hugs. Rumer and Rand climbed in and Rand implored, "Aunt Isak, do a peel-out!"

She laughed and they all waved through the open windows as Isak revved the engine, leaving a small cloud of dust and beeping her horn to a chorus of good-byes.

44

"*Now* are you ready for something to eat?" Beryl asked, turning to Micah.

"I'm starving!" he said. He called Harper, and Flannery, still panting, trundled along after her.

They went inside and, while Beryl fixed three plates, Micah lit the candles on the table and poured two glasses of wine. "Char, would you like some milk?"

Charlotte scooted onto a chair. "Yes, please."

Beryl set the plates on the table. "I'm so glad you guys are here. It would've been so depressing to have everyone leave at once and be alone in this big house."

Micah sat down next to Charlotte. "We're glad we're here too."

Beryl sat down across from them. "You must think my family is crazy."

Micah shook his head. "They're not crazy. Wait until you meet mine!"

Beryl opened her napkin. "They can't be any crazier than mine."

He laughed. "Don't be so sure."

She took a bite of her lasagna and looked skeptical. "How so?"

Micah reached for the butter and broke open his roll. "Well, we have a huge family picnic in the summertime—if you come, you can meet everyone and find out for yourself."

"Who's everyone? Charlotte, do you have a lot of cousins?"

Charlotte nodded and Micah laughed. "Actually, I don't know if *a lot* covers it!" He leaned back. "Let's see, my Uncle Isaac—my dad's brother—has four daughters; my uncle always wanted a boy, and he and my Aunt Nina kept trying, but it never happened. My dad still loves to tease him about it. Isaac wanted to keep trying too, but my Aunt Nina said the chances of having another girl were far too great and she said she didn't think he could handle it."

Beryl laughed and Micah continued, "So, then each of the girls got married and had kids, and between the four of them, there are ten offspring. It's a real hoot when we're all out at the Cape. My dad and my Uncle Isaac inherited my grandparents' house in Eastham, and when they go out there they have these great parties." Micah smiled, remembering. "They call themselves the Gin and Chowder Club. It's been a family tradition for longer than I can remember."

"What about your brother?" Beryl asked, sipping her wine.

Micah grinned. "Noah and his wife have five boys—all between the ages of seven and twenty."

"No!"

Micah nodded as he took a bite of his roll.

"Where do they live?"

"Out on the Cape. Noah is a minister, and his wife, Laney, is a teacher."

Beryl nodded, taking a bite of her lemon chicken. "Anyone else?"

Micah laughed. "I haven't *even* gotten to my mom's side!

My mom is a Carlson—did you ever hear of the Carlson Christmas Tree Farm?"

Beryl popped a piece of pineapple in her mouth and her face lit up. "Of course, we always got our tree there!"

"Then you know the area . . . up near Hancock?"

"Mmm-hmm."

Micah adjusted his glasses. "So, my mom is the youngest of eight, and every one of my aunts and uncles, except for my Uncle Tim, has between three and six kids; so, if you do the math, I have at least twenty-eight cousins . . . and all my cousins have kids, whose ages range from four to oh, let's say thirty . . . not to mention all the dogs, cats, cows, bunnies, lizards, and frogs. I can't even give you a total count, but my mom knows."

Beryl's eyes were wide with amazement. "Wow! That must be some family picnic!"

Micah nodded and took a bite of his chicken. "It is—they all live up that way. My cousins have every kind of farm imaginable, an orchard and cider mill, a sugar house, countless vegetable stands, and beehives for honey . . . and, of course, the tree farm. One of my cousins even has a dairy farm. They make their own ice cream in the summer and have a small ice-cream stand, which is a hot spot for the locals."

Beryl sopped up her plate with her roll. "So, how did your mom break away from farming and become a teacher?"

Micah reached for his glass. "My mom's older brother Tim—he was the next one up from her—had Down's syndrome, and when they were growing up my mom became very interested in working with special ed kids. She always wanted to be a teacher."

Concern shadowed Beryl's face. "How come you said *had?*"

Micah smiled sadly. "My Uncle Tim died. My mom was devastated—everyone was. He was a great guy."

"I'm sorry," Beryl said.

Micah nodded. "It was a long time ago. Most people with Down's live to their mid-fifties and Tim made it to fifty-six."

They were quiet for a while and Beryl leaned back. "Well, I had no idea your family was so big. We've known each other since high school and I never knew any of this." She smiled. "What am I getting myself into?"

"You're getting yourself into a lot of fun," Micah said with a grin. "We've had a lot of good times. My family is always there for me. You should've seen the turnout at Beth's service— everyone came. I think her family was a little overwhelmed." He looked down. "Sorry . . . there I go again."

"Micah," Beryl said softly, reaching for his hand. "It's okay. I don't mind when you talk about Beth."

He nodded, wiping his eyes and putting his glasses back on, and suddenly realized Charlotte wasn't sitting next to him. He looked around and Beryl pointed to the dog bed, where she was curled up between Harper and Flannery—sound asleep. Micah smiled and shook his head.

Beryl stood to clear their plates and Micah stood too.

"You don't have to help with this stuff, you've done enough."

"Don't be silly. I'm not leaving you with all this."

Beryl reluctantly gave in and they washed and dried the dishes; then she started to put the leftovers in smaller containers. "We finally made a dent in all this food, but there's still more—are you free tomorrow night?"

"Maybe," he teased, slipping the dish towel around her waist and pulling her toward him.

She laughed. "I'm a little busy, you know."

"Too busy for this?" he asked, kissing her neck.

"Well . . . no, I guess not," she murmured.

He playfully brushed his lips over her eyelashes. "How 'bout this?"

"Mmm-hmm. Mmm-mmm."

"And . . . this . . . ?" He pressed his lips softly against hers and, lost in the sweetness of his kiss, she barely shook her head. They stood together for a long time, gently kissing and marveling at the natural way their bodies fit together. Finally, Micah eased back. "I should go," he said softly. Beryl nodded and watched as he lifted Charlotte into his arms. "C'mon, Harp." The black Lab stood and stretched, and Flan opened one eye, but didn't make a move to get up—she was too tired.

"I'll walk out with you," Beryl said, stroking Charlotte's flushed cheek.

They went out on the porch and he reached for her hand. "Listen to those peepers!"

"I know—I love that sound!"

When they reached the car, she opened the door for Harper to hop in while Micah gently slipped Charlotte into her car seat on the other side, trying not to wake her, but when he pulled the harness over her head, she opened her eyes and blinked. "Where's Beryl?"

"She's right here," he said, stepping back so she could see.

Beryl leaned down next to her and Charlotte pointed at the sky. Beryl looked up at the silvery sliver of crescent moon and Charlotte whispered, "I love you."

Beryl smiled in surprise. "Oh, honey, I love you too!" But when she said the words, Charlotte gave her father a puzzled look and Beryl frowned. "What's the matter? Did I say something wrong?"

Micah laughed, leaned forward, and whispered in her ear. "Oh!" she said. "Can I try again?"

Charlotte smiled shyly, nodded her head, and softly repeated the words. This time, Beryl gave the correct response, and Charlotte laughed and threw her arms around Beryl's neck.

Beryl finally stood up and Micah realized she had tears in her eyes. "Why are you crying?!" he asked, reaching for her hands.

She brushed her cheek with her sleeve. "I'm not."

"Yes, you are."

"Well, it's not because I'm sad," she said, looking up at him.

He smiled and affectionately teased, "Well, that's good." Then he looked up at the house. "So, you're staying here tonight?"

"Yup . . . just me and Flan and Thoreau," she said, still wiping her eyes. "I think I'm going to let Thoreau stay here permanently; he seems to like being a country cat more than being a shop cat."

"Are you going to be at the shop tomorrow?"

"I am. I have so much to do."

"Should I tell Henry you're looking for help?"

"Yes, please. Tell him to come by whenever he has a chance."

"Okay, well, now that I'm thinking about it, he probably has track practice for a couple more weeks."

"That's fine."

"I could help until he's free."

"That would be great."

"Okay," he said with a gentle smile. "You better get to bed, then. It's back to the salt mines tomorrow."

She laughed. "My mom used to say that."

"Mine too," he said, gently entwining his fingers in hers. He paused, searching her cornflower blue eyes, and then asked softly, "Do you know that I love you too?"

She smiled, her eyes sparkling. "And I love you . . . to the moon and back!"

APPLE CRISP

This recipe was always a favorite in our house when I was growing up—and still is for my family. It was passed down from my mom (although she always credited my aunt Pete with its origin). It's yummy and very easy—especially if you don't have the time or energy to roll out pie crusts.

Ingredients

5¼ tablespoons butter (melted)
8–9 apples (I use Macs)
1 cup all-purpose flour
1 cup sugar
1 teaspoon baking powder
Dash of salt
½ teaspoon cinnamon
1 egg

Directions

Melt butter and set aside. Peel, core, and slice apples to almost fill an 11x7 baking dish. Preheat oven to 375 degrees Fahrenheit. Sift together all dry ingredients in mixing bowl and break one egg into mixture. Blend with a pastry blender until evenly crumbly and spread on top of apples. Spoon melted butter over topping in rows. Bake for 30-40 minutes or until golden brown.

Serve with vanilla ice cream! Yum!!!

MOM'S SOUR CREAM COFFEE CAKE

This recipe is another classic from my mom's kitchen. She liked to make this yummy cake to take to someone who needed their spirits lifted or just to have as a treat. It's an all-time favorite with my family, too, and, when it's my turn to host fellowship hour at church, it's always part of my repertoire!

Ingredients for Cake

1 cup sugar
¼ pound butter (softened)
1 cup sour cream
1 teaspoon vanilla
2 eggs
2 cups flour (sifted)
1 teaspoon baking powder
1 teaspoon baking soda
Pinch salt

Ingredients for Topping

½ cup chopped walnuts
½ cup sugar
1 teaspoon cinnamon

Directions

Mix topping ingredients together. Set aside. Preheat oven to 350 degrees Fahrenheit. Grease and flour angel-food cake pan. Cream together butter and sugar with electric mixer. Add eggs and sour cream and beat until smooth. Sift together remaining dry ingredients in a separate bowl and blend into mixture. Batter will be thick. Spread half the batter into the angel-food cake pan and sprinkle with half of the sugar, cinnamon, and nut topping. Spread remaining batter on top and sprinkle remaining sugar, cinnamon, and nut mixture. (I gently press down the topping with the back of a spoon.) Bake for 40 minutes or until toothpick comes out clean. Let cool and remove from pan. Enjoy anytime with a hot cup o' coffee or tea or a big glass of milk!

To request any other recipes mentioned in this book, please write to me through my Web site: www.nanrossiter.com. I'd love to hear from you!

MORE THAN YOU KNOW

Nan Rossiter

ABOUT THIS GUIDE

The suggested questions that follow
are included to enhance your group's
reading of *More Than You Know*.

Discussion Questions

1. When faced with tragedy, some people turn their back on God; others find strength in their faith—and their faith is strengthened. Why does this happen? What does Mia's unflagging faith say about her? And how does her faith influence her daughters?

2. Mia's old bulldog, Flannery, offers comic relief in an otherwise sometimes solemn story; Beryl often wonders if Flannery's presence in her life is part of God's plan to help her get through the loss of her mom. Do you think this is possible? Does God intimately intervene in our lives?

3. On several occasions throughout the book, Beryl talks about God's tapestry—Mia's colorful analogy for His way of weaving human lives together. What evidence of this is there in the story? Have you ever noticed this occurrence in your own life?

4. Mia also believed there is no such thing as coincidence and that everything happens for a reason. Do you think this is true?

5. Seeking long-term care for a loved one is always a difficult task. It's a decision fraught with guilt and heartache, and in many cases families don't agree. Some people make decisions with their heart, others with their heads. How do the sisters differ in their decision making? Who, if any, is right?

6. Sometimes it's truly amazing that siblings turn out to be so very different from one another. How do Isak, Rumer, and Beryl differ? What real-life struggles do they face

and how do they deal with them? To which sister do *you* most relate and why?

7. Mia was very much in love with her husband and even though she feels a growing attraction to David, she resolves to keep their relationship platonic. What changes? Why does she allow herself to be drawn into an intimate relationship with him?

8. Mia's relationship with David is reminiscent of the relationship between Katharine Hepburn and Spencer Tracy. What similarities can be drawn from this famous Hollywood affair?

9. What lessons—if any—do Mia's daughters take away from her memoir? How does it affect each of their lives?

10. Throughout the book, Isak seems to make the final decision on just about everything. In the end, however, Beryl stands firm in her belief that their mom would have wanted her ashes spread on David's property. How has Beryl changed? How has Isak changed?

11. Within one week of Mia's passing, Rumer's and Isak's relationships with their husbands are restored and Beryl is finding new love with Micah. It's almost as if Mia's death triggered several positive changes in her daughters' lives. Do you think there's truth to the adage "From tragedy comes good"? Where else in the story is this evident?

12. The possibility of a lasting relationship with Micah will fulfill another of Beryl's deepest hopes. What hope is that? Will she be good at it?